Outstanding praise for Holden Scott and SKEPTIC

"A truly original thriller—part medical, part paranormal, and totally gripping. Holden Scott has taken a fascinating premise, put it together with a super plot, and added intriguing characters to craft an amazing novel."
—Nelson DeMille, *New York Times* bestselling author

"*Skeptic* is riveting, and the concept of a molecular biological basis for ghosts was most intriguing. I found myself thinking about the notion repeatedly and sending up some trial balloons with my colleagues at the medical center."
—Herbert Y. Kressel, M.D., President and CEO of Beth Israel, Deaconess Hospital

"Gripping! *Skeptic* grabbed me in the first chapter and pulled me into the fascinating storyline. The medical/science premise was ingenious and based on enough scientific fact for me to accept the storyline and enjoy the ride."
—Peter G. Traber, M.D., Chair, Department of Medicine, University of Pennsylvania Health System, and Frank Wister Thomas Professor of Medicine

"Ingenious, fascinating, and thoroughly original, *Skeptic* boldly raises the bar for the medical thriller. Holden Scott ventures into exciting new territory."
—F. Paul Wilson, *New York Times* bestselling author

"*Skeptic* is a riveting adventure story in the best tradition of popular medical thrillers. Scott mines current biomedical research for highly imaginative scenarios, while his sound comprehension of the motives and workings of biomedical research institutions gives the narrative an aura of plausibility." —Thomas P. Stossel, M.D., Professor of Medicine, Harvard Medical School, and Director of the Experimental Medicine Division, Brigham and Women's Hospital

READ ON FOR MORE ACCLAIM . . .

"*Skeptic* is one of the cleverest and most exciting medical stories that I have read since Michael Crichton first appeared on the scene."   —Leonard Jarett, M.D., Simon Flexner Professor and Chair, University of Pennsylvania Department of Pathology and Laboratory Medicine

"An intriguing, high-flown scientific thesis that links new knowledge of viruses with the extrasensory capabilities and unearthly communication with the dead propels Scott's promising debut novel . . . Scott's simple action-driven prose is effective, offering bold characterization and high-concept biomedical thrills . . . an auspicious debut."
—*Publishers Weekly*

"[A] suspenseful, fast-moving espionage/mystery plot . . . Scott's novel offers the first really scientifically convincing explanation for the existence of ghosts."
—*Hartford Courant*

"Holden Scott is one of a group of new emerging young writers and the best of the lot. He is the successor to Michael Crichton . . . *Skeptic* should be required reading for believers and skeptics alike."   —Jack McConnell, M.D., Co-founder of the Institute for Genomic Research; co-founder of the Human Genome Project

"With this careful blend of paranormal, science, drama, and plain old-fashioned thriller, Scott has crafted an ingenious page-turner."   —*Tampa Tribune-Times*

**St. Martin's Paperbacks Titles
by Holden Scott**

**SKEPTIC
THE CARRIER**

THE CARRIER

HOLDEN SCOTT

St. Martin's Paperbacks

THE CARRIER

Copyright © 2000 by Holden Scott.

ISBN: 0-312-97858-8

Printed in the United States of America

St. Martin's Press hardcover edition / May 2000
St. Martin's Paperbacks edition / October 2001

St. Martin's Paperbacks are published by St. Martin's Press, 175 Fifth Avenue, New York, NY 10010.

10 9 8 7 6 5 4 3 2 1

To the women in my family,
and especially to Sandee Newman

ACKNOWLEDGMENTS

My deepest thanks to Jennifer Enderlin, my spectacular editor, for helping me become a better writer with each book. Thanks also to Matthew Shear for his continuing support; and Aaron Priest, the best agent an author could ask for.

I am also indebted to Or Gozani and Katrin Chua, Lynne Firester, Scott Stossel, Lisa Erbach Vance, Jon and Josh Mezrich, Bella Shen, Saumya Das, Drew Tulumello, Tonya Chen, and most of all, my parents.

ONE

Seven-thirty A.M. maybe closer to eight. Tiny electrical pulses traveling through braids of copper as thin as a human hair, bouncing from the ground to the sky to the ground, finally surging like an infection through a dormant patchwork of circuits, diodes, and minuscule mechanical gears.

Then the shrill, metallic cry of a portable phone.

Jack Collier's eyes came open on the third ring, sleep a swirling fog across his vision. He was still wearing his clothes from yesterday, a white T-shirt and light blue scrubs. His sneakers were on the edge of the bed by his feet, and his lab coat was curled into a ball a few inches from his shoulders, a makeshift pillow that smelled vaguely of formaldehyde, sweat, and stale junk food.

Slowly, resentfully, achingly, he turned toward the table by his bed. Twists of his unkempt, dirty blond hair fell in front of his eyes as he fumbled for the phone that peeked out from beneath a pair of dog-eared oncology textbooks. Usually, he kept the damn thing unplugged. But last night he had returned early enough from the lab to make an attempt at a delivery dinner. The unopened pizza box was still sitting on top of his dresser, grease bleeding through the cardboard and staining the antique oak.

The plastic phone felt cold against his palm, and Jack shivered, casting a glance toward the window on the far side of the room. As usual, the weather was a color, gray; and the deeper the calendar slid into November, the grayer it was going to get. The tree in front of his dorm building had already turned skeletal, its limbs casting daggered shadows across the piles of dirty laundry covering his floor.

Jack brought the phone to his ear, pretending he didn't feel a pang of hope as the fourth ring spasmed through the oblong chunk of plastic. *She hadn't called; she wasn't going to call.* He should have chucked the phone in a vat of battery acid months ago. He hit the answer key with his thumb, finally quelling the electric infection. Then he cleared his throat.

"If this is a special offer from a phone company— any phone company—I'm going to kill you."

There was a brief pause on the other end, then an angry, young, male voice.

"Jack, where the hell have you been?"

It took Jack a moment to place the mild southern accent. Daniel Clayton, a Ph.D. student who worked part time in the office of the dean of students, a tall, gangly kid about Jack's age, with a shock of bright red hair and wire-rimmed glasses. When he wasn't filing papers for the dean, Clayton worked in a lab four floors above Jack's own, chasing a neuro Ph.D. In a way that made them brothers under their scrubs.

"Hey, Clayton. Is this about tuition again? Tell the dean to relax. My grant check was late last month—"

"Jesus, Jack, this isn't about your goddamn tuition. Haven't you read the letters from the dean's office?"

Jack paused, disturbed by the frantic edge to Clayton's voice. He glanced toward the pile of unopened mail on a shelf by the door.

"There's been a problem with my mail."

"And your phone? I've left you at least ten messages."

Jack raised his eyebrows.

"I haven't had time to check my machine. I've been spending a lot of time in the lab."

Jack winced at the understatement. Twenty-hour days, seven days a week. Nearly an entire year secluded in a cinder-block coffin, where time had as much authority as an unplugged phone. Jack had completely lost touch with the outside world—but it had been a necessary sacrifice. He was within days of completing his project: *his miracle.*

He did not expect Daniel Clayton to understand.

"Is it something important?" Jack asked, chafing now that he was fully awake and wasting valuable lab time.

"Important? Jack, the proceedings started twenty minutes ago."

Jack's mind moved somewhere else—a refrigerator in a corner of his lab. Second shelf from the top, a plastic petri dish filled with tiny specks of bacteria. One more day, two at most. He closed his eyes and saw Angie, her long, dark hair and her crooked, fragile smile.

All for you, Angie. I did it all for you.

Jack's hands trembled. He wanted to hang up, but Clayton's voice continued to dribble into his ear.

"Did you hear me, Jack? You'd better get your ass over to Sackler Hall, the third-floor auditorium. Dean Cryer's already there, along with Professors Landry and Ballacroft—the chairs of the judiciary committee. Oh, and Dutton, of course. I'm sure he's in your corner—but there are specific guidelines for this sort of thing. Even Professor Dutton doesn't have enough pull to challenge the university charter."

Jack blinked, something beginning to register. A cold

feeling moved through his chest. "Clayton, what the hell are you talking about?"

There was a hiss of frustration on the other end. "OPEN YOUR FUCKING EARS AND LISTEN TO ME."

"I *am* listening. Say it again so I'll understand."

Clayton spoke slow enough for Jack to taste every word. "Jack, you're being expelled."

By the time Jack stepped through the double doors at the top of the bowl-shaped auditorium, his shock had transformed into a dull, throbbing fear. In his dorm room, amid the stench of old pizza and even older laundry, the word "expulsion" seemed laughable. But here the word was as heavy and real as a pendulum above his throat.

Sackler Auditorium smelled like Harvard—and not the diverse, glossy, laminated Harvard from the brochures. The semicircular room was vast, poorly lit, and tiled in Italian marble. Strips of crimson carpeting ran down the aisles, and huge oil paintings of long dead alumns hung from the excessively polished walls. A pair of chandeliers dangled over the raised, wooden stage, trickles of orange spilling down through matching bouquets of triangular crystal. In the center of the stage stood a long, steel conference table incongruously set between stone statues of the first two presidents of the university. The four figures seated behind the conference table seemed ghostly from Jack's distance, and the only thing he could tell for sure was that they were all men— and that they, too, smelled like Harvard.

As Jack began the lonely trek to the stage, he felt himself whirling backward to his first day as an undergraduate, nearly seven years ago. Fresh from the long bus ride from New Jersey, he had sat on a hard wooden bench along the back arch of this same theater. Drowning in a sea of strangers, waiting for the president of the university to speak, to tell him that he was privileged and chosen and bright—that he belonged.

He had looked up at the portraits on the walls, and the bearded, aristocratic faces had stared directly back at him, lips curling into mocking smiles.

Jack didn't belong. He had never belonged.

The ghosts at the conference table turned real as he reached the bottom of the crimson aisle, heading for the stairs that led to the stage. He recognized Dean Cryer immediately, a towering man with harshly combed hair and thick, black-framed glasses. Next to Cryer were the two heads of the judiciary committee, Landry and Ballacroft. Landry was Harvard's oldest English professor and looked the part: frizzy white hair, sagging, bloodhound eyes, skin like crumpled canvas. His clothes came straight from central casting: tweed jacket, red bow tie, striped blue shirt, and an ever-present handkerchief gripped tightly in his gnarled, trembling hand.

Ballacroft was more of a mystery. By title he was an anthropologist, but Jack doubted he had ever left the Ivory Tower long enough to worry the dry cleaner who managed his tailored khaki suits. Ballacroft's family was one of the richest in Boston, and there had been a family member involved with Harvard since the late seventeenth century.

Jack's feet became heavy as he reached the first step; if this was his jury, what chance did he have? Then he caught sight of Michael Dutton at the far corner of the table. Dutton was leaning forward over a stack of white paper, his windswept, auburn hair glowing in the light from the chandeliers. As usual, he was wearing an impeccable suit, and his weathered face emanated calm and control. Jack felt a surge of hope; with Dutton's help, maybe he *did* have a chance. Dutton was one of the most respected professors at the university, twice on the short list for the Nobel Prize. He was also a campus favorite, with his rugged good looks and his easy smile. Most important of all, he was Jack's advisor. He had chosen Jack as his protégé, and that made Jack his investment.

Dutton looked up just as Jack stepped onto the stage, and their eyes met. Jack saw sympathy in those pools of green—but also something else, something that sent his hope spiraling away: *pity*.

"Jack," Dutton said, and immediately every face at the table shifted toward him. "Maybe you can help us understand what's going on here. I've done my best to come up with an explanation, but I'm truly at a loss."

Jack could feel the sweat dripping down his back. He was wearing his only dress shirt, a white oxford that Angie had bought him a month before she had left. The shirt was a size too small, but he hadn't had the time to exchange it. Once Angie had run, he hadn't had the time for anything outside of the lab—because nothing outside the lab mattered. Nothing was as important as his project. At least, that's what he had thought.

"I'm sorry," Jack said, as Dean Cryer beckoned him toward an empty chair at the head of the long, steel table. "But I'm not even sure why I'm here. I haven't gotten my mail or my phone messages in some time."

Dean Cryer raised his eyebrows. "You expect us to believe that you don't even know the charges against you?"

Jack lowered himself into the chair, his face turning red. He didn't like the tone of Cryer's voice, and he had the immediate urge to lash back. Instead, he did his best to remain in control.

"Your assistant told me it had something to do with my qualifying exam."

Ballacroft pointed a manicured finger at a pair of folders on the table in front of Jack. "Why don't you take a look for yourself?"

Jack glanced at Dutton, but his advisor was looking the other way. Jack turned his attention to the folders. He opened the closer of the two and read through a paragraph of typewritten text. He stopped himself halfway down the page. He didn't need to read more—because he had written it himself.

"This is from the exam I took when I entered the biology Ph.D. program two years ago. It's an essay on the human immune system. Specifically, on the activity of killer T cells."

Jack could have rewritten the essay in his sleep. Certainly, he knew more about killer T cells than anyone at the table—except maybe Dutton. Well, even Dutton. As brilliant as Michael Dutton was, he couldn't have come close to achieving what Jack had accomplished in the lab over the past year. When Dutton found out what his charge had done, Jack wasn't sure how he'd react. Jack had been very careful to keep his work a secret for that very reason. In truth, there was no way to tell how a man like Dutton would take being upstaged by a student.

"A fine essay," Dutton commented, still not looking at Jack. "I remember telling you that I was proud to have you in my lab—in part because that essay distinguished you from the rest of your classmates."

"Ironic," Professor Landry croaked. Then he wiped his mouth with his handkerchief, and Jack couldn't tell if he was embarrassed or amused. "If you'll take a look in the other folder, Jack, you'll see what I mean."

Jack nervously reached inside the second folder and withdrew another sheet of paper. The back of his neck burned as he read the entire page. Although the words were different, it was almost the same essay. *His* evaluations of T cell behavior; *his* innovative description of immune system response. But someone else's words.

He shifted his eyes to a banner at the top of the page. There was a name he didn't recognize, followed by a date. It was a qualifying exam from seven years ago.

"This is impossible," Jack said, his voice soft. He again looked at Dutton. "Professor Dutton, I wrote this essay."

"Yes," Dean Cryer interrupted. "But someone else wrote it first. A bright student who finished his Ph.D. two years ago, then went on to teach at Stanford. His name was Albert Finsey. Unfortunately, Finsey died last year in a car accident so we were unable to speak with him. But our records are quite clear; Finsey submitted it to Professor Minton, the previous chair of biology—who has since retired. Minton can't quote the exam word for word, but he remembers Finsey and has already testified that this was his exam."

"The bottom line," Ballacroft added, his jaw tight, "is that this was not your own work, Mr. Collier. And the university has very clear rules about this sort of thing."

Jack felt his throat closing. This was insane. This was bullshit. He looked down at the two exams on the table in front of him then back at the dean and the two old men seated next to him. Then, finally, at Michael Dutton.

This was worse than bullshit. This was *deliberate* bullshit.

"Someone faked this old exam," Jack hissed. "There's no other explanation. Finsey's dead, so he can't corroborate. And Minton's as old as this fucking building—"

"Watch yourself," the dean admonished. "There's another explanation, and it's much simpler. The qualifying exam takes place in Widener Library. We don't police our students because we don't usually need to. It would have been easy for you to use the library's computer system to search previous exams. It was just that sort of search that alerted Professor Dutton to your violation."

Jack's stomach turned over. He glanced toward Dutton. Dutton shrugged, a tired expression on his handsome face. "I'm sorry, Jack. I was checking through the literature on T cells for a paper I'm reviewing. Both your exam and Finsey's old exam came up. I couldn't ignore what I had found."

The room had suddenly become an echo chamber. Dutton's voice was everywhere, and Jack felt like he was going to slip out of his chair. Dutton was supposed to be his supporter, but Dutton was the one who had aimed the gun at his head. Dutton was the one who had called this meeting. Dutton was the one who was getting him expelled.

The sick truth was, Dutton could have ignored the two papers. Or he could have come to Jack first. But he had chosen to go straight to the dean. Maybe it was proper procedure, but every lab rat in the world knew that procedure was a tool you bent to your needs.

Jack rubbed his hand over his eyes, not wanting to believe. "Give me another fucking test. Give me ten tests. I didn't cheat. I didn't *need* to cheat."

But his words were little more than air. He kept his eyes covered as the dean rattled on about the appeal process, about Jack's rights as a student, about the notification that had already been sent to his grant committee. He kept his eyes covered as the two judiciary committee members told him how hard this was for them, how they regretted the severity of the university charter, how he still had a chance to make something of himself. He kept his eyes covered as the chairs pulled back from the table, as three of the four men filed away.

He kept his eyes covered until it was he and Dutton

left alone at the long, steel table, the orange light trickling down from the chandeliers like blood.

The silence didn't last long.

"I *am* sorry," Dutton finally said. "You were a brilliant protégé. You might have made a wonderful professor."

"Why did you do it?" Jack asked, moving his hand so he could look Dutton in those fucking green eyes. There was no reason to play games now. It didn't take a *brilliant* mind to figure it out. "Why did you set me up?"

Dutton leaned back, momentarily stricken, then a dangerous smile touched the corner of his lips. "I resent the accusation. I was your biggest supporter at this university. Despite your background, I knew you had potential. It's always sad to see potential wasted."

Jack's hands shook. He wanted to grab Dutton by his fancy suit and throw him to the floor. He wanted to tear one of the oil paintings from the wall and bash Dutton's handsome face with the frame. "You doctored the old exam. You added my paragraph to the old test to make it look like I cheated. Why?"

Dutton rose from the chair, smoothing his sleeves. "This isn't getting us anywhere, Jack. I've got work to do, and you've got to pack."

Jack wanted to throw up. He tried to tell himself that it was going to be all right, that somehow it was going to be all right. He didn't need Harvard. He didn't need a Ph.D.

He had his project: *his miracle*. Even Harvard meant nothing in the face of his miracle.

"Oh," Dutton added, turning away from the table with a sweep of his jacket. "Don't bother heading to the lab for your things. Your privileges have been revoked. The lock has already been reprogrammed to reject your ID."

The words hit Jack and he doubled over, gripping the edge of the table. His face paled as he finally realized the truth. He had been such a fool. A naive, fucking fool. "My project. You know about my project."

Dutton paused, his back still turned. He could have ignored Jack; he could have simply walked away. But that wouldn't have been in character. Jack was no threat.

"It's a university lab under my supervision. You were careful but not perfect."

"You're going to steal it from me. You're going to pretend that it's yours."

Dutton raised his arms out at his sides, palms up. His face was turned toward the chandeliers. "It's the miracle that matters, Jack. Not who takes the credit."

Jack slammed his fist against the table. The sound reverberated off the marble walls. "You can't do this!"

Dutton turned to face him. For a brief moment there were wolves in his grin. "Why not? You going to blow the whistle on me? I was on the short list for the Nobel. You're here on financial aid. And now you just got kicked out of school for plagiarism."

He stepped away from the table and moved down the steps. He waited until he had reached the crimson aisle before pointing a finger at Jack's face. "Your word against mine, Jack. Who do you think they're going to believe?"

Jack leapt upward. The chair crashed to the floor behind him. "You can't do this!"

Dutton continued up the aisle. "You're a smart kid. I'm sure you'll land on your feet."

"It was my idea! It's my cure! It's my miracle!"

Dutton laughed, shaking his head. His auburn hair danced against the nape of his neck. "You're already gone, Jack."

Jack wanted to race after him. But as he moved across the stage, he felt the eyes of the oil paintings burning into him from the marble walls. Dutton was right. Nobody would believe him. This was Dutton's world, not his. Against a man like Dutton, he'd never get justice. Even after seven years, Jack didn't belong.

TWO

Two days later, Jack stood in the shadows of Michael Dutton's colonial three-story mansion, leaves swirling around his tan work boots. Even at twenty-three, he looked like a kid. Tall, angled, too pretty to be mean, but angry and tired and sick. Not physiologically; the other way, his stomach in knots and the blood pounding in his skull.

There was no turning back.

He glanced over his shoulder toward the quiet, tree-lined street ten yards away. This was the rich part of Cambridge, an upper-middle-class enclave of professors' mansions and manicured estates. The houses had names and tool sheds and visitors' parking: an affluent Brahmin enclave set just minutes from the black iron fences of the university itself.

No, god damn it, there was no turning back.

The suburban neighborhood screamed at him, and he wanted to scream back. Instead, he turned toward the colonial and focused on the window just a few feet away.

No turning back . . .

His fist hit the glass pane and there was a crack like a gunshot. The glass shattered inward, and a second later

Jack's whole arm was through and he was reaching for the latch. The window creaked as it slid upward, but Jack knew nobody was home to hear the noise. He had been watching the house for the past two days.

He carefully pulled himself over the windowsill and slid into the dark living room. His boots sank into the Oriental carpet, and there was the distinct crunch of broken glass. Jack shook the shards away as he pulled his backpack off of his shoulder, surveying the room with quick flicks of his eyes.

Dutton's tastes were urbane and expensive, and he had an incredible eye for detail. The furniture fit the architecture of the house, but the art was modern and chosen with delicate care. Elegant glass sculptures filled a cherry wood bookshelf that rose up the far side of the room, and a pair of rust-colored Louis XIV couches faced a marble fireplace, half hidden behind a silk screen. Landscape oil paintings from the colonial period hung from the walls, spaced at exactly equal, mathematical intervals. As a scientist, Dutton's obsession with precision was legendary; the running joke was that he styled his hair with a compass and a tape measure.

Jack slid past the couches, heading toward the staircase that led to the second floor. He knew exactly where he was going because he had been inside the house once before: two years ago, when he had been accepted into Harvard's biology program. Professor Dutton had invited Jack and three other graduate students to his home for cocktails. Jack had stood uncomfortably in this same living room, draped in a borrowed jacket and a cheap tie, listening in awe as the great Harvard demigod had told them they were going to be one big, happy family.

Jack's jaw clenched, as the bile rose in his throat. "One big, happy family."

Your word against mine, Jack. Who do you think they're going to believe?

Who do you think they're going to believe?

Jack's lungs burned by the time he reached the top of the stairs. A long, narrow hallway extended through the second floor, lined on either side by nondescript wooden doors. There was another staircase at the end of the hall, leading to the third floor. But Jack didn't need to go any higher.

Eyes narrowed, he plodded quietly down the hallway, the full significance of what he was about to do resonating through his shoulders. He had done a lot of crazy things in his life. He had even spent three horrible weeks in juvi when he was thirteen years old. But this was different. This was an adult crime in an adult world.

Jack stopped halfway down the hallway, facing one of the wooden doors. Sweat broke out on his forehead as he reached for the knob. He pushed the door open and stepped across the threshold of a dimly lit study. An oversized, mahogany desk rested by a window overlooking the empty driveway two floors below. Bookshelves lined the walls on either side, mostly stocked with biology texts and medical journals. A leather reading chair lounged by a photocopy machine, and an empty glass fish tank stood a few feet from the door.

Jack crossed slowly toward the desk, his eyes traveling over the smooth mahogany to the window, then over a few feet across the stark wall. His gaze settled on a green-hued painting in an ornate golden frame. Even from across the room, Jack could tell the painting was valuable. It was a forest scene, dating back at least to the late eighteenth century. Jack's mother had been an art teacher before she had died, and even though he was a child at the time, Jack knew a hell of a lot about art:

The painting was worth ten, maybe twenty thousand dollars.

But Jack was not an art thief. Jack was a scientist.

His rage returned, and he yanked the backpack off his shoulder, setting it down on Dutton's desk. His fingers trembled as he undid the zipper. Inside the main compartment were two items. A small, metallic device, about the size of a package of cigarettes. And a rolled up copy of *Science* magazine.

Jack grabbed the magazine and slammed it flat against the desk. He had picked the magazine up that very morning, at a newsstand just yards from his dorm. *Science* was the Bible of his profession, the showcase of nearly every significant research discovery of the past two decades. Jack shifted his gaze down the cover to this month's title banner, written in bright red letters: "SMART BACTERIA—THE MIRACLE CURE."

Beneath the banner was a photograph of a single-celled bacterium, a nearly transparent, elliptical creature with tiny hairs around its edges. Next to the photograph, in the same red ink of the banner, was the name of the author—the thief who had taken credit for the twenty-page paper that was resonating like a gunshot through the scientific community. Jack's lips curled back as he read the name: "Michael Dutton, Ph.D."

Jack's hands became fists and he slammed them against the desk. The sheer unfairness of it was overwhelming. Dutton had taken him completely by surprise. The magazine had come out that morning—but Dutton must have submitted the paper weeks ago. While Jack patiently ran his test samples, waiting for the proper moment to give the world his miracle, Dutton had stolen it out from under him. Every word in the fucking article had been ripped from inside Jack's brain.

It had been *his* idea to splice sections of human immune system DNA into the genome of streptococcus bacteria, turning one of nature's most vicious microbes into a miracle cure. It had been *his* idea to genetically train the strep bacteria to seek and destroy cancerous tumors. Jack had created the cure, not Michael Dutton.

Who are they going to believe?

Jack's fury intensified as he spun away from the desk. He lurched forward, grabbing the oil painting by the heavy gold frame and yanking it from the wall. He stumbled backward, staring at the steel combination safe imbedded in the plaster. He had been told about the safe a week ago by a former conquest of Dutton's, a pretty young undergrad who washed test tubes in his lab. Dutton had bragged about his hidden plunder—the undeclared result of a decade of gambling, of precise mathematics played out in the sport of cards—while feeding his more widely known, quietly tolerated, addiction: his penchant for young, naive women. Now he was going to pay for both his vices. Most of all, he was going to pay for ruining Jack's life.

Jack reached into his backpack and retrieved the small metallic device. It was rectangular, with an LCD screen across its front and two red wires hanging from its base. The wires ended in tiny, circular acoustic pads. Jack had built the device himself last night, working from a design he had first tested while in high school: a sonar receiver attached to a microchip that could distinguish between the different metallic tones of combination tumblers.

He quickly unrolled the wires from the base of his sonar device and attached the leads to the surface of the steel safe, bare centimeters from the combination dial. Then he carefully turned the wheel. When the first tumbler loosened, a tiny black dot blinked across the LCD screen. Jack noted the number, then twisted the dial in the other direction, waiting for the next black dot.

Less than a minute later, there was a series of clicks and the lock jerked open. The safe door swung outward, and Jack blinked, hard. *Christ!*

He had never seen so much money in his life. Stack after stack after stack, stretching at least three feet back into the hollow safe. Fingers trembling, Jack reached forward and touched one of the stacks. Hundred-dollar bills. He counted with his fingers: one hundred bills, held together by two rubber bands.

Ten thousand dollars. Jack's mouth went dry as he quickly totaled the stacks in the safe. Exactly two million dollars. Dutton's boasts had not been idle. Jack thought about scooping it all into his backpack: but he was not a thief. He was a scientist. And he intended to be fair.

Because of Jack's research, Michael Dutton was going to win the Nobel Prize. The prize was worth close to a million dollars; some of that money Dutton deserved, because Jack's work *did* profit from his reputation and certainly his lab. Jack would not be greedy—in fact, he would take less than he deserved and only as much as he could easily carry. The Nobel Prize wasn't really about money, and neither was this: Dutton's loot was going to be a means to an end.

His heart racing, Jack reached into the safe and began to count out twenty-five stacks.

Forty minutes later, Jack's boots clicked against the sheer cement floor of a dark lab tucked in the basement of Harvard's McCaffrey biology building. He moved quickly through the familiar maze of porcelain counters, equipment racks, and stainless steel sinks. The backpack was heavy against his shoulder, bulging with the twenty-five stacks of Dutton's money. His skin felt hot, sweat running in thin rivers down his back. He had spent two years of his life in this basement labyrinth, yet now he was a trespasser. As Dutton had threatened, his ID card had not worked on the level-two air lock that separated the lab from the rest of the building, and he had been forced to override the electronic lock by shorting the cadmium battery in his sonar safecracking device. Forced to break into his own lab, to gain access to his own research.

His miracle cure. Jack slowed to a stop in front of a steel refrigerator set atop a sterile marble counter. He could see himself reflected in the steel, and he suddenly looked much older—but somehow not as angry, not as tired, not as sick.

He pulled open the refrigerator door, bathing in the cold blast of supercooled air. Four degrees Celsius, the optimum temperature to contain the growth of bacteria. Jack looked down the horizontal racks that lined the refrigerator, finally settling on the pair of plastic petri dishes on the second shelf. He could see the yellow agar bases through the clear, circular plastic, and the tiny white dots growing on the agar.

Inadvertently, he smiled. He knew how bizarre his reaction was: smiling at the sight of bacteria—and not just any bacteria. streptococcus A, one of the fiercest, hungriest creatures in the microbe world. So fierce that the popular press even had a name for it: flesh-eating. Or the even more ominous scientific term: necrotizing fascitis. Responsible for thousands of vivid, vicious deaths a year.

Jack reached forward and lifted one of the petri dishes out of the refrigerator. No gloves, no mask, no Racal bodysuit. Nothing but the plastic case separating him from what was formerly one of nature's most deadly killers. Jack peered through the clear plastic, turning the dish in his hands. Then he sighed.

It *had* been a brilliant idea. Turning a killer into a

cure. Teaching a microbe to hunt tumors instead of normal, organic cells. Using his own DNA, a sample of his own blood—the blueprint for his own immune system—to train strep A to search and destroy an interloper: cancer.

He unzipped the front compartment on his backpack and pulled out a small, steel cylinder. The cylinder was three inches high, with a top like a child's thermos. There was a compression switch on the side, and Jack made sure it was off before he unscrewed the top. Then he carefully placed the petri dish inside. Once the top was back in place, he pressed the compression switch. There was a sharp whistling sound, as a tiny, battery-powered pump expelled every molecule of air, turning the container into a miniature vacuum.

His fingers trembling, Jack returned the container to the front compartment of his backpack. Although not as stable as refrigeration, the vacuum would keep his bacteria in an arrested state for at least a week. Hopefully, that would give Jack enough time.

Jack reached back into the refrigerator and retrieved the second petri dish. Staring down at the white specks of bacteria, his thoughts turned immediately to Angie. He wondered if she had read the *Science* article. Without Jack's name on the cover, it would have been meaningless to her, just another inflated claim, like all the others. She would never have guessed that it was real, that the tiny bacteria in the picture was her salvation. And that Jack had created it for her—for her alone.

Dutton would never have understood the truth. The *Science* article, the Nobel Prize, the fame, the money, even Harvard, none of that had ever mattered. There was only one reason why Jack had dedicated the past two years of his life to finding a miracle cure. He had done it all for Angie.

Ovarian, Jack. Stage four. You know what that means.

Eyes closed, he could hear the phone call as if it were yesterday. He remembered how her voice had sounded so small, far-away.

Three years at the outside, Jack. Surgery, chemo, they won't make any difference. I've got three years. And I'm not going to spend them in a hospital.

I'll come with you, Jack had said. I'll drop out and come with you. But her voice had suddenly grown strong.

I'm not going to let you, Jack. I won't ruin your life with mine.

Angie, he had pleaded. My life *is* ruined without yours.

Please don't try to find me.

And then the phone had gone dead. With it, Jack's heart.

It had taken every ounce of willpower not to go after her, but there had been no choice. Jack knew the statistics. If he had followed her, it would only have been to watch her die.

Now things were different. Now he could save her. If his name had been on the *Science* article, she would have seen it and come to him. Instead, he would have to find her.

His fingers tightened against the plastic petri dish. All Dutton cared about was the glory of the discovery—and what it would do for his career. He didn't even know about Angie.

Jack had the sudden urge to toss the second petri dish to the floor, to crush it with his boot, to rip the entire lab apart, destroying everything he had created. As brilliant as Dutton was, it would take him years to recreate what Jack had done. As he struggled to truly understand Jack's work, the scientific community would begin to wonder, perhaps to suspect. Maybe the truth would come out.

Jack sighed, lowering his eyes. He knew he couldn't destroy his cure. As much as he hated Dutton, his cure was too important. Not just for Angie, but for the millions of other people who were going through hell.

He carefully placed the second petri dish back in the refrigerator. As he pulled his hand away, he felt a strange tingle run up his forearm, a dozen invisible spiders racing across his skin. He guessed that even his nervous system recognized the significance of the moment. The old Jack was gone.

He shut the refrigerator and reached for his backpack. Then he bent to one knee, opening a cabinet beneath the marble counter. He retrieved a small green duffel bag, packed months ago for the road. He had always been ready to chase after Angie; he just didn't know when. It hadn't been hard to decide what to take with him; all of his clothes were basically interchangeable, and other than his boots, he didn't have any real possessions. In retrospect, he'd been ready to run most of his adult life.

He moved easily through the lab, the backpack over one shoulder, the duffel over the other. Only when he reached the enormous blackboard hanging a few feet from the air lock did he pause, his lips curling into a grin. He found a piece of bright blue chalk, and scrawled a quick note across the slate. Something Dutton was sure to understand. Then he dropped the chalk and headed for the air lock.

Two hundred and fifty thousand in hundred-dollar bills. A petri dish full of bacteria. And a bag full of clothes.

Jack Collier was no longer a scientist. He was a fugitive on a mission.

And it was time to run.

THREE

"Brad, come on. This is crazy. Not here. The elevator's going to open any second."

Brad Kershaw ran his tongue up the soft curve of Jill Lawler's breast, then took her nipple between his lips. He had her pressed against the elevator doors, his hands down the back of her scrubs, her lab coat open, and her T-shirt up all the way to her collar bone. He could feel her moistening through her thin white panties, and there was no way in hell he was going to stop now. He didn't care that they were in an elevator on their way to the basement of the McCaffrey Building.

"Jill," he whispered, "there's no one around. It's nearly nine-thirty. And it's the Wednesday before Thanksgiving. We're probably the only ones left on campus." Brad slid his hands deeper into her pants, cupping her ass with his palms. He could feel the elevator doors vibrating against her back, and he knew she was right, they had almost reached the basement. But nobody was going to be down there. Hell, *they* shouldn't have been down there either. Professor Dutton had some nerve, calling Jill from his fucking cell phone and asking her to run an errand in the middle of the night.

"It just doesn't feel right," Jill said, squirming out of

Brad's grip. She put her hands on his chest and shoved him back, then pulled her T-shirt down over her breasts. Brad exhaled, yanking his hands out of her scrubs. He stepped back, watching her fix her lab coat. Even disheveled, Jill looked fantastic. Tall, athletic, with long, blonde hair and upturned, Protestant features.

"You're no fun." Brad kicked dejectedly at the oversized plastic cooler by his feet. "You drag me out here, make me lug this thing all over campus, and now you're going to deprive me of one of Harvard's traditional rites of passage?"

Jill rolled her eyes. "First, you told me we had to do it in the library stacks. Then on the banks of the Charles. Now we have to do it in the elevator in the bio building?"

Brad ran his hand through her long, blonde hair. "Either that or on the floor of Dutton's lab. Your choice."

Jill turned just as the elevator doors whiffed open. "You're a hell of a romantic, Brad."

"Well, I'm no Mike Dutton, but I try."

Brad regretted the words as soon as they left his lips. Jill glared at him, then stepped out into the basement hallway. Brad sighed, scooping up the heavy cooler, and starting after her. He knew it was a topic he should have left alone. His nagging suspicion that something was going on between his girlfriend and their professor was causing a major rift in his relationship. But Dutton was a notorious Lothario; a lesser member of the Harvard pantheon would have been sent packing if even half of the Dutton legend was true. Worse yet, Dutton seemed perfectly comfortable calling Jill at her dorm, even in the middle of the night. Brad figured he had a right to be suspicious.

"You've got to admit he's quite the prick, making us

come out here. Like this couldn't have waited until after Thanksgiving."

Jill was moving quickly between the cinder-block walls, heading toward the air lock at the end of the narrow hallway. Brad's comments were obviously gnawing at her because her voice tightened, jumping up an octave. In her eyes—along with most of the scientific community—derisive comments about Dutton were akin to blasphemy.

"Actually, no, it couldn't wait. With all the excitement concerning his miracle cure, he wants to move his project to the new lab as quickly as possible. It's a real honor that the university is transferring us upstairs—and I think you ought to show a little more respect. You know Professor Dutton's success is going to help us both with our careers."

Brad kept his mouth shut as they approached the air lock that led to Dutton's lab. Despite the professor's breakthrough, he wasn't sure he *wanted* Dutton on his résumé. So maybe he had cured cancer. That didn't change the fact that he was probably fucking Brad's girl-friend.

Brad kept his thoughts to himself as he watched Jill run her security card through the slot next to the air lock. A second later she glanced at him, her eyebrows raised. "Something's wrong. The door's not working."

"Try it again," Brad said, shifting the heavy cooler between his arms. Jill ran her card through the slot a second time. The electronic lock showed no signs of life. Jill shrugged, putting her hand against the steel air lock. To Brad's surprise, the door swung inward.

"Looks like someone was here earlier," he said. "Maybe the janitor shorted out the electronic lock."

Jill nodded, stepping into the dark lab. She hit the light switch and there was a loud clang as the fluorescent ceiling panels went on. The lab was rectangular, with high, sheer walls and a smooth, cement floor. There was a distinct, antiseptic scent in the air and a constant background hum drifting from the self-contained ventilation system. The huge room was divided into dozens of work areas by parallel rows of marble counters, test-tube racks, and sink stations.

Brad followed Jill through the maze, keeping his gaze pinned to the firm curves beneath the penguin tail of her lab coat. If his evening was going to be ruined by Dutton's last-minute errand, at least he could try to make the best of it. "So how much shit do we have to cart upstairs?"

"Just the bacteriological samples," Jill responded, turning a sharp corner into the center portion of the lab. "Both dishes of tailored Strep A, as well as the control samples. Oh, and he also wants us to take anything we find that belonged to Jack."

Brad raised his eyebrows. "He wants Jack's work brought to the new lab? What the hell for? Jack's expulsion became official this morning."

"Look, that's what Professor Dutton said. I didn't ask why." Jill came to an abrupt stop in front of the steel sample refrigerator. Brad placed the cooler on the floor next to her feet and leaned back against a marble counter.

"Seems pretty strange to me. What does the prof want with Jack's research? Dutton didn't lift a finger to help Jack out when the grant committee—"

"Brad," Jill interrupted, yanking the refrigerator open. "Let's just get this over with as quickly as possible. Open the cooler."

Brad dropped to one knee as he went to work on the cooler latch. It *did* seem pretty strange. Dutton had found the cure to cancer; what the hell did he want with research materials from a kid who'd just gotten himself expelled? Then again, God only knew what Jack Collier had been working on. The kid was a complete loner and definitely brilliant. Too bad he was also such a fuck-up. Brad shrugged the mystery away, flipping open the empty cooler. Out of the corner of his eye he watched Jill reaching into the refrigerator—and then suddenly she jerked her hand back.

"Christ!"

"What?" Brad looked up, startled. Jill had stumbled back a few feet from the refrigerator, holding her right hand in front of her face.

"Jill?"

Her face had turned ash white. Brad shifted his eyes to her hand, and his throat constricted. There were bright red sores all over her palm. The sores were circular, almost burnlike, with rough, dark edges. As Brad watched, the sores began to grow. "Oh, my God! What the hell?"

Suddenly, Jill was screaming, waving her hand in the air. Brad leapt to his feet, grabbing her by the wrists, shouting for her to stay calm, when he felt a sharp pain on the skin of his left arm. He looked down, then recoiled in horror.

There was a dime-sized sore on his skin, just above his own wrist. Then he saw a second sore, a few centimeters away, and a third! Sharp pain tore up his arm, like a thousand stinging insects were ripping into his flesh. He crashed back against the marble counter, his arm out in front of him.

Jesus fucking Christ! The first sore was now the size of a quarter. Its center was so deep, he could see the white glint of bone. A scream tore through his lungs, and he whirled, his eyes searching for Jill.

And then he saw her, on her knees next to the plastic

cooler. His vision swirled as his gaze tracked toward her face. Even through the haze of pain, he could tell that something wasn't right. Realization hit him, and he let out a soft moan. No, it wasn't right at all.

Jill's face was gone.

But that wasn't the worst part.

FOUR

Suburbia looked a hell of a lot better at ninety miles per hour. Michael Dutton nursed the accelerator with his foot, navigating his metallic blue BMW through the loping curves of the posh, tree-lined neighborhood. Despite the fact that it was just past 3:00 A.M., he felt alive, sharp, like an addict on a cocaine high. He had dropped five thousand dollars at the blackjack tables in Foxwoods, and still it had made no difference. Gambling was an obsession of precise odds, and the odds were *always* in his favor. Not just in gambling—but in life.

Dutton laughed, tapping his fingernails against the steering wheel. Then he reached for his cell phone. He had already made three calls during the two-hour trip from the Connecticut Indian casino, all to young women with connections to his lab. Nobody had seen or heard from Jack Collier since the expulsion verdict had come down, and there was a good chance the kid was already on his way back home to Shitsville, New Jersey. Still, Dutton had taken the extra precaution of having Jill Conway move all of the important samples to his new lab on the third floor of McCaffrey. At this stage, paranoia was in order.

Dutton punched at the cell phone keypad as he turned

onto Brattle Street, then waited for the connection. It was past midnight in LA, so he wasn't surprised when his agent's voice mail picked up on the third ring. He waited for the tone, running a hand through his hair. The sleeve of his Armani shirt brushed his cheek, and he felt an electric charge as the cool silk touched his skin.

"I've thought it over, Aaron, and *Dateline* seems like the best place to start. Then *20/20* then the talk shows. And I've looked over the revised PR sheet; I like what you've done. I'll be at home all day tomorrow, so give me a call."

Dutton hung up the phone, exhilarated. A bio professor with a Hollywood agent—he could imagine the envy gnawing at his colleagues. The feeling was not new; he had been at the top of the Harvard food chain since the second year of his tenure, when an article on tumor blood flow had sent his career skyrocketing. But this time, the rise would not stop at a short list or a special commendation from the Academy of Science; this time, he had a clear shot at immortality. Everything he had achieved in his entire life paled in comparison to the miracle cure. This time the Nobel would be his—and with it, a true place in history.

A shadow crossed Dutton's cheeks, and he quickly shook it away. It wasn't important how it had happened; the results were what mattered. It was the greatest scientific advance of the decade—and who better deserved the accolades?

He pulled into the circular driveway in front of his Brattle Street mansion. He needed a drink, something to calm him down. He hadn't slept much in the past few days, and he was beginning to worry that he was getting a bit manic.

As he stepped out onto his driveway, a strange thought hit him. *Maybe this is what guilt feels like.* Then he laughed out loud. The sound was high pitched, slicing through the silent, suburban night. What the hell did he have to feel guilty about?

He had chosen Jack Collier out of a sea of biology students. He had generously given the little shit free reign in his lab. Then, like a good supervisor, he had kept out of the way, nurturing Jack's research from the sidelines. No easy task—Jack had done his best to keep his project a secret, coming to the lab late at night, purposefully mismarking his samples, even hiding slides in his dorm room. But Dutton had always been there, watching over the kid's shoulder, making sure he stayed on track. And when the moment had come to step in, Dutton had done what any good scientist would have done. Jack was just a kid; he was in no position to handle the ramifications of his discovery. Dutton had the reputation and the respect to make the most of the miracle cure. The scientific world *expected* something like this from him, and he did not intend to let them down.

A second later he stepped into the dark front hall of his home. He pulled off his weathered suede jacket and dropped it on the floor, then headed toward the living room. He knew there was a bottle of Glenfiddich hidden beneath one of the couches, a leftover from his older brother's recent visit. Evan was a recovering alcoholic and did not understand that even social drinkers sometimes liked to drink at home. Just as he didn't understand that gambling was an intellectual sport, a show of mathematical control, not a sickness. That was the way it was with Evan; everything had to be black and white.

Dutton breathed heavily as he stepped through the entrance to the dark living room. He thought about what Evan would say if he had known the real story behind the *Science* article. No doubt he would have condemned his own brother. He would have called his actions corrupt and unfair. He certainly wouldn't have understood.

Dutton slowed his pace, his eyes trained on the couch just a few yards away. Well, was it fair that Jack Collier had come up with the idea in the first place? Was it fair that Dutton had landed twice on the short list for the Nobel, never quite making the grade, while some punk kid from an alabaster ghetto stumbled into greatness at the age of twenty-three?

Dutton's thoughts were interrupted by a sudden crunching sound, and he froze. It took him a few seconds to gauge where the noise had come from. He finally looked down toward the rug—and something sparkled up at him. *Broken glass.*

Dutton's eyes widened. He felt a cool breeze pulling at his silk shirt, and he turned toward the window. The window was wide open, a section of the glass pane missing.

"Oh, fuck!" Dutton raced across the living room, nearly colliding with one of his antique couches. He reached the stairs and leapt upward, his knees crying out at the effort. He had never been much of an athlete, and since his forties his body had softened considerably; now his charm was all in his chiseled jaw and his green eyes. By the time he reached the second floor, his eyes were blurry from the effort, his cheeks flushed.

Barely breathing, he barreled down the hallway. His stomach dropped as he approached the open doorway that led to his study. He was sure he had shut the door when he had left for Foxwoods two days ago. He dove through the threshold of the study then came to a dead stop.

"Fuck! Fuck! Fuck!" The oil painting was lying face down on his desk, and the safe was wide open. Whoever had broken into his home had known exactly where to look. Dutton pressed his fists against his eyes, cursing himself. God only knew how many young women he had told about his stash. God only knew how many whispered rumors of the university idol's gambling treasure had spread across campus. It was ridiculously stupid, but Dutton had never been able to control his tongue, especially around irrelevant young women.

Shoulders sagging, he stumbled forward. When he got to the other side of his desk, he paused again, his eyebrows rising. There were still many stacks of hundreds inside the safe. *Who the hell would break into his home, crack a safe, and leave money inside?* It didn't make any sense. Slowly, he began counting the remaining stacks.

A minute later he stepped back, his thoughts swirling. Exactly twenty-five stacks were missing: $250,000. The thief had left $1,750,000 behind. It was utterly bizarre. Dutton felt like shouting for joy. He was still a rich, rich man. It didn't make any sense—but there it was, right in front of him.

The question remained, who had broken into his home? What sort of fool would leave behind so much money? And what the hell could Dutton do about the burglary? The two million dollars were unreported earnings from twenty years of gambling. He had never declared the money to the IRS, had never paid a penny of taxes on the stash. He couldn't call the police; he couldn't even mention the theft to his own brother.

He paused, now facing his desk. His gaze had drifted downward, to the oil painting lying face down on the mahogany. Sticking out from under the painting was the edge of a glossy magazine.

Curious, Dutton reached forward and slid the magazine free. He looked at the cover, and his heart froze.

"You goddamn piece of shit. I should have guessed."

Jack Collier hadn't gone home. Jack Collier had broken into his study and stolen $250,000 from his safe. Why he hadn't taken the rest, Dutton could only guess. Maybe something had scared him off. Maybe he was planning to return. It didn't matter. For a kid like Jack, $250,000 was a king's ransom. And there was nothing Dutton could do about the theft. Jack was smart, that was for sure, a regular fucking genius.

Suddenly, Dutton had a horrible thought. What if Jack was after more than money? There was no way the kid could prove that he was the real source of the miracle cure; Dutton had made sure of that. But Jack could still destroy what he had created.

Horrified by the thought, Dutton headed for the door.

The first thing Dutton noticed as he stepped through the open air lock was the smell: gaseous, similar to methane, but more noxious than anything he had ever smelled before. The scent seemed almost liquid, permeating every inch of air. As Dutton moved through the aisles of his former lab, the scent grew even stronger.

What the hell had Jack done? Lit some sort of sulfur bomb? Vandalized the lab? Dutton grimaced, covering his mouth and nose with his silk sleeve. He wouldn't put it past the kid. He had read Jack's file; he knew all about Jack's childhood. His juvenile record had been part of the reason it had been so easy to make the plagiarism rap stick. In fact, Jack's record had been Dutton's inspiration to get him kicked out of Harvard in the first place. The kid was a fuck-up after all.

Dutton turned a corner, winding deeper into the maze. The smell became so strong his gag reflex began to react. He heaved, swallowing down bile, but still he forced himself forward. He maneuvered around the last corner, sliding past a pair of steel sinks, then turned to face the sample refrigerator—and his eyes went wide.

He blinked, both hands racing to cover his mouth. *Holy mother of god!* His throat constricted, his lungs frozen. He stumbled back, staring. "Jesus Christ!"

There were two bone white skeletons lying on the floor just a few feet in front of him. One of the skeletons was curled into a fetal position, its back against the steel refrigerator. The other was jackknifed against a marble counter, arms splayed out at its sides. Both skeletons were garbed in light blue scrubs and white lab coats. Neither had the slightest hint of flesh or muscle, not even an inch of human skin. They looked as though they had been scoured clean.

For a brief second, Dutton wondered if it was some sort of sick joke. And then he saw the hair. Next to the skeleton lying against the refrigerator, a pile of beautiful, long, blonde strands. Dutton recognized the golden hair. He had run his fingers through it, had smelled its fragrance. *Jill Conway's hair*.

Realization flickered down Dutton's spine. He shifted his gaze to the skull, to the craters where Jill's eyes used to be. A thick, mucouslike liquid dripped from one of the sockets. There was a quiet hissing, and tiny bubbles appeared in the surface of the mucous.

Dutton's mind went blank with fear. He spun away from the horrible sight and dove forward, crashing into a rack of test tubes. Glass exploded in front of him but he barreled on, oblivious. His mouth was wide open, a scream caught in his throat. He careened through the maze, taking the turns at full speed. As he closed in on the open air lock, he inadvertently caught sight of the blackboard hanging from the nearby wall. There was something written on the dark slate, a scrawl in bright blue chalk. *My God!*

Dutton's knees gave out, and he crashed to the floor,

staring up at the blue scrawl. His lips trembled as he
read the words again and again.

> *It's called karma, Professor.*
> *I hope it eats you alive.*

FIVE

"Could be worse, Dr. Ross. I could be home with the family, like last Thanksgiving. Thank God for the FBI." Martin Caufield winked as the elevator doors whiffed open. Tyler Ross looked past him at the chaos engulfing the basement hallway, and a painful expression swept across her nordic features. *Here we go again.*

She placed a hand on the burly tech's shoulder. "If this is the better option, Mr. Caufield, I hope I never meet your family."

She stepped past him out of the elevator, squaring her shoulders. A palpable hush swept through the crowd, heads turning in her direction. Tyler felt a rush of nerves, but her face remained stiff, her gaze practiced. At five-eleven, she had long ago grown used to the attention, though at the moment, the stares had more to do with her status than her stature. The shiny silver badge affixed to the lapel of her dark gray, cashmere jacket shone like a beacon in the hall filled with white lab coats, green tech jumpsuits, and standard blue police uniforms. As usual, Tyler outranked everyone within view, which meant she could never blend in—even if she had wanted to. It didn't help that she was a woman. A *tall* woman. With cropped blonde hair and azure eyes.

"The control board is just about ready," Caufield said, coming out of the elevator behind her. He was a large man, short in comparison to Tyler but built like a fire hydrant. His face was round and wide, his features puggish. "The probe is inside, fully operational."

Tyler nodded, getting her bearings. There were at least thirty people in the hallway, most of them technicians from the FBI's Sci-Ops Department. A handful of uniformed officers from the Boston Police Department watched from a few yards down the hall, keeping a healthy distance from the plastic tenting that had been wrapped around the open air lock entrance. Next to the sheer transparent sheets was the control board, a rectangular steel cabinet set atop eight fixed iron wheels. The board bristled with levers, dials, and buttons, and rising out of the center of the steel cabinet was a three-foot-tall TV screen. Tyler noted that the screen was the newest "flat" model, barely an inch thick. At the moment, the screen glowed a soft blue, broken only by a tiny red time code in the bottom right corner.

"What about the professor?" Tyler asked, as she approached the board. A pair of technicians in matching jumpsuits moved aside, giving her a direct line to the screen. "Michael Dutton—the man who found the bodies?"

Caufield pointed toward the ceiling. "We've got him in a makeshift quarantine on the third floor, along with a campus security guard and two officers from the BPD. They're the only ones who've been inside the lab; as per procedure, we sealed it up as soon as we got the call from the local bureau. All four subjects have already gone through preliminary questioning—"

"I read the file on the airplane," Tyler interrupted. Twice, actually, first in the limo that had rushed her from Quantico to the Dulles airfield, then again during the short shuttle flight into Logan. "Pretty horrifying."

She said the words without emotion. At thirty-six, she had been with the FBI's Biological Investigation Unit for nearly ten years. She did not like to think of herself as hardened, but it was impossible to do what she did without gaining a certain *perspective*. Lately, however, she had noticed that it was becoming more and more difficult to keep her edge, especially when the cases went bad. Her last serious boyfriend had told her she was softening with age, but age had only a small part to do with the change.

"Well, it's much worse up close," Caufield said, and Tyler was immediately troubled by his tone. An ex–football player from the Deep South, the burly tech was far from squeamish. "I think we're definitely looking at something new."

Tyler controlled her thoughts as they reached the control board. Caufield slid next to her, his thick hands immediately jumping to the levers and dials. A few seconds later the screen shivered and the blue glow was replaced by a black-and-white picture. The resolution was excellent, far clearer than any commercially available video.

"The probe is about ten feet from the discovery point," Caufield said, unlocking a plate halfway up the console. A three-inch-long joystick popped upward on pneumatic springs. "The place is a fucking labyrinth. It was a bitch navigating the sucker this far. The old 280 would never have made it. But the 290 is one sweet piece of machinery. Thank God for the IRA."

Tyler smiled. Caufield was always thanking God for something. In this case, Tyler had to agree. The probe was probably the only good thing that had come out of the decades of violence in Ireland. Basically, the probe was a tank-style robot, about the size and shape of a small kitchen trash can. Radio-controlled and armored in titanium, the probe sat atop four separate treads and contained thirteen state-of-the-art rotary propulsion motors. It was outfitted with two fiber-optic video cameras and a retractable, robotic arm. The probe had originally been designed by the British military for bomb defusement, and models were now in use in nearly every city in the United States. Tyler's predecessor, Arthur Feinberg—now an assistant director in the Bureau and her direct supervisor—had been the first to suggest the probe's use in biohazard situations such as this. Like all of Feinberg's suggestions it had made perfect sense; there was no reason to put an agent at risk when a few million dollars of steel and microchips could do the task just as well. The actual sample collecting still had to be done by agents in Racal bodysuits, but the initial investigation could be done from as far as a hundred yards away.

"She's all yours," Caufield said, gesturing toward the joystick. Tyler noted that the hallway had gone still behind her, every eye trained on the flat screen. At least the attention was no longer on her. Her shoulders relaxed as she touched the joystick with her fingers.

The screen trembled, the probe jerking forward. It took a few seconds before Tyler had the machine moving smoothly, at a pace slightly slower than a gentle stroll. The lab opened up on the screen in front of her, and she did her best to take in every detail. The setting was extremely familiar; she had spent most of her adult life in biology labs. First during her college years at Yale, then during two years of graduate school at Columbia. After that had come her stint at the FBI Academy in Quantico, nearly four years spent huddled in Arthur Feinberg's specialized laboratory on the sixth floor of the Sci-Ops building. There was something warm and comforting about the narrow aisles on the screen in front of her.

The warmth evaporated as the probe skirted around a tight corner and came to a dead stop. Tyler yanked her hand back from the joystick, her eyes widening.

Caufield had been right; it was much worse in person. The two skeletons splayed out on the floor of the lab were straight out of a horror movie. Completely devoid of flesh, shorn of muscles and organs. The only potentially organic material dripped from the eye sockets of the two skulls, a viscous, bubbling liquid. Something dark, of unknown origin.

Tyler rubbed her own eyes, tension riding up her spine. On the outside, the change was imperceptible; but inside, she could feel herself winding into knots, like a spring feeding on the tension, tightening with each twist in the developing case.

She quickly reminded herself that the entire hall was watching. It was up to her to set the tone of the investigation. She had to remain strong on the outside—the tough FBI agent they had all grown to respect. She exhaled, slowing her pulse. "Okay, we'll need a sample of the secretion coming out of those sockets, also bone chips and marrow taps. And we need to sequence everything that's inside that refrigerator, especially anything bacteriological."

Caufield nodded, parroting her orders to a pair of techs in lab coats behind him. The Racal bodysuits were waiting in a changing room on the first floor, along with sample containers and sequencing equipment. Tyler knew that the next few hours were crucial; in a case like this, the answers came quickly or they didn't come at all.

She turned back to the skeletons, breathing deeply, trying to imagine what sort of microbe could have done this. She knew all about Professor Dutton's work; in fact, she had read the *Science* article long before she had ever gotten the call from the Boston Bureau. Dutton's work was the reason she had come to the scene in person, rather than giving the case to one of her underlings at Quantico.

Staring at the bone white victims, she had a sinking suspicion that Dutton's miracle cure had just gone seriously ugly. That thought affected her more than she'd ever let Caufield or any of the others know. She set her jaw, then used the joystick to move the probe a few feet closer to the nearest skeleton.

"You ever seen anything like this?" Caufield asked, his voice low. Tyler shook her head. She had seen many things in her past ten years with the FBI. She had watched people die in horrible ways, their bodies tortured by viruses, bacteria, and chemicals. But she had never seen a victim reduced to nothing but bone.

"Do we have an ID on the victims?"

Caufield nodded. "The security guard checked their scrub pockets before we had a chance to seal the place up. Both of the victims were Ph.D. students who worked in the lab. The male skeleton—the one by the counter— was a kid named Brad Kershaw. Big kid, good-looking; his family's from Belmont. He was barely twenty-six years old."

"And the other victim?" Tyler asked, her chest heavy. Her younger brother was just a few years older than the two dead scientists. She quickly pushed the thought away: The minute this truly became personal, she would have to walk away—from the case and probably from the FBI.

Caufield cleared his throat. "Well, here's where things get interesting. The victim by the refrigerator was female, five-seven, twenty-five years old. Her name was Jill Conway."

Tyler did not recognize the name. She glanced at Caufield, waiting for him to continue.

"Jill Conway was the daughter of Tom Conway, *Senator* Tom Conway."

Tyler leaned back from the control panel. *Shit.* Senator Conway was a third-term Republican from California, an extreme conservative with strong ties to the religious right. He was a decorated officer, who had served in both Korea and Vietnam—a huge supporter of the military, both financially and through his Senate votes. He was also a personal friend of Hale Fairbanks, the director of the FBI.

"Well, I guess we know what this means," Tyler said. The burly tech nodded, his thick lips curling down at the corners.

"Eyes in the sky."

It was departmental code for the cases with involvement from the highest levels. Tyler had to assume that Quantico was going to be watching her investigation very carefully; furthermore, there was a good chance Senator Conway would get personally involved. It was the worst way to begin a case, and Tyler felt the rope winding tighter inside of her.

"All right," she said, finally turning away from the television screen. She noted that the crowd quickly went back to work, preparing for the sample collection and the full-scale sanitation process. The lab would be sprayed with over twenty different antiviral and antibiological agents, then bombarded with radiation. "Let's get this investigation going. I assume we've got a War Room set up somewhere in the building?"

It was FBI procedure to work as closely to the site of a biothreat as possible. Caufield stretched his arms above his head, the packed muscle in his shoulders shifting under his green jumpsuit. "Fifth floor, a converted conference room. The coffee and donuts arrived over an hour ago. I'm guessing the turkey won't show until mid-afternoon."

Tyler laughed, letting out some of her internal tension. "On Christmas the donuts were red and green. I wouldn't expect much more effort from the Bureau on Thanksgiving. Has my opposite number arrived?"

As per protocol, a case like this was headed by two team leaders. Tyler was in charge of the scientific aspects of the case; her job was to figure out exactly what had happened in the lab and whether it was a continuing threat. It was her partner's job to take care of any criminal issues that arose. In other words, he was in charge of apprehending the suspect or suspects and bringing the responsible parties to justice.

"Waiting for you upstairs," Caufield said. "His staff has been setting up shop since five A.M."

"Good," Tyler noted. "It sounds like we'll get off to a running start."

"Well, I wouldn't celebrate just yet."

Tyler did not like the change in his voice. "Mr. Caufield?"

Caufield sighed. "They've brought in Vincent Moon. Flew him here on the director's private jet with a dozen of his black-suited goons."

Tyler closed her eyes. She had never met Vincent Moon, but he was a Quantico legend. In fact, his reputation extended well beyond the walls of FBI headquarters. If even one-tenth of the stories were true, Tyler could think of no greater mismatch for a case like this. *Christ, this is just what I need.*

"Tell Mr. Moon I'm on my way." She sighed, turning

toward the elevator. "And ask him not to shoot anybody until I get there."

Caufield had not been kidding about the black suits. Tyler felt incredibly out of place as she crossed the threshold of the L-shaped conference room on the fifth floor. There were fourteen agents huddled around the long, steel table that took up the main leg of the room—all men, all impeccably groomed, and all wearing black. The oldest looked to be about thirty, and more than a handful seemed just out of training. Kids, really, some younger than the two victims in the basement laboratory. Their fresh, excited faces seemed a stark contrast to the bone white skulls lying against the laboratory floor.

Tyler shook the thought away, stepping farther into the conference room. The place was brightly lit, two fluorescent ceiling panels accentuating the natural orange light spilling in through the enormous picture window that took up most of the far wall. Aside from the steel table and a refreshment counter beneath the window, the room was devoid of furniture. Tyler had made it halfway to the nearest group of agents when a gruff voice jabbed at her from the far end of the steel table.

"Welcome to the War Room, Dr. Ross. If you'd take your seat, we can finally begin."

Tyler was caught off guard by the officious tone, and she quickly shifted her gaze across the rectangular room. She immediately caught sight of the well-built man standing at the head of the table. He was at least six foot three, balding, with wire-rimmed glasses and a jutting, square jaw. He looked to be in his late forties to early fifties, and there was a slight stoop to his wide shoulders. Still, he was an impressive sight, built like a heavyweight boxer.

"Mr. Moon," Tyler acknowledged, crossing the room

toward the one empty chair at the opposite end of the long table. Despite Moon's brusque greeting, she decided to try to begin on the right foot. "It's a pleasure to finally meet you, though of course the circumstances could be better. I hope our two teams can work smoothly together to bring this case to a proper close."

Vincent Moon watched her from behind his glasses as she headed toward her seat. The other agents in the room had gone dead silent, well-trained dogs waiting for their master's cue. Finally, Moon nodded. "I'm sure we'll do just fine, Dr. Ross. I've read your file, and I'm confident in your abilities. I was especially impressed by your handling of the situation in Atlanta two months ago."

Tyler paused, only halfway into her seat. Two months ago she had headed up a team investigating a religious cult that had been stockpiling sarin nerve gas in warehouses just outside the Atlanta city limits. Barely three days into her investigation, she had learned that the cult was planning an attack on one of the city's largest indoor malls. She had been forced to order a raid on the cult's headquarters. Seven cult members had died in the gunfight that erupted, and two federal agents had been critically wounded. Tyler considered it one of the worst outcomes of her career. In fact, after Atlanta she had spent three weeks on personal leave, deciding whether or not it was time to move on to a different career. It was then that she had first noticed the changes going on inside of her—the general breakdown of the external walls that protected her from the pressures of her job.

For a brief moment, she wondered if Moon's comment had been meant as a jab. Then she realized that the compliment had been sincere. From what she knew about Moon, seven casualties meant nothing to him.

Moon flicked a hand toward one of the dark-suited

men seated to his left. "Let's bring Dr. Ross up to speed. Craig, distribute the updated file so we can get started."

In a flash, Moon's lackey was out of his seat, a stack of manila folders in his hands. He quickly moved around the table, handing a folder to each of the seated agents. Tyler watched him with curiosity; he was handsome, young, with bright blue eyes and a near crew cut—the kind of agent they photographed for the FBI recruitment brochures. According to the rumors, Moon handpicked his people barely two months into the first semester at Quantico, so he could better indoctrinate them to his way of doing business. His team was considered the most loyal and insulated of any team in the FBI.

As the young man reached Tyler's seat, she shifted her gaze to the bulge beneath the right side of his jacket. Her own Beretta 92F automatic was locked away in the safe in her hotel room. She would not strap it to her body unless the case deteriorated to the point where there was no alternative. Certainly, she would never have considered arriving armed to the War Room. The young man smiled at her, then placed a thick manila folder on the table in front of her.

Tyler tried to push her growing sense of anxiety away as she opened the folder and stared down at a stack of five-by-seven photographs. She recognized the first picture immediately; it was a close-up shot of the two skeletons in the basement lab, taken by the probe's high-resolution digital camera.

"Dr. Ross," Vincent Moon said, leaning back in his chair at the head of the table. "Please enlighten us. What the hell are we looking at?"

Tyler took a deep breath. Looking at the skeletons, she was only sure of one thing. Whatever had done this was hungry. *Ravenous.* She slowly shook her head. "It's much too early to say. My team has just started collecting samples from the scene."

Moon nodded impatiently. "This lab was the site of research involving a dangerous form of bacteria, isn't that right? A cancer cure created from a mutated strain of streptococcus A?"

Moon pronounced the word carefully, as if to emphasize the fact that this was not his area of expertise. Tyler laced her fingers together. "That's correct. Professor Dutton recently published groundbreaking research on the use of a mutated form of the bacteria that could seek and destroy cancerous tumors. According to Dutton's BPD interview, two petri dishes containing samples of his mutated strep were kept in the refrigerator seen in this photograph."

She stopped, unwilling to go any further. After Caufield had analyzed the samples from the scene, she'd have a better idea of what they were facing. Until then, she did not want to jump to any conclusions.

But Vincent Moon obviously wanted to press ahead. "Isn't strep A also known as flesh-eating bacteria?"

A murmur moved around the table, and Tyler quickly raised her hands. She wasn't going to let this turn into a panic session. "The popular media has sensationalized the condition considerably. It is true, however, that strep A is responsible for necrotizing fascitis—a destructive infection of skin, muscles, and fat. The disease usually presents as a violet discoloration, blistering, and eventual gangrenous state at the site of transmission. Certainly, strep A has never caused anything like what happened to the victims in the lab."

"But it has to be more than a coincidence," Moon continued to a chorus of nods from around the table. "This necrotizing fascitis—how is it spread?"

"Usually by direct contact with the skin of an infected

carrier or via aerosolized droplets from a carrier's nose or mouth. It can also pass directly from a culture sample; there have been a few reported cases of lab students contracting the disease from bacteria growing in agar."

Tyler paused, watching Moon digest the information. One of the agents to her right was tapping keys on a tiny laptop, while another scratched notes onto an electronic pad. Tyler felt her anxiety again begin to rise. "As I said before, it's much too early to come to any real conclusions—"

"But if you had to guess?" Moon asked. "Based on what you've seen so far?"

Tyler looked at the photograph of the two skeletons, her lips curling down. She hated to make guesses, but she knew she had to give Moon something. "It's possible that this is somehow related to strep A. But the bacterial activity has been enormously accelerated. And it's unlikely that this is a naturally occurring mutation; no microbe could change its behavior so drastically. We need to reinterview Professor Dutton—"

"Of course," Moon said, waving his hand. "As soon as we're done in here. Keep in mind, piecing together what happened in that lab is only half of this case."

Moon turned back to the manila folder. Tyler raised her eyebrows, annoyed. She did not like being cut off. She considered saying something, then decided it wasn't worth it. It seemed inevitable that she and Moon were going to butt heads repeatedly during the case, but she thought she might at least start out civilly.

She calmed herself, flipping to the next photograph. She immediately recognized the blackboard and the two-sentence scrawl of blue chalk. Her pulse roared as she reread the words. By itself, the cryptic note made little sense. But when added together with what had happened in the lab, the words became graphic and disturbing.

"Handwriting analysis checks out with Dutton's story," Moon said. "And we've already isolated four separate fingerprints at the scene."

He paused, then dramatically flipped to the next picture. He glanced around the table, his gaze skipping past Tyler. "And here, gentlemen, is our target."

Tyler turned to the next picture and found herself staring at a yearbook photograph of a waifishly handsome young man, with bright blue eyes and unkempt, dirty blond hair.

"Jack Collier," Moon continued, speaking in a near monotone. "Twenty-three years old. Recently expelled from Harvard's biology department for plagiarism. Don't let his choirboy looks fool you; this kid is no angel. Arrested twice for car theft, three times for B and E. Spent a week in juvenile detention in Patterson, New Jersey."

Tyler was barely listening, her attention pinned to the photograph in front of her. There was something compelling about Jack Collier, even beyond his looks. Tyler couldn't tell if it was anger, passion, or pain; but it was there, an intensity she could not immediately define. Jack Collier was no ordinary kid.

"According to Dutton," Moon said, holding Jack's photograph in front of him like a menu in a fancy restaurant, "Collier was intensely jealous of his professor's success. After his Ph.D. grants were rescinded, he made a number of threats—including a promise that he would somehow sabotage Dutton's research. It's obvious Jack Collier found a way to carry out that threat. In the process, he murdered two young scientists. He stole one of the petri dishes containing Dutton's mutated strep. And now he's on the run."

Tyler looked up from the photograph. She watched as Moon leaned forward, quietly conferring with the agent to his left. The War Room filled with sound, as the other members of Moon's team began to discuss the different aspects of their hunt. Tyler caught snippets of conversation, something about a national APB and FBI deployment in all major train stations, bus depots, and airports.

A sudden thought pricked at her: *This was moving way too fast.* Jack Collier was a kid, a few years younger than her brother. His life had been turned upside down—and sure, he was probably pretty angry about it. But did that make him a killer?

Tyler shifted in her seat, her gaze moving back to Collier's picture. She had read Dutton's interview with the Boston Police Department. She knew all about Collier's expulsion and his misdirected anger toward his professor. She also knew about his criminal record, if one could call it that. Collier had been thirteen years old, raised in a working-class neighborhood by a foster family. The kid had made mistakes, and he had paid for them. Then he had earned himself a free ride through Harvard University. Even if he *had* cheated his way into graduate school, did he really have the heart of a murderer?

Tyler didn't know. But she didn't like the direction the case was moving. Moon was jumping to a conclusion based entirely on Dutton's BPD interview—a conclusion with enormous implications. It just didn't seem right. They needed to slow down, to take this step by step.

"Hold on a moment," Tyler finally said, a little louder than necessary. She waited until the room had gone quiet before continuing. "Even if Jack Collier did somehow sabotage Michael Dutton's research, that doesn't automatically make him a killer. This could very well have been some sort of accident—"

"Dr. Ross," Moon interrupted her again, pushing back

from the table. "You've seen the note he left on the blackboard. Collier had been kicked out of Harvard. He threatened Dutton personally. He was out for revenge."

Tyler reached for the photograph of the two skeletons, her anger rising. If Moon kept cutting her off, she was going to jump down his throat. "You really believe *this* was intentional? How? You've already said that the forensics show there was nobody else in the room when this happened."

Moon shrugged his bearish shoulders. "Some sort of booby trap, I assume. Timed release or proximity. Now he's got the second petri dish with him, so that makes him armed and immensely dangerous."

Tyler squinted. The idea that Collier was carrying the petri dish around as some sort of bioweapon seemed one hell of an assumption. "And what evidence do you have to support this theory?"

Vincent Moon partially rose from his chair. It was obvious from his expression that he was not used to being challenged. The agents closest to him seemed to cower, their young faces darkened by his hulking shadow. "We have Collier's fingerprints. We have a very clear motive for revenge. And we have Collier's own confession, written in chalk on a blackboard at the scene of the crime: 'It's called karma, Professor. I hope it eats you alive.' We've got all the evidence we need."

Tyler felt her face getting hot. She did not like to be bullied. She also pushed herself out of her chair, rising to her full height. "We can place Jack Collier in the lab sometime before the two deaths. Beyond that, we've got nothing concrete. I agree that we need to bring Collier in for questioning, but it sounds like you're ready to convict him of murder."

Moon paused, surprised by her vehemence. "I would think that you, of all people, would resist sympathy in this case. Aside from murdering two of his classmates, this terrorist has purposefully sabotaged a miracle cancer cure. A lot of people are going to suffer because of Jack Collier."

Moon's eyes shifted for a brief second down toward Tyler's chest. Her cheeks automatically reddened, and she resisted the urge to yank her cashmere jacket closed. She wasn't sure what her FBI file contained about her six-month ordeal back in 1993, but it was none of Vincent Moon's business. Still, his comment had hit a nerve. Despite her attempts at objectivity, this case did affect her in a very personal way. But she refused to let her emotions cloud her investigation.

She finally responded, her voice low. "My personal life has nothing to do with this. I am a federal agent, the same as you. I'm only trying to keep our perspective trained on the facts of the case."

Tyler could tell by the silence in the room that her words were useless. Vincent Moon had been specifically brought into this because he *didn't* listen; that wasn't his job.

In FBI parlance, Moon was a shooter. He handled the roughest cases—the violent fugitives, the serial killers, the heavily armed terrorists. In over thirty-six cases, he had only made three clean apprehensions. The rest had involved body bags. There was no reason this case was going to be handled any differently.

Moon put his huge palms flat against the table. "Until someone proves otherwise, Jack Collier is a killer. He's murdered two people with an unidentified biological weapon. He is on the run, and he is dangerous. Now *those* are the facts of the case, Dr. Ross."

Tyler looked around the room, at Moon's eager young men in their matching black suits. Her internal spring had wound so tight, she felt like she was about to explode. She knew exactly what was going on. The Eyes in the Sky had stacked the deck from the very beginning. Tyler Ross and her team of Sci-Ops specialists were little more than window dressing. Vincent Moon was running the show. And that meant only one thing.

Guilty or not, Jack Collier wasn't going to get out of this alive.

SIX

"In just a few minutes, we will be entering New York's Penn Station. Please make sure you have all your belongings as you exit the train. ESPECIALLY YOU, WITH THE TWO HUNDRED AND FIFTY THOUSAND DOLLARS OF STOLEN MONEY . . ."

Jack lurched forward, his eyes snapping open. For a brief second he had no idea where he was. Then the soft rumble of the train's wheels against the tracks chased the last vestiges of his sleep away. He made sure the backpack was still balanced against his lap, one strap tied around his left arm. Satisfied, he glanced around the crowded car, his vision adjusting to the dull orange lighting.

The train had already entered the labyrinth of tunnels that led into the station, and people filled the aisles, pulling bags down from the overhead racks. It was crowded for a red-eye, even on Thanksgiving morning; Jack had been lucky to get two seats to himself for the five-hour trip. Still, he was surprised he had managed to fall asleep. The few paranoid minutes he had spent waiting for the train to pull out of South Station had been the longest of his life. Even now, he half expected the train to lunge to a sudden stop, armed SWAT teams crashing in through the windows.

He shook the ridiculous thought away. Even if Professor Dutton had returned from Foxwoods and discovered the missing money, there was nothing he could do about it. He sure as hell wasn't going to call the police. Jack was free and clear, and the farther he got from Harvard Square, the more likely it was he'd never see Dutton's face again.

Jack stretched his long legs beneath the seat in front of him. Fuck Dutton. *Fuck everyone.* He felt good, for the first time in years. He was well rested, free, and rich. More importantly, he had begun his search for Angie. After a long, tortured year, he was going after her. And it felt *right.*

Still, he had a long way to go before he'd get to hold her in his arms again. Angie wasn't in New York—Jack was certain of that. She hated the city. But he was almost as certain that she had *been* in New York; her brother, Justin, had an apartment in the city, and she would have gone to him for money before heading anywhere else. Not that Justin Moore had any money to speak of; as far as Jack knew, he had never held a steady job in his life.

But he was Angie's big brother, and also Jack's childhood friend. She'd have gone to him and that made him Jack's first source of information. The faster he got to Justin, the closer he'd be to finding Angie. And he had to find her soon—before the strep in his backpack started to die.

With the money he had stolen from Dutton's safe, he could have booked a first-class airplane ticket and saved himself four precious hours. But Jack wasn't stupid; and even though he was on a deadline, he didn't intend to take any chances. You had to show your ID to get on an airplane; and if you paid cash for a ticket, people were likely to remember you. The Amtrak was different. You could walk through Penn Station in your underwear, and nobody would remember you the next day.

The liquid squeal of pneumatic brakes interrupted Jack's thoughts, and he reached under his seat for his duffel bag. Another minute and the train would enter the station. He slung the backpack over his shoulder, then rose to his feet. The floor trembled beneath his boots, and he imagined the great steel wheels throwing sparks off the tracks. He turned toward the window to his right and watched blue light play off the stone tunnel wall. His face went numb in the glow. It was a familiar feeling, and it had nothing to do with what he was running from or where he was running to. It was something much simpler than that.

Jack's father had welded tracks for Amtrak for more than twenty years. A French Canadian immigrant, he had spent most of his life in the steel foundry just outside of Patterson. Honest, brutal work, for which he had an immigrant's pride. Jack was quite certain he would have happily welded tracks for another twenty years if one of the damn things hadn't fallen off a crane and cracked his skull open.

Jack blinked as the numbness turned into something worse—a memory. It was a Friday, two days before his seventh birthday. They had brought Jack home early from school, and he couldn't figure out why there were so many people milling around his house. Then he had found his mother, sitting at the kitchen table. She was crying, which was impossible because she never cried. Standing next to her, hand on her shoulder, was the man from Amtrak. He had a check in his pocket for ten thousand dollars. That was what your family got when a track fell on your head.

At the time, it had seemed like a lot of money. Six months later, Jack's mother had her first heart attack and her first extended hospital stay. The ten thousand dollars was gone in a matter of weeks, and Jack's mother didn't last much longer. He ended up being handed over to foster care without so much as a suitcase.

Jack blinked again, another flash of bright blue sparks. The glow was like an ache, deep behind his eyes. God damn it, he had lost so much already.

His body rocked forward as the train finally slowed to a complete stop. The line of passengers started down the aisle, and Jack allowed himself to be swept forward. He could feel the dank tunnel air, heavy with the scent of New York's underground. His eyes narrowed as he reached the end of the car and stepped out onto the crowded platform. There were two hundred people between him and the escalator that led up to the main floor of the station. The anonymity warmed him, and the numbness thawed away. His mind came alive, and he made a snap decision. He suddenly slid to his right, angling his way through the crowd.

A tall man in a gray suit glared at him as he shoved past, and he fought the urge to glare back. He didn't want to make eye contact with anyone who might remember him. He kept his head down until he reached the edge of the platform. The concrete dropped away suddenly into a deep gully containing another set of tracks. On the other side of the gully was a cement maintenance stairwell. The stairwell looked deserted, and there was no sign of any oncoming trains. *Perfect.*

Jack waited until the crowd had passed behind him, then carefully lowered himself down into the track gully. The hair on the back of his neck stood upright as he waited for someone to shout at him, but nobody was watching; he was alone with his paranoia. He moved quickly across the tracks, ignoring the sound of the rats scurrying out of the way of his boots. His nostrils filled with the scent of burnt oil, and a cool, underground breeze licked his flesh. Ahead of him, the dark tunnel looked like an open, toothless mouth, and he wondered where it led. Probably Philadelphia, beyond that Washington, beyond that a thousand places where you could easily disappear, especially if you had money to burn.

When he found Angie, that's exactly what they'd do. Take the money and disappear. Maybe end up on a tropical beach somewhere; Mexico or an island. Somewhere far away.

Jack reached the maintenance stairwell and leapt quietly up the steps. The stairs wound around like a convulsing snake, then ended in a propped-open steel door. The heavy sound of Penn Station echoed through the stairwell: a thousand mingled voices, squealing baggage carts, and scuffling shoes—a symphony of mass transit. Above the bray came the train announcements, a voice reminiscent of rusty gears: "Bridgewater, Track Thirteen. New Jersey Coast, Track Twelve. Washington, Track Eleven. Now arriving Track Ten, Boston, Massachusetts."

Jack pushed open the door, his gaze darting through the sea of people. He saw the sign for Track Ten hanging above the surging escalator, barely twenty yards away. He recognized a few people from his train as they rose, bleary eyed, from the underground. He was about to turn away when he saw something that made his heart freeze.

There was a pair of uniformed police officers standing a few feet from the top of the escalator. Not transit cops, the real deal, NYPDs. Next to the two cops stood a large, well-shouldered man in a dark suit. The man was scanning the faces coming off the escalator, all the while talking into a cellular phone. He looked young, barely older than Jack, with a crew cut and serious blue eyes. When he shut the cell phone and shoved it back into his pocket, his jacket fluttered and Jack caught sight of a leather holster strap.

Christ. The man in the dark suit was either a federal agent, a bounty hunter, or an NYPD detective. He was scrutinizing the passengers arriving from Boston, with the two NYPDs as backup.

Jack's face drained. Was the black-suited man looking for him? It seemed impossible. He reminded himself that this was New York—the fugitive capital of the world. Still, he was glad he had crossed the tracks to the maintenance stairwell. He did not like the nervous expressions on the cops' faces or the way their hands rested on the butts of their holstered .38s. Whoever they were looking for, they had been told he was dangerous. And there was no creature more dangerous than a scared New York cop.

Jack moved quickly in the opposite direction, angling along the back wall of the main waiting area. The station opened up ahead of him into a cavernous atrium, filled with hundreds of people. The morning travelers were focused on the big Amtrak board hanging from the ceiling in the center of the vast room; nearly every eye was trained on the revolving tiles that announced the tracks a minute before the PA system croaked to life. Those sixty golden seconds were priceless; they meant the difference between a comfortable seat with a window and a view, and a six-hour trip lodged like a human clot in an overcrowded aisle. Jack felt invisible as he wound beneath the board; his backpack could have been a machine gun and still no one would have noticed.

Halfway across the room, Jack glanced back. He could no longer see the uniformed cops or the man in the black suit. The crowd had closed behind him, an ocean of urban migrants. Most were college age, dressed in sweats, jackets, and jeans. Jack blended right in: ratty

Levi's, brown work boots, gray sweatshirt, thick gloves, and an oversized tan windbreaker. As he continued forward, he tried his best to forget what he was carrying, to walk with the same sense of careless ease as the kids around him. Criminals got caught when they acted like criminals; the key was to convince yourself that you hadn't committed a crime at all.

Jack smiled as he reached the far side of the waiting area. Fitting, that he was dredging up Justin Moore's advice on criminal etiquette; especially considering that the last time he had followed Angie's brother's advice, they had both ended up in Juvenile Hall. Back then Jack had worshipped Justin, had wanted to be just like him.

Jack sighed as he crossed through the wide entrance to the station's public bathroom. The bathroom was shaped like the hollowed-out inside of a horseshoe, tiled in porcelain and reeking of antiseptic cleansers. There was a row of sinks to the right and a dozen box-shaped urinals to the left. Most of the urinals were occupied; a homeless man in tattered clothes slept peacefully beneath the last three, his body wrapped in a half-dozen dirty blankets. Someone had dropped a five-dollar bill on the floor in front of him, and now it was covered in wet footprints, molded to the porcelain tiles by a thin film of grime and urine.

Jack headed past the last urinal to the stable of stalls that lined the back of the bathroom. The first three were locked, the fourth open but obviously broken, the air emanating from the rectangular space thick with the scent of old shit, puke, and God only knew what else. Jack skipped the next two, finally choosing the last available booth.

Once inside, he shoved his gloves into his pockets, then hung his backpack from the hook on the door. Crouching in the confined space, he delicately propped his duffel on the tops of his boots. He lowered his pants down around his ankles and sat gingerly on the open toilet seat, trying not to think about the army of germs finding solace in the warm cracks between his epidermal cells. Once you started down that path, it was a short hop to OCD and, beyond that, schizophrenia. The world was a dirty place; your ass wasn't supposed to stay clean.

Someone was humming a few stalls down, something Jack recognized but couldn't quite name. The man's baritone harmonized with the sound of the duffel's zipper. Jack dug beneath a second pair of Levi's and retrieved a small black notebook. He opened the notebook against his bare knees, then leafed through a handful of regional U.S. maps that were paper-clipped to the front page. He had ripped the maps out of half of the atlases in Widener Library, assuming that he'd probably need them. Before she got sick, Angie had often talked about traveling west; it was something they were going to do together. Jack assumed it was something she had ended up doing alone.

Jack's chest grew heavy, and his fingers moved beneath the atlases to a postcard that was clipped to the edge of the notebook. He pulled the postcard loose and looked at the picture on the cover. Two kittens in a basket, mischievous gleams in their eyes. A sappy, sentimental, ten-cent piece of crap that sent daggers straight into his heart. He turned the postcard over.

The postmark was from Chicago, Illinois, and the date was a little over six months ago. There was no return address, no signature, no name. But Jack had known the minute he had seen the kittens who it had come from:

I'm still okay, and I miss you. Sometimes I think it was a mistake to leave. Sometimes I hope you haven't

*moved on, found someone else. Sometimes I pretend
that I'm not dying, that I'll be coming home any day
now.*

I love you, Jack

Jack's fingers shook as he placed the postcard back
into the notebook. She was such a fool. Did she really
believe he was going to move on? Find someone else?

*How do you chase moths, when you've held a butter-
fly in the palm of your hand?*

He pictured her as he had last seen her, asleep in his
bed the morning before she disappeared. Her long, sable
hair, her full, serpentine lips, her long body curled beneath the blankets like a fragile child. He was supposed
to have been able to protect her. He had promised her
that much when she had followed him to Harvard.

Jack tried not to think as he turned back to the maps,
shifting through the pages until he found New York
City. He searched out a junction of two streets in Chelsea, maybe ten minutes from where he was squatting.
He had gotten Justin's address from Angie's diary before
he had sealed it in the box with the rest of her belongings. The box was in a corner of the basement of his
apartment building in Cambridge; maybe he and Angie
would send for it one day. Then again, they wouldn't
need to. With Dutton's money, Jack would buy her
everything she needed. Brand-new clothes, new shoes, a
new diary, maybe a pair of kittens in a little fucking
basket . . .

Jack felt the tears running freely down his cheeks. His
hands balled into fists and he cursed at himself. Then he
cursed at Angie. Why the hell did she have to leave? He
could have tried to be strong. *He could have tried.*

He rubbed the tears away. No, Angie was right. If she
had stayed, he would have died with her. And he would

certainly have never found his miracle cure.

Jack took a deep breath, then closed the notebook and returned it to the duffel bag. He stood, flushed the john, then quickly fixed his pants. It was time to get moving. He slung his backpack over his shoulder and hurried out of the stall, nearly colliding with a middle-aged businessman in a light blue suit. The man was overweight and bald, his thick jowls glistening with sweat. He glared at Jack, gesturing rudely with his hands.

"Watch where you're going, asshole."

"Sorry," Jack mumbled, pushing past. He could feel the man's eyes burning holes in the back of his neck, but he didn't turn around. "Have a nice shit, asshole."

This was New York, after all.

SEVEN

Steve Myers slammed the stall door shut behind him. The nerve of some people. Fucking pretty boy, traipsing around the city like he owned the place. Who the hell did that kid think he was anyway? And why did they make these stalls so damn small?

Myers grunted as he struggled out of his jacket, his elbows bouncing against the steel walls on either side. Someone cursed at him from the stall to the right, and he cursed right back. City was full of assholes. The place was going straight to hell, despite Mayor Giuliani, the Wop. Teach manners to these animals? *Yeah, right.*

The jacket finally came free, and Myers hung it from the hook on the door. Then he started on his belt buckle. The clasp was some strange European design, and it took him a minute to figure out how the damn thing worked. His wife had given him the belt last night, a belated forty-sixth birthday present, something she had picked up in one of those fancy stores on Madison. He hated the thing; he knew it was another one of her stupid attempts to dress him up like her hip downtown friends, the long-haired fags who worked with her in the art gallery on Prince. Myers was only thankful it was Thanksgiving and that the offices at Morgan were closed, along with the market. He would have been laughed right off the trading floor.

He finally got the clasp open and yanked his pants past his knees. He grimaced as he caught site of his thighs; huge, pasty white, and crinkled like cottage cheese. He kept promising himself that he'd get to the gym, but there was never any time. The longer he waited, the more daunting it seemed. He had been gaining weight at a steady pace since his college football days, his body expanding like one of those floats from the Macy's parade. Myers grunted, picturing himself floating down Fifth Avenue, tethered to a bunch of idiots in oversized Santa Claus suits—with his wife's huge, fag belt buckle exposed for all the world to see. Just his luck, he'd run into some self-absorbed pretty boy float coming in the other direction. *Have a nice shit, asshole.*

Myers heaved himself around in the confined space, then lowered himself onto the cold porcelain seat. The toilet creaked beneath him as he rested his elbows against his knees. His shirt clung sweatily to his back, and he knew he was going to look like crap by the time he reached his folks' house in Jersey. Still, it could have been worse. He could have been on his way to Florida with his wife. He could have spent the entire weekend with his in-laws in that asylum they called a retirement community.

Thank God the market was open on Friday. Otherwise, he'd be jammed in an airplane lavatory instead of luxuriating in the relative comfort of the Penn Station john. He grinned, shifting his weight against the seat— when something sharp dug into his left buttock.

"Fuck," he cursed. It felt like he had just sat on a piece of broken glass. He shifted again—and felt another sting, a few inches away from the first. Before he could react, the feeling multiplied, jabs of intense pain spreading across his naked flesh.

He leapt up from the toilet seat. Now the pain was spreading down the backs of his thighs. He reached around with both hands, swatting at his skin with his palms. His face turned pale as he realized that his skin didn't feel right. His ass and upper thighs felt pockmarked and sticky, as if chunks of his flesh had been torn away. He brought his palms quickly back in front of his face and watched, horrified, as a bright red sore erupted in the center of his right hand. *What the fuck?*

The pain went from acute to unbearable, daggers tearing into his flesh in more than a dozen different places. His mouth came open and a scream tore through his chest. The sound echoed through the bathroom, followed by a sudden, dramatic silence.

"Help me!" Myers shouted, "Oh my God, help me!"

He teetered forward, his ankles caught in his lowered pants. His shoulder hit the stall door and the steel buckled. The hinges flew off, and Myers crashed out into the bathroom. His knees hit the floor, and his body toppled forward. Now the sores were everywhere; growing red blotches covered every inch of visible skin. The pain was so horrible his muscles began to convulse, and he struggled forward, his elbows and knees jerking against the tiled floor. He could hear footsteps moving around him, but he couldn't tell if people were coming to help or running away. Using all his strength, he raised his head and realized there was something wrong with his eyes. The room had gone blurry; it was as though he was staring through melted glass. He could barely see the ring of people that had gathered around him, their faces pale, eyes wide.

"Jesus Christ," someone whispered.

"Please," Myers coughed through the pain. He

watched a man in a tan overcoat kneel next to him, felt
a hand against his shoulder. A second later, the hand
jerked away. But Myers barely noticed. His face crashed
back to the floor, and there was the distinct sound of
bone scraping against porcelain. Then the sound was
drowned out by screams.

It took Myers his last second of life to realize that the
screams were coming from someone else. . . .

EIGHT

The pig was curious. And hungry, of course, but he was always hungry. He rose up on his haunches, his snout twitching as he sniffed at the crisp, sterile air. There was something there, an intriguing, moldy scent; he couldn't tell yet if it was food. He grunted once, then brushed against the door to his chain-link cage. To his surprise, the door swung open.

Excited, he started quickly across the lab, his little hooves clicking against the shiny floor. He knew the lab was empty because he had watched the strange, bulky, bright orange creatures exit through the air lock on the other side. The creatures were unlike anything he had ever seen before; thankfully, they had left him alone in his cage, and he wasn't even sure they had known he was there. As far as he could tell, the creatures didn't have faces, and that meant they didn't have eyes, or ears, or even snouts. He wasn't sure how they stayed alive at all, but in truth, he really didn't care. It wasn't his problem. He was only a pig.

He paused as he reached the center of the lab, his pink ears perked into tiny triangular points. He could see the transparent plastic dish sitting on the low stool five feet away, right where the orange creatures had set it down just a few moments ago. He sniffed at the air again, noting that the moldy scent had grown stronger. His stomach gurgled; the smell was definitely coming from the dish, and that was a very good sign. He had been finding food in dishes of varying sizes and shapes for as long as he could remember.

His heart thudded with anticipation as he pattered ahead. He reached the stool, noting happily that it was set at just the right height. He sniffed at the air one more time, then leaned over the plastic dish.

There was something spread across the bottom of the dish, something yellow with white spots. It didn't look like anything the pig had eaten before. But he was a good sport. He was willing to try anything once.

He tilted his head to the side, reaching out with his tongue.

"Oh God," Professor Dutton whispered, his face turning white. "Oh dear God."

Tyler watched his reflection in the Plexiglas observation window. There was no doubt in her mind; his reaction was genuine. His body seemed to melt against the back wall of the small viewing room, his arms limp at his sides. His hair was drenched in sweat, and there were thick dark rings beneath his green eyes.

She turned her focus back to the scene on the other side of the window. There was a dull feeling in her stomach as she watched the pig jerking against the floor. Most of its skin was already gone, especially around the face and head. The eyes had melted away, replaced by the same black ooze they had found in the other victims. The bones of the animal's skull were clearly visible, ivory white in the fluorescent glow of the sealed lab.

In another twenty seconds the jerking stopped, and what was left of the pig lay still against the floor.

"Three minutes," Vincent Moon commented from Tyler's right. He was leaning against a metal stool, a sea of files spread out on a low counter behind him. His expression had not changed during the entire experiment; it was like looking at a face that had been chiseled into a stone wall. "One hundred and eighty seconds from first contact to total annihilation. Interesting way to cure cancer."

Tyler threw him a sharp look, but he had already gone back to his files. She turned back to Dutton, who was rubbing at his eyes with both hands. He looked like a man on the verge of collapse. Tyler felt a pang of sympathy. She could imagine what he was going through. He was watching everything he had worked for crumbling away right in front of him.

"Professor Dutton," she said, her voice soft, "do you need a moment? We could send down for some coffee."

Dutton looked at her, his eyes watery. She noticed that his lower lip was quivering, and she wondered if he had slept at all in the past twenty-four hours. Despite his frazzled state, he was a handsome man. Tall enough, with wide shoulders and windswept, auburn hair. Though he was at least fifteen years Tyler's senior, she did not deny a subtle attraction. She had always been a sucker for genius. And Dutton's brand of genius hit home in a very personal way.

She gently met his gaze, remembering the burst of excitement she had felt when she had read his article in *Science*. She had wondered if it was really possible—if this really was the end to the fear she had carried with her for the past six years. Like many times before, her hopes had been dashed; but that wasn't Dutton's fault. In a way, he was a victim, just like her.

"No thank you," he finally responded. "I've already

had enough coffee to kill a labful of rats. Right now, I'd just like to go home."

Tyler smiled. "I completely understand. But we feel it's best if we keep you under medical supervision for at least another twenty-four hours. In the meantime, I'd like to ask you a few more questions."

Dutton glanced at Moon, who was still buried in his files. "I've already told Agent Moon everything I know about Jack Collier. How he threatened to sabotage my research—"

"I know," Tyler interrupted, moving away from the observation window. She headed toward the bulbous water cooler that stood by the door, the only piece of furniture in the spartan room that had not been painted an institutional shade of yellow. "Actually, I'm more interested in your research itself."

Dutton eyed her as she filled a paper cone from the cooler's dispenser. "Are you a cancer specialist, Dr. Ross?"

Tyler saw Moon's head rise a few inches. She ignored him, offering Dutton the cone of water. He accepted with trembling fingers.

"Not exactly," Tyler answered. "My Ph.D. is in microbiology, and my FBI training is in the realm of biological hazards—viral as well as bacteriological. But I have a basic understanding of oncology, and I try to keep up with the latest advances in the fight against cancer."

She felt a tingle move down the right side of her chest as she said the words. She thought about adding more, perhaps a mention of her own experience with the disease, but decided it wasn't necessary. As she had told Moon, this wasn't personal.

She perched against a stool at the far end of the counter where Moon sat. She could hear Caufield and his techs moving about the lab on the other side of the observation window in their bulky orange Racal body-suits. Again, gathering samples. Her business was all about samples.

So far, the samples had told them very little about the deadly disease that had sprung from Michael Dutton's miracle cure. They knew it was bacteriological in nature, and that it was somehow related to Dutton's tailored strep A. It was incredibly fast-acting; the strange bacteria devoured live tissue at an alarming rate, feeding on cellular proteins while disrupting all major cell function. Upon exhausting its source of food, the bacteria quickly died, leaving behind a harmless, if repellant, conglomerate of bacterial shells—the black ooze they had found coming out of the victim's eye sockets. Caufield had come up with a simple theory for the location of the ooze; the skull contained the last pocket of edible tissue—the brain. In its ravenous quest for food, the bacteria followed the spinal column upward through the medulla, then rapidly starved to death once the brain had been consumed.

The ooze itself was not contagious; nor was there any living bacteria found on the skeletons or in the vicinity of the initial infection. In truth, the mutated bacteria was a very poor survivalist; it destroyed its prey so quickly, it did not have much of a chance to find a new source of food. The only real mode of infection seemed to be direct contact, as in the case of the pig and the contaminated agar base. As for the two lab students, the forensics implied that the infection had spread from one to the other by direct touch. Tyler had no reason to believe that secondary contact could distribute the bacteria. As far as she could tell, there had to be flesh-to-flesh contact.

From her research, Tyler still had no way of knowing whether or not Jack Collier was responsible for the mutated strep A or for the two deaths. But she certainly had not found any new evidence that would lead her to call it murder. According to Forensics, Collier had not been in the room at the time of the deaths. It's doubtful he could have known for sure that the two Ph.D. students would touch the petri dish—or, once infected, each other.

Still, if Collier had sabotaged the experiment, that made him criminally responsible. And if he had sabotaged the experiment in an attempt to injure or kill Dutton, then it was a case of murderous intent. For now, it was Tyler's job to figure out if a pissed-off twenty-three-year-old could really have manufactured such a deadly bacteria. To do that she had to start at the source of the deadly scourge.

"I've read your article in *Science*," she began, focusing her attention on Dutton's handsome face, "and I understand the basic science behind your cure. But I was hoping for a more detailed explanation of the tailored bacteria you created—the tumor-seeking strep A."

Dutton rubbed his jaw, glancing around the room. He seemed jittery, anxious, and Tyler again wondered how long he had gone without sleep. She knew from the BPD's interview that he had just returned from a weekend of gambling at a Connecticut Indian reservation when he had discovered the bodies. She also knew there was a chance he was hungover, having read Moon's file on him. As was standard procedure, in the past two hours Moon's lackeys had already begun an extensive background search, including preliminary phone interviews with many of Dutton's colleagues. Not surprisingly, there was a fair amount of jealousy among the renowned professor's coworkers, and a few had relished the opportunity to point out Dutton's flaws.

Tyler knew the man was no saint. He drank too much,

he gambled, and he had a penchant for female grad students. The university had been willing to overlook these vices because, in truth, they did not make him any less the genius. Strangely enough, his demons didn't make him any less attractive either.

Tyler had been drawn to bad boys most of her adult life. She assumed it had to do with her parents; her father, a former air force pilot who had investigated crashes for the National Transportation Safety Board (NTSB) until his retirement four years ago, had a reckless spirit that had never really been suited to family life. When her parents divorced during her senior year of college, Tyler had never wondered why; the real question was how her mother had tamed Billy Ross in the first place.

Tyler had inherited that urge to tame from her mother. It was probably the main reason she was still single at thirty-six. When she looked at Michael Dutton, she saw a project—and that bothered her as much as it turned her on. At her age, with what she did for a living, she didn't need a project.

She listened intently, trying to focus, as Dutton began to talk. "If you know anything about cancer, Dr. Ross, you understand that every form of the disease, from the most treatable brand of skin cancer to the most deadly astrocytoma of the brain, is a product of the same essential disorder: unrestrained cell growth. Cells reproducing without limitation, immortalizing themselves at the expense of the mortal tissue surrounding them. When these frenzied, savage cells reach a certain magnitude, we call them tumors. It's the tumors that define cancer. It's the tumors that kill."

Tyler shivered, her hands clenching involuntarily against her dark slacks. Even the word made her sick to her stomach. *Tumors*. When she closed her eyes, she could see them: black, pulsing masses of cells, tearing through innocent tissue as they grew, unstoppable and unrelenting. The fucking beasts would keep on growing until there was nothing left but tumor, spreading through the circulatory and lymphatic systems to different organs, building little circulatory systems of their own to keep them well fed, growing and growing and growing. "It has to come off," the surgeon had said. "There's no choice but to take it off." "Well, then, take the damn thing off," she had responded. *Take the damn thing off.*

Tyler felt her jaw tighten. She angrily forced the memory away. Damn it, this was not the time or place. "So that's where you focused your research: the tumors themselves."

Dutton nodded. His eyes drifted for a moment to the lab on the other side of the viewing window where one of the Racal-suited scientists was bending over the pig's skeleton. "My project actually took the form of two groundbreaking discoveries, and each was worth a Nobel Prize of its own."

He said it without the slightest hint of swagger. It was a fact, nothing more. Still, he seemed exhausted by the statement, as if speaking about his triumph was almost as draining as the triumph itself. He ran his fingers through his hair. "It begins with the immune system, Dr. Ross. Specifically, with killer T cells."

Tyler nodded impatiently. She wanted to show him that he didn't need to talk down to her, especially with Moon still sitting quietly in the room. At the same time, she realized, she wanted to impress him. "The T cells are the body's most important line of defense. Their job is to recognize and destroy anything foreign to the human body."

Dutton downed his cone of water, his full lips glistening as he crumpled the paper cup and dropped it to the floor. "Correct. T cells contain tiny receptors that fire off when they come into contact with specific ligands— sequences of proteins—present on the surface of foreign cells. In other words, when a T cell encounters a ligand that it recognizes as foreign, it sends a signal through the immune system that something needs to be done— immediately."

Tyler noticed that Moon had raised his head from his files. He was half-listening to Dutton speak, his face still expressionless.

"About two and a half years ago," Dutton continued. "I found a previously unknown ligand shared by more than ninety percent of cancerous tumors. A tiny sequence of proteins present on the exterior surface of the tumorous cells."

Tyler tried to imagine the excitement Dutton had experienced when he had made this incredible discovery. On its own, it was enough to set cancer research ahead by decades. But Dutton had taken the discovery and compounded it with true brilliance.

"And then you turned back to the immune system," she said, her voice a near whisper, "back to the killer T cells."

Dutton nodded, obviously pleased by her awed reaction. "From there, it seemed academic. I cloned a receptor from my immune system, which recognized this ligand as foreign. I took killer T cell DNA from my own blood, placed the sequence into a plasmid, and incorporated that plasmid into strep A bacteria. Once the killer T cell DNA was expressed within the strep A at a high enough level, it became a receptor for the bacteria."

What had seemed "academic" to the professor was actually an ingenious use of genetic engineering; he had combined one of the building blocks of the human immune system with a single-celled bacterium, creating a genetic hybrid: part strep A, part killer T cell.

"Of course, the bacteria replicated like crazy," Dutton continued, waving his hand like he was chasing a fly, "as bacteria do. Soon a perfectly random mutation caused the receptor to tie into the bacterial system of pathogenicity."

He paused for effect. It was obvious he had rehearsed his part—not altogether surprising, since he had obviously been on the verge of international celebrity before the tragic deaths.

"As you're both well aware," he finally finished, "strep A's pathogenicity is to eat cells. My new, tailored strep A contained a receptor for a specific type of cells—cancerous tumor cells. In other words, my strep A was biologically conditioned to eat cancerous tumors: a miracle cure."

He crossed his arms against his chest, glancing toward the clock that hung above the door. Moon cleared his throat. "And that's where Jack Collier enters the picture, right, Professor?"

Dutton looked from Moon to Tyler. His cheeks were red with anger. "The bastard couldn't handle my success. He'd been kicked out of school, and he was filled with rage. He did something to my cure. I don't know what. I don't know how. But he did something and created—that." Dutton extended a hand toward the observation window.

Caufield, garbed in a Racal suit, was gingerly wrapping the pig's skeleton in transparent plastic. Tyler understood Dutton's anger, but she intended to remain objective.

"Before we're ready to lay blame," she said, more for Moon's benefit than for Dutton's, "we need to begin the process of sequencing the mutated bacteria. With your help, Professor, we'll figure out exactly how it changed back from a cure to a killer, an *accelerated* killer. Obviously, the strep A is no longer getting its cues from the human immune system—"

She stopped, a sudden question crossing her thoughts. "Professor, why did you choose to use killer T cell DNA from your own immune system?"

Dutton was barely paying attention, his focus still on the other side of the Plexiglas. Moon had risen from the counter and was noisily gathering up his files. His hunched shoulders quivered with impatience. Too much talk, they seemed to say. Time to go out and shoot somebody.

"I already explained this," Dutton responded. "Killer T cells seek out foreign objects—"

"No, that's not what I'm asking. Why did you use your *own* blood? Isn't it normal procedure to use screened blood from a sample bank for laboratory research?"

Dutton paused. For a brief second he seemed nervous, as he searched for an answer. Then his calm returned. "I guess I was in a rush when I reached that phase of the experiment. It seemed more convenient to use my own blood."

Tyler looked at him, but he avoided her gaze. There was something odd about his answer; not in the explanation itself, which seemed reasonable, but in the way he had seemed to think of it on the spot. She had the sudden feeling that he was hiding something from her.

The feeling bothered her. She had learned a long time ago to trust her instincts. Still, she admired Dutton, she was attracted to him, and she wanted to take him at face value. Perhaps he was just being wary. She knew how competitive science could be. She knew that secrecy was an important concern, especially in the arena of cancer research. Maybe Dutton was just being careful. *Or maybe he did have something to hide.*

Tyler was about to follow up with another question when a shrill ringing echoed through the room. She and Dutton both whirled toward Moon, who was already reaching for the cell phone strapped to his belt. Barely a minute after the phone touched his ear, he was racing toward the door. His eyes had gone bright behind his glasses.

"The Karma Killer's struck again."

It took Tyler a second to realize what he meant. It was common FBI practice—depersonalizing a suspect, turning him into a cardboard villain. Tyler hated the custom. *You depersonalized someone you intended to kill.* "Mr. Moon, what happened?"

"A public restroom in Penn Station, New York. Seven people dead—all reduced to skeletons in a matter of minutes."

Tyler felt her throat tighten, as she rose from her stool. But Moon wasn't finished.

"It gets better," he said, and there was pleasure in his tone. "Three eyewitnesses IDed our boy from his photo. He came in on the train from Boston, barely ten minutes before the outbreak. Is that enough proof for you, Dr. Ross, or do you still think we're chasing a little angel?"

Tyler closed her eyes. The knots were tightening inside of her. This was rapidly becoming a nightmare. Seven more skeletons, and Jack Collier spotted in the vicinity. Whether he was responsible or not, he was certainly involved. Worse yet, the case was no longer confined to a Harvard laboratory.

The scourge had hit New York.

NINE

The realtors had a trick they used in this part of Chelsea. They only showed apartments when the wind was from the east. When the wind was from the east, the rental prices seemed incredible; Brooklyn rates for large, lofty two-bedroom apartments with hardwood floors and bay windows, barely two subway stops from downtown Manhattan. A quiet, safe enclave of modern concierge buildings and older town houses, an oasis unmarred by the army of homeless beggars that laid siege to the rest of the city's streets.

It was when the wind changed that the prices—and the lack of vagrants—suddenly began to make sense. Jack felt the breeze turn angry as he moved up the front steps to Justin Moore's building, and he quickly pressed a gloved hand over his nose. Even so, his eyes started to water, and he struggled against the urge to retch. The scent was unmistakable, and it conjured up a sudden, repellant image: row after row of bleeding, bloated carcasses hanging from massive steel hooks.

He glanced down the block, toward the low skyline of box-shaped buildings with oversized chimneys and vertical steel doors. It was an immensely disturbing sight. On the map in his duffel bag, it was nothing more than three ugly words: meat-packing district. But in reality, it was civilization at its most barbarous, a rank nightmare of systematic brutality. Three fetid miles of refrigerated warehouses and chopping plants, stretching from this corner of Chelsea all the way to the Hudson River.

Jack coughed into his glove as he reached the door to Justin's building. It angered him to think of Angie climbing those same steps, gagging on the noxious air. Then again, he doubted she had stayed here very long. Not only did she hate New York, she was an ardent vegetarian.

He hit the buzzer for Justin's apartment, then waited for a response. A few seconds passed in silence, and he pressed the buzzer again, surprised. It was Thanksgiving, but that shouldn't have made any difference. When Angie's father had thrown them both out of the house—something to do with a stolen car, a visit from the Patterson Police Department, and a fistfight between father and son—Justin had headed for New York; that's where Jersey kids went when they ran out of options. Last Jack had heard, Justin was working part-time for one of the chopping plants. *Bright lights, big city.* Still, it beat a steel warehouse in Jersey.

Jack gave it another minute, then reached into a small compartment on the side of his duffel bag. He retrieved a pair of steel tweezers and a miniature screwdriver. He looked over his shoulder, though it was hardly necessary. It was now a little after ten, and most people were at home with their families. Anyone who happened to stroll by would be too concerned with the stench to notice a kid playing with a pair of tweezers.

Thirty seconds later, Jack was inside the building's front entrance. Not quite a personal record—the lock was a newer model—but close enough. Jack grinned, remembering how he had impressed his roommates his freshman year by breaking into Widener Library at 4:00 A.M. with a half-chewed toothpick from the dining hall. At the time, he had thought it was crazy: two straight-A Harvard kids who could play Mozart from the age of twelve impressed by a juvenile delinquent from Jersey because he could beat a twenty-year-old pin tumbler. Well, maybe that's what the brochures meant when they rattled on about the benefits of "diversity." By senior year, both of his roommates could break a pin tumbler in under two minutes. And Jack could recognize the *Jupiter* Symphony in fewer than three bars.

He pushed through the inner door and started up the narrow steps toward the fourth floor. He could hear voices drifting through the thin walls of the apartment complex, along with the clink of silverware and the rush of running water. As he rose higher through the building, the air grew warmer and the smell from outside finally began to dissipate.

Jack was sweating by the time he reached the top floor. He opened his jacket, then slipped off his gloves and shoved them deep into his pockets. He didn't see any numbers on the doors that lined the fourth-floor hallway, but he recognized the beaded doormat in front of the last door on his right; Angie's mother had been obsessed with the damn things, giving them to everyone in the neighborhood. The one in front of Justin's door had a picture of a bright red, charging bull above a colorful Spanish phrase: *Seek your destiny.* Jack wondered if Angie's father had told his kids the same thing when he had kicked them out of the house.

Jack rubbed his feet against the mat, then rapped his knuckles against the door. To his surprise, the door swung inward. There was soft Latin music coming from somewhere inside and beyond that, the constant beep of a cheap alarm clock.

"Justin, you home?"

Jack stepped through the threshold of the one-bedroom apartment. Another short hallway led to a small, rectangular living room. Jack's eyes widened as he took in the chaotic scene; the upended furniture, the stained carpeting, the broken beer bottles, the over-turned, broken lamp fixture sticking out of the shattered center of a glass coffee table. Jack first assumed that the place had been robbed; then he saw the half-eaten cartons of Chinese food in the far corner beneath the drawn window shades. Not even the most brazen burglar stayed for Chinese.

Jack dropped his duffel bag on the floor by the door and quickly moved through the living room. He passed a small bathroom, glancing inside to see the same level of chaos: more beer bottles, more broken glass, and a puddle on the floor that was dried vomit, or urine, or both. Then he reached the entrance to the bedroom. The smell was almost as bad as outside: beer, piss, body odor, and smoke. There were dirty clothes strewn everywhere, and someone had written all over the walls in magic marker. Most of the words were intricate slang, and Jack recognized a few verses of poetry from Justin's journals, the ones he had kept hidden from his parents. The poems were as good as anything Jack had ever read in any book; but when he had tried to tell Justin they deserved to be published, his older friend had shaken his head, laughing: *Only room for one genius in Patterson, brother, and you've got that spot locked solid.*

Jack remembered how he had felt, hearing those words from his hero. He had realized that the real world was much bigger than Patterson, that Jack would soon be leaving Justin and everyone else behind. Jack had hated the idea. He had felt like a deserter. When Angie had joined him, crashing on his dormitory floor, he had felt like he had stolen her away too, the only rose from the foul garden of their childhood.

Justin had felt the same way at first. He had come after his sister, swept up in a fit of jealous rage. He and Jack would have come to physical blows had not Angie stepped between them. It was *her* decision, she had shouted at her brother. It was *her* life. And though Justin had finally accepted what he could not change, Jack had always felt remorse for taking Angie away.

His feelings of betrayal multiplied as he caught sight of his former hero, lying shirtless on a bare mattress in the far corner of the bedroom, head back, mouth partially open, arms and legs twisted like the limbs of a dying insect. His skin was remarkably pale, and there was a two-day beard growth covering his jaw. God, he looked awful; for a brief second Jack wondered if he was alive—until he saw his bony chest rise and fall, his fingers twitch, and a dribble of spit slide from between his full lips. He was alive; he just looked like death.

"Man, you've really gone to hell," Jack commented, expecting Justin to wake up. But his friend just lay there, unmoving. Jack was about to raise his voice when he saw something that sent chills down his veins.

There was a yellow rubber tube tied around Justin's upper arm, just above his elbow. Below the tube, Jack saw a line of tiny red dots, leading all the way to the edge of a tattoo that sprawled across the inside of Justin's forearm. The tattoo was of some sort of bird, with curled talons and a sharp, scimitar-shaped beak. Lying a few inches from the beak, on a stained portion of the mattress, was an empty syringe.

"Shit, Justin," Jack groaned, leaning back against a

warped, junkyard dresser at the edge of the room. "Weren't things bad enough?"

Justin stirred, his legs sweeping slowly against the mattress. He looked at Jack with glazed eyes. A dull smile crossed his lips. "Hey, Jack. Home for the holidays. Pull up a syringe and join the party."

His eyes closed again, and a tremor moved through his limbs. Jack cursed to himself. He had never suspected Angie's brother was an addict. When the two of them were sent to juvi, an older kid had tried to get Jack high, and Justin had beaten the kid so badly, all three of them had ended up spending the rest of the week in isolation. So what the hell was Justin doing with a yellow tube tied around his arm?

"You've got to clean yourself up, man. Let me help you."

Jack moved forward, then stopped himself. What gave him the right? He had left Justin behind a long time ago.

And though Justin used to be his hero, that wasn't why he was here. He had to keep focused; Angie was out there, dying every day.

"So you're an angel, ey, Jack?" Justin mumbled. "Come to take me away."

"I'm looking for Angie. I need to find her as soon as possible. It's about her disease."

Justin seemed to perk up at the mention of his sister. It was obvious, even in his doped-up state, that Angie was everything to him, the only rose in his fucking garden too.

"She was here," he mumbled, his words slurred, "for a while. But she left."

Jack nodded. He had guessed right. "I got a postcard from Chicago, about six months ago. But there was no return address. Do you know where she is, Justin?"

Justin's head drifted back against the mattress, his eyelids drooping. He looked like he was about to nod off.

"Damn it!" Jack half-shouted. "Justin! Chicago! Come on, man, stay with me. This is about Angie's health."

Justin's eyes came open again. "Angie's health. Angie's dying, Jack. Shows what the whole fucking world is about. Cancer, Jack. Cancer's gonna get us all eventually. Eat us all up."

Jack started to shake. Even though Justin was high, he was suddenly making a lot of sense. *Cancer's gonna get us all eventually.* When Angie had gotten sick, Jack had wondered how life could have conspired against him. But then he had looked more carefully at the statistics: 38 percent of women got cancer at some point in their lives; one in six found a lump; one in twenty, like Angie, had some aspect of their reproductive system turn to poison. The newspapers went on and on about AIDS—but cancer was the real scourge, the one that affected everyone at some point.

Except now Jack had found a way to fight the scourge. He squeezed the strap of his backpack. "Justin. Is she in Chicago?"

Justin looked right at him. For a brief second, he seemed completely sober. "A clinic. Some sort of alternative medicine clinic. Helio Cancer Research Foundation. I saw her fill out the application."

Jack nodded, excited. It made sense; she had gone after an alternative cure. The medical community had given her a death sentence, so she had decided to seek a different avenue of treatment. Most cancer patients went alternative when they realized that traditional science didn't have all the answers.

"The alternative lifestyle," Justin murmured, falling

back against the mattress. "That's where it's at, Jack. Just pull up a syringe . . ."

Jack took a deep breath, some of his excitement tapering away. He looked at Justin. Angie he could save, but her brother?

Jack shut his eyes and suddenly found himself in a hospital room, holding Angie's hand moments after her first biopsy. She was in that shadow state between asleep and awake, and her words had trickled out like snippets of her brother's poetry.

I understand it all, Jack. I finally understand.

What's that? What do you understand?

Balance, Jack. It's all about balance. Acts and repercussions. Goods and bads. When something goes wrong, Jack, you've got to make it right. Karma, Jack. It's about karma.

Karma. Innocent and dying, Angie could somehow cling to the belief that there was such a thing as justice. She believed that somewhere, somehow, her death would be balanced by something good, something true. And a big part of Jack wanted to believe that the world could be that simple.

Jack's jaw tightened, and again he was staring at Justin. For Angie's sake he had to find some way to set things right.

The only option came to him, and he unzipped his backpack and carefully counted out five of the twenty-five stacks. Then he turned and opened the top drawer of the wooden dresser. He was placing the money underneath a layer of boxer shorts when his fingers came against something hard and cold. His eyes widened as he withdrew a .38-cal. pistol. The gun was heavy and smelled vaguely of powder. He looked back at Justin, lying semi-conscious on the bare mattress. The thought of the .38 in Justin's thin fingers sent chills down his spine. He shoved the gun into his backpack, then shut the drawer.

"When you come down," he said, turning around, "you're going to start a new life. And this one's going to be a lot more fair."

Jack watched Justin for a long moment. He wished there was more he could do, but the money would have to be enough. Angie was waiting for him.

He quickly left the bedroom, eyes locked straight ahead. If he turned around he knew he'd break down. Just as he reached his duffel, he heard a noise behind him. At first he thought it was Justin. Then he saw the cat, pawing its way around the broken coffee table. It was a mangy creature, its fur a dozen different colors, and it eyed him curiously as he slung his duffel over his shoulder. He bent to one knee, holding out his bare hands. The cat came a few inches closer, then paused, bothered by something in the air. Jack shrugged, rising back to his feet.

"Take care of my friend," he said, heading for the door. He was outside in the hallway when he noticed that the curious animal had followed him. He smiled, reaching down. The creature pulled back, then finally let him scratch the fur behind its ears.

"See," Jack said. "I don't bite."

The cat looked at him, then suddenly reared back on its hind paws, hissing fiercely. It spun around and raced back into the apartment, sending beer bottles flying.

Jack stared after the animal, then shook his head. *Neurotic little beast.* He pulled his gloves out of his jacket and slid them over his hands. Then he started down the stairs.

Twenty minutes later, Jack sat in a crowded corner of the Port Authority Bus Station, his baseball cap pulled down low over his eyes, his backpack braced, guardedly, on his lap, his duffel under his knees. He had never seen the place so packed; the rumor disseminating through the room was that there was something wrong at Penn Station, some sort of gas leak that had the place completely closed down for the first time in years. Personally, Jack couldn't have asked for a more fortuitous turn of events. He had intended to take the bus anyway; he still couldn't risk flying, and the way the schedules worked, the bus would get him to Chicago three hours before the train. Also, the bus somehow seemed more anonymous, safer. Especially today.

Because of the crowd, there had been no problem slipping past the cadre of blue-clad police officers gathered by the main entrance to the sprawling station; likewise, Jack had used the crowd to keep a fair distance from the three crew-cut men in dark suits standing by the ticket station, alternately speaking into cell phones and shouting orders at the irritated cops.

If they weren't looking for him, they were certainly looking for someone. He was convinced now that it was some sort of major operation; he could read the cues in the invisible tension lines running between the dark suits and the blue uniforms. The young men with the cell phones had authority over the NYPD, which meant they were federal—FBI or DEA. Either way, they had to be avoided at all costs.

In the mob scene of the waiting area, that had been an easy task. First, Jack had worked his way to an innocuous corner, seeking out an empty seat next to three elderly women with bushy white hair and colorful winter coats. As he neared the seat, he had put on an exaggerated limp, dragging the duffel and backpack behind him as he struggled the last few yards. Finally plopping down onto the hard chair, he had made eye contact with the closest of the three women. When she smiled sympathetically in his direction, he gently cleared his throat.

"Excuse me, ma'am. I'm sorry to bother you. But I was wondering if you could do me a favor—on account of my leg."

A moment later, she was on her way to the ticket counter for him, two hundred of his stolen dollars clutched in her wizened right hand.

"See," he had told her two friends, a grateful expression on his face, "I knew New York was a friendly place after all."

Now that he had his ticket zipped tightly in his jacket pocket, there was nothing to do but wait for his bus to be called. He spent the time glancing through his atlases, tracing the interstates along the thousand-mile bus route that led to his next stop. He was electrified by the distance, by the number of regional maps he was going to traverse as he slipped into the Midwest; he had never been off the East Coast in his life, and it thrilled him to think that by tomorrow morning he would be hundreds of miles away from everything he knew. He and Angie were going west together after all, though she didn't know it.

He was so swept up by the feeling of adventure, he nearly missed the announcement filtering over the station's intercom system. The elderly woman touched his sleeve, smiling warmly. "Your bus. Bay eighteen. I hope you have a nice time in Chicago."

Jack thanked her, gathering up his atlases. As he trudged toward the correct bay, his eyes inadvertently focused on a tall young woman moving in the same direction a few feet ahead of him. He was struck by her height and the way her long, dark hair spilled down her back. For a brief, foolish second he thought it might be *her*: an excited sweat broke out all over his body, and his mouth went dry. Then he realized how idiotic the thought was. Angie was still a thousand miles away.

He wondered what it would be like when he really did see her again. Would he know what to say—or would he just stand there, staring, his heart in his throat? Would he curse at her for leaving? Or would he scoop her up in his arms?

He swallowed, pushing the questions away. As he passed out of the station onto the crowded, concrete bus platform, he lost sight of Angie's clone. He was glad because now it hurt too much to look at her. He waded through the mob toward the huge, tinted Greyhound, handing his ticket to a bored man in a wrinkled white shirt. Then he was aboard, the warm, recycled air against his cheeks, fighting his way down the narrow aisle. He finally found a seat in the last row and slung his duffel into the overhead rack. He plopped down, his backpack landing on his knees. Then he shook his head. The aisle was still full, twice as many people as there were empty seats.

"This is going to take all morning," he mumbled, mostly to himself.

"What's the rush?" a voice asked from his left. "You wanted for murder or something?"

He turned and his heart fell. She was tall. She was beautiful. And she was sitting right next to him.

TEN

"Well, you don't see this every day."

Vincent Moon was developing one hell of a sense of humor. Tyler glared at him through her Plexiglas face mask as she carefully maneuvered past the line of urinals. She caught a sudden glimpse of herself in the mirror across the bathroom and paused, momentarily startled. The Racal bodysuit made her look like some sort of bright orange alien, with bulky limbs and a sheer, reflective face. The twin oxygen canisters attached to her back weighed at least ten pounds, and her heavy plastic boots were cumbersome, slowing her progress to a near crawl. Even though the suit was probably unnecessary, it brought home the seriousness of the situation. Likewise, in light of the direction the case had taken, Moon's perpetual wisecracks concerned her; people were dying, and it just didn't seem to bother him.

She wondered if that's the way she used to be: a hardened agent, able to crack jokes in a bathroom full of skeletons. At the moment, things didn't seem funny at all.

"We're lucky the outbreak was relatively contained," she commented, her voice reverberating through her helmet. "Seven deaths could easily have turned into a hundred more if one of these men had lived long enough to make it out into the waiting area."

She stepped over an outstretched, clawlike, skeletal hand, using the top of the last urinal to steady herself. She had almost reached the line of stalls where the out-break had begun. Moon was a few feet ahead of her, directly in front of ground zero—the stall at the end with the door ripped off its hinges. Moon's favorite lackey— Craig Densmore, the youthful, carbon copy, brochure agent Tyler had met in the War Room—was to her right, leaning over what looked to be the first victim, a skel-eton in a light blue business suit, pants down around his ankles. Someone from the forensic team had taped a yel-low plastic notecard on the dead man's lapel, with a dark vector showing the direction the outbreak had traveled. A similar notecard was attached to each of the six other victims, in the order that it was presumed they had died.

From Tyler's point of view, it seemed that the foren-sics team had done a good, detailed job. The team, con-sisting of fifteen experts from Washington and three more borrowed from the NYPD, had moved out of the bathroom to give her and Moon room to work; the trail they had left behind of white chalk marks and sealed Baggies was easy to decipher.

Staring down at the forensic evidence, then at the skeletons stretched across the bathroom floor, Tyler was again struck by the speed at which the infection had traveled. She could imagine how the scene had gone down: the businessman crashing out of the stall, sores tearing across his flesh. Another man reaching out to help him—flesh-to-flesh contact—and the chain reaction beginning, the microscopic killer leaping from body to body. No shared needles, no exchange of bodily fluids, no open wounds—nothing but the slightest touch of skin against skin.

"Not much question," Moon commented, "this is certainly the same bacteria that killed the Ph.D. students. Would you agree, Dr. Ross?"

Tyler nodded, her unwieldy helmet clunking against her collarbone. "The first victim must have contracted it inside the stall. Then he carried it out into this area—Agent Densmore, please be careful. You're standing on a piece of evidence."

Densmore jerked a heavy boot into the air. An expensive Cartier watch, probably from the wrist of the businessman, lay crushed against the tiled floor.

"Sorry," Densmore mumbled, his voice seeming exceedingly high-pitched coming through the speaker near Tyler's ear. "I'm not used to the suit yet."

"You never get used to the suit," Tyler responded. She watched as Moon pushed his way into the last stall. "Mr. Moon, do you see any signs of a delivery system?"

There was a moment's pause, then Moon's voice crackled through her helmet. "Not on first inspection. According to our eyewitnesses, our perp was moving through the waiting area just minutes before the outbreak. He might not have used a delivery system; he might have placed the bacteria in here himself, then sat back and watched the fireworks."

Tyler bent over the dead businessman, her eyes drifting to his shiny belt buckle. The buckle looked complicated. "You think he spread the bacteria on a toilet seat?"

Moon came out of the stall, his loping gait accentuated by the Racal suit. "That's what it looks like."

"Why?" Tyler asked, half to herself.

Moon held out his gloved hands. "Maybe it was a test of his weapon in a non-laboratory setting. Maybe he knew one of these seven men. Or perhaps he was just getting his kicks."

Tyler considered his answer. She doubted Jack Collier knew any of the men in the bathroom; that would have been too much of a coincidence. And there was no way to evaluate the third possibility—that Collier was simply a psychotic, who killed for pure pleasure.

The idea of a test run, however, was certainly plausible. The religious cult in Atlanta had tried out their sarin delivery system in a boarded-up warehouse on the edge of the city. They had used a half-dozen dogs from the local pound as test subjects. Still, this was a totally different situation.

"If he's testing a weapon," she said, "he picked a strange place to do so. Usually, a test run is done in a private facility to keep the likelihood of discovery to a minimum. This is hardly private."

Tyler thought of the veritable sea of reporters that had gathered outside the front entrance to Penn Station; the story she had made up about a gas leak and the possibility of contamination had hardly mollified the crowd. And when she had finally stepped inside the cleared out station and heard her voice echoing off the cavernous walls, she had realized what a media nightmare this was going to be. When it had just been a lab at Harvard, they had been able to a keep a tight rein on all of the elements involved. Dutton wasn't going to talk; this was his miracle cure, after all. And very few others had seen the bodies of the two Ph.D. students.

But this was Penn Station. This was New York.

"Maybe he's not trying to keep this a secret," Agent Densmore tried. "He left a note on the blackboard, after all. He probably wants publicity. He's trying to create a scare."

Tyler shook her head inside her helmet. "It just seems too uncontrolled. He would have to have taken enormous precautions to keep himself from getting infected; this bacteria seems to jump from skin to skin at an amazing rate. I just can't see how he could have spread it on a toilet seat without endangering himself—"

"Well," Moon interrupted, impatient, "no matter how he managed it, I think it's clear we're dealing with one sick individual. And we'd better find him quickly—or we're going to be looking at a lot more of these skeletons."

Once again, Tyler felt like Moon was discarding her opinions. He was so eager to go after Collier, he was willing to ignore the facts. For the moment, Tyler had no choice but to let him lead the show. She could not yet interpret the evidence, and that meant she had little more than her intuition.

She did not believe that what had happened in this bathroom was as simple as murder or as complicated as psychotic rage. But she simply didn't have any proof.

"Craig," Moon continued, "have we dredged up any New York leads from Collier's background check?"

Densmore nodded, his motions exuding the excitement of a trained dog, even through his suit. "One New York phone number came up a few times on his dormitory phone bills. We've traced it to an apartment in Chelsea, rented by a twenty-nine-year-old named Justin Moore. Moore grew up in the same hometown as Collier; in fact, he and Collier spent a week in juvenile detention together."

Moon was leaning over one of the sinks, resting his shoulders. Tyler wondered for the first time if his stoop was the result of some sort of past injury. There was nothing in his file about being wounded in action but he had spent six years in the military before joining the FBI.

"Interesting," Moon commented, looking at his reflection in the mirror. "Perhaps our perp's come to New

York to get back together with his old partner. Perhaps they're planning something big together."

Tyler raised her eyebrows, incredulous. "Partner? I've read the file, Mr. Moon. They were thirteen years old when they ended up in juvi. They stole a neighbor's car and were caught two blocks away, stuck in a ditch by the side of the road. Let's not get carried away."

Moon did not turn away from the sink. "Dr. Ross, I'd appreciate it if you took this a little more seriously."

Tyler stared at him, shocked. "Excuse me?"

"You seem to be going out of your way to trivialize our adversary and the violence he's committed. I don't know if it's some sort of motherly instinct kicking in or a romantic crush, but you refuse to see our perp as the monster he obviously is."

Tyler felt her face blanch beneath her helmet. She had the sudden urge to tear a hole in Moon's suit. The chauvinist fuck. She could just picture the grin on Densmore's face. Her hands shook as she jabbed a finger in Moon's direction.

"You've gone way over the line, Mr. Moon. I haven't trivialized anything; I'm simply attempting to understand the evidence in this case. You, on the other hand, don't seem to give a damn about the evidence. If anyone has a hard-on for Jack Collier, it's you. Now I think you owe me an apology."

Moon pushed away from the sink. Although he was only a few inches taller than Tyler, he looked enormous in his Racal suit. "Frankly, Dr. Ross, I don't care what you think. And you can cry about the evidence all you want. But remember, you're in charge of the test tubes and microscopes. I'm the one who's going to bring Collier in. So do us both a favor and stay the fuck out of my way."

He stepped past Tyler, heading for the door. "Craig,

send a team to pick up Justin Moore. And make sure they take full precautions: he and the Karma Killer might be in on this together."

Tyler watched the two men from behind her face mask, fury rising through her chest. Moon had thrown down the gauntlet. He had come at her at full bluster, and he obviously expected her to back down. He had sorely underestimated her.

Tyler had once looked a man in the eyes, and told him to cut off her left breast. She wasn't afraid of Vincent Moon.

She clenched her shaking hands into fists and stormed after him.

Forty minutes later, Tyler was still fuming as she followed Moon toward the cell-like interrogation room on the third floor of the Chelsea police station. They had taken separate cars from Penn Station, and Tyler had spent most of the short ride on the phone with Arthur Feinberg, her direct superior at the Bureau. Feinberg had confirmed her suspicions: Moon had been appointed to the case by the director of the FBI himself. Any conflict between the two case team leaders would automatically be decided in Moon's favor. In other words, Tyler could not expect any help from Washington. She was going to have to handle Moon on her own.

Feinberg's mood had been sympathetic but curt. A small, amicable man in his mid-sixties, Feinberg had been head of the FBI's Science Operations for nearly thirty years. He understood the politics that drove the Bureau and had long ago chosen to sequester himself in the labyrinthine basement labs of Quantico rather than deal with men like Moon out in the field. Sometimes Tyler envied his reclusive lifestyle. One day, perhaps, that's how she would end up, surrounded by test tubes and plastic-wrapped samples for the rest of her life.

Halfway to Chelsea, the discussion had shifted from Moon to the scientific aspects of the case. Feinberg had confirmed what Caufield had already told her. The genetic sequencing of the mutated strep A had given them little information about the killer disease. At its core, the bacteria was indeed Dutton's modified strep A. But long, unidentified strips of genetic material had somehow inserted themselves into the bacterial genome, changing its structure. It was still unclear how the strips of DNA had turned the strep into such a fierce killer.

Tyler's call was interrupted before she could ask Feinberg if he thought a twenty-three-year-old Ph.D. student could have modified the bacteria in such a manner. She had been momentarily irritated to hear Densmore's voice on her second line; then he had begun to relate the report from the team at Justin Moore's apartment, and she had instantly given him her full attention. It was obvious the New York lead had paid off. Along with more fingerprints belonging to Collier, the investigating team had made a bizarre and chilling discovery. There had been another casualty of the mutant bacteria. And this time, even Moon was at a loss to explain the choice of victim.

The two team leaders had exchanged few words during the elevator ride to the third floor of the police station. Tyler assumed Moon was as confused by the team's finding as she was, but as usual, the man's face could have been chiseled from stone. He barely acknowledged the small group of black-suited agents waiting on the other side of the elevator, who fanned out behind him like a dark cloak as he loped toward the interrogation room at the end of the hall. Tyler had to rush to stay next to him or risk becoming a part of his entourage.

When they reached the unmarked door at the end of

the hall, Moon finally turned to look at her. The distaste was evident in his gaze. "When the team found him, he was doped up on heroin. We've given him two doses of Narcan and a shot of epinephrine, so he's going to be a little jittery. If he gets violent, stay behind me."

Tyler did not respond. She didn't need Moon to protect her. She had gone through boot camp at Quantico. Still, she felt a rush of adrenaline as Moon unlocked the door and moved inside.

Everything about the twenty-foot-by-twenty-foot room was harsh, from the bright halogen strips beaming down from the ceiling to the bare cement walls. The air was oppressive with the smell of sweat and fear, and Tyler's excitement waned as she took her seat next to Moon. She had been in a hundred different versions of this interrogation cell before, but somehow things felt different. Maybe it was the case, or Moon's antagonism, or the fact that this was New York; the intense setting seemed to have been stripped of every level of pretense. *This room was designed to break men down.*

Tyler tried not to show any signs of sympathy as she looked at Justin Moore. The kid was seated behind an oversized steel desk in the center of the room, his bony arms crossed against his chest. His jet black hair, still wet from the cold shower they had forced upon him when he had arrived at the station, was slicked back against his head, sweeping out behind his oversized ears like tar-coated snow drifts. He was dressed in a light blue smock tied at the waist, the pants and sleeves loose around his long, thin limbs. His street clothes were locked away in a plastic bag in the evidence room; they would be tested for DNA samples, along with everything else in his Chelsea apartment.

"Good afternoon, Justin," Moon said, without any hint of sarcasm, as he lowered one hip onto the edge of the desk a few feet from where the kid was seated. "I'm Agent Moon of the FBI. This is my associate, Dr. Ross. We're here to ask you a few questions about the dead cat we found in your living room."

Justin's beady dark eyes moved from Moon to Tyler. She did not look away as she leaned back against the cold cinder-block wall. She could tell, just from the kid's eyes, that he was scared to death. But he was trying his best to hide his fear, and his lips changed to a near snarl as he turned back toward Moon.

"I want a lawyer. I get a lawyer."

Moon nodded, but he didn't move from the desk. "That's right, Justin, you will get a lawyer. After our little chat."

Tyler watched Justin's face turn pale. He had been arrested before and knew his rights. But this situation was different. This was the FBI, and the investigation involved the possibility of biological terrorism. In a case like this, the rules could be bent.

"I don't got nothing to tell you," Justin tried, his voice cracking. "I don't know what happened to my cat. I was sleeping when your goons broke into my apartment. I didn't know about the cat until they showed it to me."

Tyler clasped her hands behind her back. She tried to read the expression on Justin Moore's face. It seemed to her that he was telling the truth. But Moon obviously felt differently.

"Sure, Justin. And I bet you don't know a thing about the bacteria either."

Justin stared at him, arms still crossed against his chest. "What the fuck are you talking about?"

Moon rose from the desk. His hulking form cast a shadow across the pale-skinned kid. "Where's Jack Collier, Justin? What's he planning to do with the bacteria? Why did he kill your cat?"

A bewildered look crossed Justin's face. Moon slowly paced around the corner of the desk. Tyler could feel the tension rising in the room. Her heartbeat was loud in her ears.

"And what about the money, Justin? The fifty thousand dollars we found in your dresser. What's a fuckhead like you doing with that kind of money? Are you and Jack going to sell the bacteria? Is that what this is about?"

Tyler shifted to her right, to get a better view of Justin's reaction. Again, his expression could only be described as mystified.

"Fifty thousand dollars," he repeated, struggling with the idea. "In my dresser? Are you fucking with me?"

Tyler cleared her throat. It was obvious they were not going to get anywhere with intimidation. "Justin, you need to understand that this is an extremely serious situation. I know you want to protect your friend, but you're not going to do Jack any favors by lying to us. If you want to help Jack, you need to tell us what's going on."

Justin lowered his eyes toward the desk. The top drawer was slightly open, and it seemed as though the kid wanted to crawl inside the empty space and disappear. "I swear to God I don't know what the fuck is going on. I was taking a nap in my room. A bunch of FBI fucks in weird suits break in and drag me here. They show me a skeleton in a plastic bag and tell me it's my cat. Then this asshole tells me you found fifty thousand dollars in my dresser. You know how much smack I could buy with fifty thou?"

The kid met Tyler's eyes. She knew in that instant that he was telling the truth. *But not the whole truth.* "Justin, we know Jack Collier was in your apartment this morning. What did he want? And where is he now?"

Justin stared at the wall. "I ain't saying another thing without my lawyer."

Tyler sighed, frustrated. "Justin, if you don't talk to us, you could be charged as an accessory to murder."

"I said I ain't got nothing to say."

Tyler glanced at Moon. It looked as though they weren't going to get any more from the kid. But Moon wasn't ready to give up quite yet. He moved to the edge of Justin's chair. Without a word, he leaned forward and grabbed Justin's wrist and turned his arm over. Tyler could see the colorful tattoo running up the kid's porcelain skin.

"This gang ink, Justin? You and Collier running with some of your old friends from Jersey?"

There was a frozen pause. Then Justin grinned up at Moon. "Yeah. We fuckin' kill cats, then skin 'em. It's how we get off."

Moon smiled back. Suddenly, he twisted Justin's wrist around and shoved his hand into the open desk drawer. A second later Moon's knee shot forward, slamming the drawer shut. There was a horrible crack, and the room echoed with Justin's screams.

"Goddamn you! I don't know anything! I swear! I don't know anything!"

Tyler leapt forward, stunned by Moon's sudden violence. Now Moon had his hands on Justin's shoulders, pushing him back in his seat, his face inches from the boy. "You'd better stop lying to us. You've still got another hand."

Tyler stood in the middle of the room, every muscle contorting as she tried to control her voice. "Mr. Moon. Outside. Now."

She turned and walked to the door. Her neck burned as she waited for Moon to follow. Finally, she heard his heavy, uneven footsteps. She yanked the door open and barreled into the hallway. Densmore was standing with a group of uniformed NYPD officers by a closed-circuit television screen linked to a surveillance camera hanging from the ceiling of the interrogation room. When they saw Tyler's face, they quickly dispersed. Tyler waited for Moon to shut the door behind him, stifling Justin Moore's anguished moans.

"I will not be a party to torture," she finally said, barely in control. "I don't care how powerful your friends are at the Bureau; I will not stand by as you brutalize this boy."

She was not naive. She knew that there was a time and place for controlled violence, especially when innocent lives were at stake. She had taken part in a handful of fairly brutal interrogations during her years as an agent. But never anything as blatant as what had just happened in the interrogation room.

Moon rolled his eyes behind his glasses. "That punk was toying with us. He knows where his friend is. He knows about the bacteria."

"I don't care what he knows. If you so much as touch him again, I will resign from this case and present a report on your behavior to Internal Affairs. Is that understood?"

Tyler's entire body was shaking. She had never felt such hatred for a colleague before. She could still hear the crack of Justin Moore's wrist reverberating in her ears.

Finally, Moon shrugged. "Fine. I'll lay off the prick. But when Collier kills again, it will be on your shoulders."

Tyler wanted to slap Moon across the face. Instead, she took a deep breath. "If Justin Moore knows where Collier is, he isn't going to tell us—no matter how hard you lean on him."

"And what about the money?" Moon asked. "And the cat? You think Justin Moore is telling the truth when he says he doesn't know anything at all?"

Tyler looked at the television screen. Justin was sobbing quietly, his shattered wrist cradled against his chest. Tyler felt suddenly nauseous. "Yes, Mr. Moon, I do. The dead cat doesn't make any sense. And if the money does have something to do with Collier and the bacteria, Justin Moore doesn't know about it."

Moon took off his glasses and rubbed them against his shirt. "You're making this much more complicated than it needs to be, Doctor."

Tyler clenched her jaw. "And either you're being purposefully obtuse, or you're just plain stupid. If you think Jack Collier and Justin Moore—two kids from New Jersey—cooked up this scheme to make money—"

She stopped, noticing that Moon's attention had shifted to the closed-circuit TV screen. In the interrogation room, Justin Moore was on his feet, glaring directly into the camera. His dark eyes brimmed with defiance.

"I don't know why the fuck you're after him," he shouted, his voice crackling as it spewed through the TV's speakers, "but you ain't gonna catch him! You can send the whole damn FBI after Jack, and he'll outsmart every last one of you!"

Moon placed his glasses back on his face, then looked at Tyler. "Jack Collier isn't just some kid from New Jersey. And I'm not being stupid, just objective. Now if we're finished out here, can we continue our interrogation?"

Tyler's eyes flashed angrily. "After we set his wrist. And get him a lawyer."

Moon paused then shook his head. "The lawyer will have to wait. This kid's a violent drug addict. As you can see, he's already hurt himself resisting arrest; we wouldn't want to put a public defender in danger, would we?"

Tyler stared at Moon in disbelief. *Objective, my ass.* Moon was a psychopath, pure and simple. The stories she had heard about him were all true. Tales of unarmed suspects gunned down during routine arrests, of interrogations turned into bloodbaths, then covered up by Moon's friends in the Bureau. And one story from two years ago that chilled Tyler to the bone.

It had been a case out of Portland, Maine, involving a drug dealer named Alex Turner who had taken three hostages during a standoff in a local hardware store. Moon and his black suits had taken control of the scene, ordering the SWAT team back beyond the safety perimeter. Moon himself had entered the hardware store— alone—with a sawed-off shotgun strapped to his lower back.

Ten minutes later, Turner was dead, both legs and both arms blown free from his torso, his head smeared against the back wall of the store. Forensic evidence had showed that the final shotgun blast had been fired from less than ten inches from the back of Turner's skull.

Shortly after the standoff had ended, two of the hostages had come forward, claiming that Turner had tried to give himself up before Moon had opened fire. One of the witnesses had painted a grim picture of the final moment: Turner on his knees, begging, while Moon approached with the shotgun, unwilling to accept the surrender.

The Bureau had considered suspending Moon for his actions, when both hostages had suddenly, and unexplainedly, changed their stories. Tyler could only imagine what a late-night visit from a pair of dark-suited agents could do to one's memory.

And now that she had seen Moon in action, she had no doubt that Moon's capacity for violence was not exaggerated. He saw violence as a necessary and acceptable component of his job. Now he had set his sights on Jack Collier—and nothing was going to stand in his way.

Not even two pieces of evidence that made no sense: a dead cat and a stack of hundred-dollar bills.

ELEVEN

The highway was a two-laned shaft of black asphalt, bordered on both sides by trees. The sun was just beginning to set, and the bus's bulbous, tinted windows had turned a strange burnt orange color, nearly the same shade as the whiskey they were both drinking. The two bottles were from her backpack, liberated somewhere west of Pittsburgh, and since Cleveland they had been matching drinks like kids on their way to a high school prom.

Her name was Kate, she really was beautiful, and it was almost six hours of drinking and talking and sizing each other up before she finally asked the question. "If she loved you, how could she leave?"

Jack closed his eyes, sinking back into his seat. The bus rumbled beneath him.

"Jack?" Kate said, her perfume mingling with the bus fumes. "If you don't want to talk about it, you don't have to."

Jack rubbed a gloved hand over his eyes, then took another sip of his whiskey. The whiskey burned going down, a sharp contrast to the cool breeze licking his cheeks. Someone had propped a window open against the bus fumes, which had only served to make things cold and noxious, but Jack was too fucked up to care.

Still, he didn't think it was the alcohol that had allowed him to get this close to a total stranger. Nor was it just the physical similarities, the accidents of cartilage, skin, and hair that made him think of Angie. And it wasn't the way her eyes smiled even when she was trying to be serious, or the way her lips seemed stuck in a permanent pout. This girl *wasn't* Angie; she was a good deal younger and even more fragile. She had told him her life story before they had reached the Pennsylvania border, and sometimes it seemed as though she was a few bare words from breaking down.

Well, perhaps that was the reason he was letting her get so close. It had been so long since he had felt so in control.

"I mean," she continued, because he hadn't yet told her to stop, "didn't she want to stay with you until the end?"

Jack thought for a long moment. If this were a movie and he was Leonardo DiCaprio and they were on an airplane or a cruise ship or the fucking space shuttle he would have given her a pretty, clichéd answer, something like: It was *because* she loved me that she left. But the truth was, he was on the fucking Greyhound and the answer wasn't quite that pretty.

"Cancer," he finally said, and it sounded like a non sequitur, but it sure as hell wasn't. "It changes you, Kate. You feel the disease, and I don't mean the pain. I mean you feel *diseased.* And everyone else pretends you're still the same but you're not."

His voice sounded strange in his ears. He was drunk and he was bound to say something stupid, but he didn't care. It was good to be able to talk, even to a total stranger. For two years he had kept it all bottled inside.

"You could be the most beautiful, loving person in the world, but the minute you find out you have cancer, you learn how to hate."

"But why did she have to give up so easily?" Kate asked, naive, not cruel. "Why didn't she check into a hospital, at least give it a try? What was there to lose?"

Jack shook his head. She didn't understand. She had bought into the crap that had been spoon-fed to the American public by the hopeful and misled media. "There are only three accepted ways to treat cancer: cut, poison, and burn; surgery, chemo, and radiation. If the cancer is too advanced or lodged in organs that are too important to destroy, it doesn't matter what you do, you're going to die. Angie knew that. And that's why she ran."

Kate was silent for a moment. The bus eased between lanes, and Jack saw a sign for Ann Arbor. Chicago was getting closer by the minute.

"Is that what you were studying at Harvard?" Kate asked. "Cancer?"

Jack touched the backpack beneath his knees, felt the bulge of money and the hard plastic of the vacuum-packed petri dish. His cheeks burned from the whiskey and his feet tapped against the bus floor. "Sort of. I was already interested in the human immune system. When Angie got sick, I sort of became obsessed."

Kate looked at him, then out the window. "You make me feel lucky. My parents can't even be in the same room for five minutes without throwing punches, I spend half my life shuttling between my dad's apartment in New York and the motel my mother owns outside of Gary, I haven't kept a boyfriend for more than two weeks since I was sixteen, and *I'm* fucking lucky."

Jack smiled. He liked this girl. Then he cautioned

himself: This is the road; this is temporary. This is drunk on a bus in the middle of nowhere.

She tapped the window with a long finger. Now it was getting dark, the trees bleeding together, the headlights cutting across the highway like reflections from a shattered disco ball.

"Listen, Jack, I want to help."

"This is something I should do on my own," Jack responded. He thought about the stacks of hundred-dollar bills and the vacuum-packed bacteria. He couldn't involve anyone else in his journey. "It won't be hard to track down the clinic in Chicago. I'll be with her by tomorrow morning."

Hopeful words. He was following the directions of a heroin addict and a postmark that was over six months old. But if Angie was in Chicago, he would find her.

Kate wasn't going to give up so easily. "You could crash at my mom's motel. I've got a Jeep. It's a piece of shit, really, but it will get you to Chicago. I can drop you off tomorrow morning. You need to sleep, Jack. At least for a few hours. You haven't seen her in two years."

Jack caught a glimpse of himself in the window and realized she was probably right. He did need to sleep. The alcohol wasn't helping; his eyes looked swollen, his lips puffy. He didn't really give a shit how he looked, but he'd have to be sharp when he hit Chicago. Maybe the girl had a point.

"Your mom won't care that you're bringing some stray home for the night?"

Kate raised one corner of her lips, a Mona Lisa smile. "My mom won't be home for two days. The motel's being renovated, and she's with her new boyfriend in Hawaii. We'll have the whole place to ourselves."

The smile changed, slightly. Jack felt something stir,

pretended not to notice. The girl didn't seem quite so fragile anymore. Jack wondered if his sense of control was little more than illusion.

A moth, he reminded himself. *Not my butterfly.*

The motel was a two-story, ranch-style structure, extending for a hundred yards along a desolate stretch of single-lane highway. There were a pair of bulldozers parked perpendicular to one another in a corner of the vast parking lot, and sheets of canvas covered nearly one-fourth of the first floor. A pile of bricks rose up next to the bulldozers, lit from behind by a blinking neon sign: SLEEPY HOLLOW MOTEL: CABLE TV IN EVERY ROOM.

"It's true," Kate said, as she staggered across the parking lot. She was wearing jeans and a heavy, white, long-sleeved shirt. "You might be stuck in the middle of butt-fuck Indiana, but at least you've got cable."

Jack laughed, steadying himself with a gloved hand on her shoulder. His backpack and duffel seemed to weigh a thousand pounds. "Seems like an odd place for a motel. Doesn't look like there's much traffic around here."

They hadn't passed a single car during the twenty-minute walk from the bus stop, itself a desolate kiosk of brick and wood at the edge of a field. After Boston and New York, Jack felt like he had been deposited on the surface of a dying star. The silence was impossibly dense, the air so heavy with the scent of nature Jack could feel his lungs struggling for some hint of smog.

"In two years," Kate said, sweeping her arms out as if to embrace the entire parking lot, "this place is going to be swarming with people."

"Your mother have a crystal ball?" Jack asked, as they passed through the shadow of the bulldozers.

"Better than that. Her new boyfriend is on the city building commission. They're putting in a commuter airport just twenty miles down the road. Right now, it's not much of an airfield—just a way station for Midwest drug couriers and salesmen too cheap to fly commercial. But soon that will change. People will be coming for the planes and staying for the cable TV."

Her left foot caught on a brick and she lurched forward. Jack caught her sleeve, nearly losing his own balance. As she righted herself, her bottle of whiskey slipped out of her shoulder bag, shattering against the pavement.

"Shit," Kate said. "Seeing as you already finished my other bottle, that was going to be breakfast."

Jack didn't think she was kidding. He looked past her, toward a pair of Japanese lanterns that lit the front entrance to the motel. To the right of the entrance, he saw Kate's Jeep, parked next to a low bank of shrubs.

"Just give me a second," Kate said, pushing ahead. "I'll get us a room key from my mom's office. Too bad the honeymoon suite isn't finished yet. We could have christened the hot tub."

She saw the shocked look on Jack's face and smiled. "Kidding. It's not that sort of motel. And my mother taught me never to share a hot tub with a stranger. Everyone knows, those tubs are breeding grounds for bacteria. Be right back."

She squeezed his glove, then skipped ahead. Jack waited next to the Jeep, his duffel resting on the front hood. He saw a light go on in a window next to the front door, then watched the shadows play against the drawn window shades. Five minutes later Kate returned, a heavy set of keys dangling from her left hand.

The room was an entire corner of the second floor, though that wasn't saying much. There were two double beds, a wooden dresser, a minibar, and a mirrored door that led to a small, brightly lit bathroom. The entire floor was covered by a dark green carpet, and the bedspreads were a surprisingly luminous shade of aquamarine. It took Jack a moment to realize that the glow was actually **caused by trickles of neon drifting in from the sign above** the parking lot; the bedspreads were actually much closer to beige.

Kate dropped her shoulder bag on the carpet, then leapt onto the center of one of the beds. Her body looked much longer stretched out horizontally, and Jack felt suddenly warm in his jacket and gloves. He removed them, then cautiously set his backpack and duffel on the other bed. The floor seemed to be shifting beneath his feet, and he really wanted to lie down. Instead, he headed for the bathroom. He could see Kate crawling beneath her bedspread in the mirrored door. Her heavy white shirt slipped up above her jeans as she yanked at the blanket, revealing even whiter skin. Jack took a deep breath, then locked himself in the bathroom.

Leaning over the sink, hands against porcelain, face in a pool of ice cold water, Jack started to sober up. He opened and closed his mouth like a fish drowning on dry air. When he yanked his head back, the icy drops dribbled down the back of his neck. He took a towel from the rack on the wall, and furiously dried his hair. Then he turned to the toilet, lifted the seat, and emptied his bladder.

What the hell am I doing here? He guessed he wasn't the first person to ask the question in a ratty motel bathroom. He tried to tell himself that he was still simply playing the game. If they had been looking for him in New York, they'd also be looking for him in Chicago. The main bus station would be as dangerous as Grand

Central. Kate had a Jeep; she could drive him right to the clinic's front door.

But he knew these were just rationalizations. He could feel the heat rising up his abdomen. He had spent two years in a laboratory, and there was a beautiful drunk girl in the next room. It was shallow and weak, but it was also human. He could go into the bedroom and pretend he was with Angie, before the cancer and crying and the fear. Angie, when she was happy, when her smile lit up his dorm room and made the outside world disappear.

He remembered how they used to pretend that their bed was a raft in the middle of the ocean, a thousand miles from land. They'd keep the lights off when they made love, and sometimes Jack could actually hear the waves, could smell the salt air in the sweat that dripped like tears down the curve of Angie's breasts. Nobody can bother us here, she'd tell him, because nobody else exists. She'd pull him tight against her, their naked skin sealing together in the heat of sex, and he'd truly *see* that fucking ocean lapping at the sides of his bed.

It would never feel like that with anyone other than Angie.

Jack's jaw tightened, as he thought about the girl in the other room. Disgust filled his soul. Pretend she was Angie to fill a meaningless moment in a meaningless place like this? It was the sort of thing Michael Dutton would do. *Not Jack Collier*

He opened the bathroom door. His gaze tracked to the bed closest to the door and relief flowed through him. Only her head was visible above the covers, her eyes closed, her sable hair flowing down across the white pillows like oiled silk. She had passed out. No awkward conversation, no difficult words of rejection. Just a little petty theft.

He crossed to her shoulder bag and dug inside for her car keys. Then he found the phone on a nightstand by the dresser, and dialed information. Two minutes later, the operator had connected him to the Helio Clinic in Chicago. The receptionist asked no questions, she simply gave him the address and wished him good luck. That was, after all, the alternative way. He thought about asking about Angie, then decided there was no point. If she was there, she wasn't going by her real name; she was stubborn, and she knew what it meant to disappear. If she wasn't there anymore, he was going to have to find out where she had gone next.

He retrieved his jacket and gloves, then his backpack and duffel. He had made it halfway to the door when his eyes once again moved to the sleeping girl. He had a sudden feeling of remorse—or regret? He paused, feeling the weight of her car keys in his right hand. Then he came to a decision.

He opened his backpack and retrieved one stack of hundred-dollar bills. He moved to the edge of her bed, and placed the stack next to the bulge of her slumbering body. Then he leaned forward and gently touched his lips to hers. He lingered a second longer than necessary, then headed for the door.

As he stepped outside onto the second-floor landing, he thought he heard a sound from inside the motel room, a light thrashing mingled with a series of sharp, intense moans. But then a stiff wind hit him from across the parking lot, tearing the motel door out of his gloved hand. The door slammed shut behind him, and he shrugged, starting toward the Jeep.

Meanwhile, on the other side of the motel door, the stiff gasp of wind swirled across the dark green carpet, catching a corner of the beige bedspread and sending the stack of hundred-dollar bills spinning into the air. The bedspread undulated upward, then lifted free—revealing a snow white skeleton and a pile of long, black hair.

TWELVE

Duke Baxter rolled an unlit cigar between his lips as he navigated his bright yellow pickup truck down Route 23. He was about forty minutes out of Gary, frantically chasing dawn while the police scanner on the seat next to him squawked in his bad ear. The scanner had awakened him a little after four, and an hour later it was still going strong. Duke smiled around the cigar, his yellowed partials making room for the stiff Cuban, right up near the gum line—where the taste had a straight shot all the way to the brain. Goddamn, he wanted to light the fucker. But a promise was a promise, and even though Marta had passed on more than five years ago, Duke had never broken a promise to the old sore. He sure as hell wasn't going to start today.

He drummed his gnarled fingers against the steering wheel as he rounded a curve in the road. His excitement rose as he caught sight of the neon sign in the distance, a good two shades brighter than the rising Indiana sun. He cautioned himself against getting too worked up; he had always believed that hope was the highway to disappointment, and at sixty-six he had already lived through his fair share. Two failed marriages before the old sore had come along to save him, at least a dozen journalism jobs that had never ended up anywhere except on his résumé, and finally the successive demotions at the Gary *Gazette* that had left him sleeping next to a police scanner—holding onto the vague belief that perhaps life owed him something after all. No shame in mediocrity, the old sore had often consoled him, and he'd never had any reason to give her much of an argument. But he'd kept his ears open just the same—and today there was a chance, just a chance, that his stubborn streak had finally paid off.

His pickup jerked upward as he caught the edge of the curb on his way into the parking lot. He cursed, hoping he hadn't hurt the alignment. It seemed his driving was getting worse every day; he blamed it on the thirty-year-old Ford engine, not his sixty-six-year-old eyes. His son, Ronnie, by his first marriage and not the old sore—whose fallopians were tied tighter than a hangman's noose—had been trying to get him to sell the yellow eyesore for years. But Duke would never part with his truck; he dreamed that one day he'd keel over in the front seat, and they'd bury them both together, like some ancient Egyptian pharaoh and his loyal steed. A mediocre pharaoh, not one of the big ones; no pyramid necessary, just a few stones in the cemetery next to the old sore, god rest her ornery soul.

"Well, this is a sight," Duke mumbled, as his truck rolled across the parking lot toward the neon sign. At the moment, the neon was overkill; the parking lot was lit up like Mardi Gras. Duke counted a half-dozen cop cars, two ambulances, and a truck from the local fire department. A group of uniformed deputies from the Gary Sheriff's Office stood by a pair of bulldozers a few yards from the front of the motel. Duke squinted through the windshield and saw that the deputies were talking to a pair of men in light gray construction jumpsuits. Duke guessed these were the two workers who had called the thing in. According to the scanner, they had arrived at 4:45 to do some beam work on the motel. A funky smell had led them to the room on the second floor, and the frantic 911 call had come soon after.

Duke pumped the brake as his pickup neared the crowd of deputies. There was a high-pitched squeal as the yellow truck came to a tortured stop, and the crowd turned in his direction. He waved, and a couple of the cops waved back, smiling. Good Gary boys, every last one of them.

"Smooth ride, Scoop?" one of the deputies called, a young man named Purdue who'd gone to the same high school as Duke's son. "Shade a' yellow makes a man want to puke. 'Specially this morning."

"Same color as my fake teeth," Duke echoed back through his open side window. He carefully took the cigar out of his mouth and placed it on the seat next to the scanner. He looked at the unlit end wistfully, then sighed, reaching for the glove compartment. He removed a small pad of paper and a denture-marked pencil.

Purdue came over and opened the door for him. Duke's knees cried out as he stepped down onto the asphalt, but he'd long ago learned to ignore the pain. Another of the old sore's sayings came to mind: *Arthritis is just God's way of reminding you that you're still alive.*

"Guess you heard the story on the scanner," Purdue said, thumbs curled beneath the strap of his belted holster. "Some pretty bizarre shit. Sheriff Carlson's been in there for forty minutes with the coroner; still ain't got no clue what the fuck happened."

Duke raised his bushy white eyebrows. "I thought the dispatcher told the officers to stay away from the scene until the feds got here. Thought the whole thing would be sealed up by now."

Purdue laughed. He was a good head taller than Duke, even back when Duke's old spine had been straight. When Purdue laughed, his wide shoulders arched outward like pterodactyl wings. "You think the sheriff was going to let the feds have all the fun? He figured since the construction workers seemed okay, it was safe to poke around. The rest of us opted to stay out here—secure the area, so to speak."

Duke felt the wind pull at his stringy white hair. "You mean keep the press away?"

Purdue winked. "Exactly. Wouldn't want to stir up a panic, not before the feds can tell us what the hell is going on. Last thing we need is a bunch of old-timers from the *Gazette* sticking their noses in here."

Duke shoved his notebook into the pocket of his dark green bowling shirt. Purdue slapped a big hand against his shoulder. "Course, there's nothing wrong with one of the sheriff's bowling buddies dropping by. Just so long as he doesn't put anything in the paper before we've had a chance to sort things out."

Duke nodded. He understood the routine. His relationship with the sheriff had kept him on the *Gazette*'s staff five years past retirement, and he wasn't about to screw things up by embarrassing the Gary Police Department with a premature scoop. Carlson would let him know when it was time to go to print. With Purdue and his good ol' boys standing guard out here, Duke could be sure he'd have first shot at the story.

And maybe, just maybe, his hunch would pay off and this time, he'd earn himself more than a column in the Wednesday police blotter. If what he'd heard on the scanner was true—he stopped himself mid-thought. He could see the old sore shaking her head. *You're an old man, Duke. Leave the dreaming to those with reason to dream.*

Duke smiled softly at Purdue, then headed toward the front entrance to the motel. As he passed through the crowd of deputies he exchanged a few nods and handshakes, but he could tell the mood was uniquely subdued. The two construction workers looked almost green in the light of the police cars and neon sign; Duke reminded himself to get their statements when he was done inside. As for the rest of the young men gathered by the bulldozers, it didn't look as though any of them had gotten sick; still, from their faces, it seemed a fair bet that not a one would be ordering a big breakfast this morning. It was a bit like the scene of a homicide; though according to the scanner, it seemed much more likely an act of God. It fit his modus operandi, after all.

Duke grinned at his own joke as he reached the front door. Then his grin dissipated as the smell hit him. His eyes started to water, and he coughed, the sound rattling through his chest. No wonder the construction workers had decided to check on the upstairs room.

The stone stairwell ran up the center of the building, partially enclosed by a stucco wall. There was a strip of yellow police tape halfway across the second-floor landing, and Duke grimaced as he bent down to get underneath. The stiff collar of his shirt got caught on the sticky side of the tape, and he had a brief Laurel and Hardy moment as he struggled to get free. Then he was moving across the second-floor landing, breathing hard as he patiently tried to catch his breath. Five years since his last cigar, and still his lungs hadn't gone back to normal. Still, was a little emphysema such a bad trade-off for a really fine Cuban? Emphysema aside, a promise was a promise—god damn it.

"I thought I saw Ol' Yellow pull into the parking lot," a gruff voice called from down the landing. "Hell of a morning, Duke. You'd think it was Halloween."

Duke caught sight of the sheriff leaning halfway out of a motel room doorway just ten yards ahead. He had a white surgical mask pulled down over his nose and mouth, and his uniform was open at the neck, revealing a burst of silver chest hair that matched the wiry mess leaking out from beneath his wide-brimmed trooper hat. He beckoned Duke forward with a gloved hand.

"Try and breathe shallow while we get you a mask," Carlson said, as Duke stepped through the threshold after him. "And don't touch anything. The feds are already gonna go apeshit when their forensic boys try and count the depressed footprints in this ugly fucking rug."

Duke could hear the tinge of glee in Carlson's voice. Like any good small-town sheriff, he hated the FBI. He saw them as a bunch of overeducated lab rats with huge expense accounts and even bigger heads. Sort of the same way Duke thought of the journalists at the larger papers, the guys from the *Sun* and the *Times* who always seemed to get the good scoops—and then the cushy editorial positions, the television production spots, the press passes, and the best tables at the fancy fucking restaurants. Duke hated 'em all, and wished to God he was one of them. Same as Sheriff Carlson.

"Like it really matters," Carlson continued, as a young man in a blue paramedic's uniform handed Duke a white mask. "I don't care how good the FBI forensic boys are; how the heck are they going to explain this?"

He pointed at the bed, just a few feet away. Duke's stomach constricted, and for a brief second he thought he was going to puke. Even though he had heard it all on the police scanner, it was a hell of a thing to look at.

"I guess it ain't some sort of a prank," he tried, tying the mask behind his head. "I mean, it looks pretty real from here."

"It's real all right," Carlson responded. "Two paramedics and a coroner confirmed it. Didn't take long to figure out who it used to be either. The hair was a dead giveaway."

Duke blinked, wanting to look away but unable to do so. The coroner was standing at the foot of the bed, snapping pictures with an oversized evidence camera. The paramedic was leaning against the wall, a helpless look on his face.

"Kate Matti," Carlson continued. "Eighteen years old. Her mother owns the place. Parents divorced; father lives in New York. We found pictures of the family in a drawer in the motel office."

"Does the mother know?" Duke asked. He thought of his son in Passaic, wondered what it would be like to get the phone call.

"She's in Hawaii. Someone at the station is trying to locate her, but it will take some time. Not such a bad thing, considering. We've left a message for the father, but we haven't heard back."

Duke's eyes drifted down toward the floor. His pulse was racing, not only because of the repellant thing on the bed, but because he knew, now, that his hunch was not far off. This might very well be The Story—the one that pushed him beyond mediocrity, that finally launched his career.

You're sixty-six, he heard the old sore's voice in his ear, *what do you mean launch?* He ignored her, something he had practiced for many, many years.

He was about to ask Carlson another question about the dead girl's family when he caught sight of something on the floor by his feet. He bent forward, squinting, not because of his vision, damn it, but because the object was just about the same color as the god-awful rug.

"Is that a hundred-dollar bill?"

Carlson nodded. "They're all over the place. About

ten thousand dollars in total. We've also found traces of whiskey on her clothes, and a broken bottle out in the parking lot. Seems she had a little party before—well, before. And we think there was someone else here with her."

Duke raised his head. "What makes you say that?"

Carlson gestured toward the bathroom. "Toilet seat is up. How many girls you know lift the toilet seat when they take a piss?"

Duke felt his lips twitch upward, despite the setting. "You're a regular Sherlock Holmes, Sheriff."

"Tell that to the feds. Chartered a jet in New York; they're going to be here within the hour. You can be sure they're going to try to bust my country ass."

Carlson's jaw had gone as square as John Wayne's. But Duke's ears had perked at something his friend had said. "New York? Why aren't the feds coming in from Washington?"

Carlson shrugged. "Seems they've seen something like this before. Got two hotshot investigators already working on the case. I assume their last lead was in New York."

Duke felt like clapping his hands. His hunch had been right.

"Sheriff," he finally asked cautiously, "you hear about the shit that went down in Penn Station yesterday?"

Carlson had turned back toward the skeleton on the bed. "Penn Station? Sure. Seen it on the news. Some sort of gas leak. Sad thing to happen on Thanksgiving."

Duke tried to read his friend's voice, but got nothing. "Strange thing about that gas leak. You know my son, Ronnie, lives in Passaic, New Jersey. Well, Ronnie works for Con Edison. Supervisor of half the tri-state area; doing real good for a kid from Indiana."

Carlson was looking at him now. "Real good, Duke. Hell of a kid."

"Right. Anyway, Ronnie called me last night, just checking in. Been doing that every week since Marta died. Well, last night I decided to ask him a few questions about that gas leak. And he told me a funny thing. Turns out, there aren't any gas pipes anywhere near that bathroom in Penn Station. So after I hung up with Ronnie, I called the NYPD for more information. I was immediately transferred to the FBI. Now why was the FBI involved in a gas leak in Penn Station?"

Carlson paused. "Maybe it was some sort of terrorist thing, or maybe they just happened to be in the area."

"Maybe," Duke said, nodding. "Except there's one other thing. After I got off the phone, I couldn't get back to sleep. Since Marta went, the bed just seems too damn big, know what I mean? So I started dialing. Reached a buddy of mine, an old pal from college who works for the Long Island Railroad. I asked him about the gas leak. He passed on a rumor that scared the shit out of me. And it scares me even more right now."

Carlson could see that Duke was much more thrilled than scared. "What sort of rumor, Duke?"

Duke lowered his voice so only the two of them could hear. "A rumor about skeletons, Sheriff. Seven of them, strewn out across a bathroom floor."

Carlson's eyes widened. He looked at the thing on the bed, then back at Duke. "Well, that's something, Duke. That's really something. A newspaper story like this— it could really put someone on the map, couldn't it?"

Duke grinned so wide his partials nearly fell out of his mouth. "Hey, I'm just a bowling buddy, Sheriff. What do I know about newspapers?"

Inside, Duke's bones were on fire. And for once it had nothing to do with his arthritis. A little more digging

and he was going to be ready to break the biggest story
of his career.

The minute he read the byline, he was going to light
that damn Cuban—promise or no promise. The old sore
would have to understand. Then again, she probably
wouldn't.

Duke guessed that was just part of her charm.

THIRTEEN

"So this is a stakeout. Somehow, I always pictured it much more gritty."

Tyler rose out of her seat in the back corner of the café and held out both her arms. Her brother leapt around a waiter and grabbed her in an immense bear hug, lifting her a full three inches off the hardwood floor. She gasped, the wind knocked out of her by his enthusiasm. When he finally let go, she quickly made sure her cell phone was still sitting on the black lacquer table next to her tall glass of orange juice.

"The gritty part is going on two buildings away," she said, her voice low. "Thirty men in black suits staking out a clinic, another thirty in Racal protective gear waiting in vans parked behind the McDonald's next door."

David Ross raised his eyebrows, then lowered his pudgy body into the cushioned chair on the other side of the table. The café was both quiet and quaint: black tables, oak floor, exposed brick walls, and a trendy clientele, most dressed in business suits and drinking coffee from oversized ceramic mugs.

"So you weren't just kidding about the scale of this thing. Jesus, Tyler, shouldn't you be out there with the rest of them?"

Tyler sat down across from him. She didn't want to stare, but he looked much heavier than when she had last seen him. His hairline had receded a few centimeters, and his skin seemed pale, almost anemic. Still, his eyes had that glow of youth, and his smile hadn't changed a bit. Big enough to engulf an entire hospital ward, the nurses at Bethesda had said when he had visited her after the surgery.

"Caufield is right next to Moon in the command center across the street from the clinic. If they spot our target, this phone will ring and I'll be over there in two minutes. It's less than thirty yards outside that door."

In truth, Tyler doubted she'd be running down the street any time soon. The present lead was tenuous at best. Shortly after they had arrived at the motel outside of Gary, they had traced a call made late last night to the Helio Clinic. A receptionist at the clinic had confirmed that she had given a young man on the other end of the line the address; and though it was partially a hunch, both Tyler and Moon had agreed that the clinic was a good place to start.

After the horrible scene at the Sleepy Hollow, Tyler was glad for the time to decompress. The mysteries were building by the second, and she was still no closer to cracking the case. A part of her truly wished she could just walk away, just hand the damn thing to Caufield and return to Washington.

David shook his head. "The old you never even stopped to sleep during a case. Now you're having OJ with your brother right in the middle of a takedown."

Tyler watched as her brother signaled the waiter, ordering himself a vitamin drink to match her orange juice. It was true, this moment would have been unthinkable seven years ago. She had been tough, and she had been driven. Now every second of the case seemed a struggle.

She wanted to believe it was just the circumstances—the viciousness of the disease they were chasing—but she knew the circumstances were only part of the story.

"So how was your last scan?" David asked, as if reading her mind.

Tyler glanced around the café, then turned red as she realized how foolish she was being. Even in front of her own brother it was difficult to talk. As if her cancer was one big secret; as if the knowledge of what she had gone through would make everyone look at her differently.

"The scan was clean," Tyler said, the words resonating in her skull. "Still one hundred percent cancer-free. At this point, it's considered a cure. I've been off the tamoxifin for nearly two years, and my lymphatic system is perfectly clear."

"Fantastic," David said, reaching across the table and squeezing her hand. He had always been physically affectionate, even when they were little. It was the first clue Tyler had picked up on that he was going to be different from the other boys in the neighborhood. Still, it had taken her by surprise when he had finally told her the truth nearly ten years ago. "I wish I had similar good news about Jasper. Last week we had to check him back into the hospital."

Tyler's heart swelled as she watched David's smile flicker, then return. He had been dating Jasper on and off since college, but the relationship had not turned serious until after Jasper had been diagnosed with HIV.

"Is it the pneumonia again?"

David nodded. "His T cell count dipped and the PC came back with a vengeance. I was with him at the hospital all last night."

He paused and Tyler wished there was something she could say. She had always seen herself as David's protector; and when he had finally told her he was gay, he had moved far beyond the reach of her wings.

"He's weak," David continued. "But he's going to pull through. I can see it in his eyes. He's got another five years at least."

Tyler squeezed the glass of orange juice, feeling the cold condensation on her palm. "And, of course, you're being very careful. You've been careful all along?"

David stared at her, then clasped his fingers together. "That's got to be the stupidest thing you've ever asked me, Ty."

Tyler met his gaze. She was embarrassed, but she couldn't help herself. "I'm sorry. You're right. I'm your big sister and I have no choice but to say dumb, over-protective things. It's in my genes."

"Of course we're careful. We were always careful. And I get myself checked every month. I'm in more danger from the grease pits they call restaurants in this town than from my boyfriend."

Boyfriend. The idea that David had a boyfriend still seemed strange to her. But at least he had someone who loved him. It was more than she could say. For some reason, the image of Michael Dutton flashed across her thoughts, and she laughed at herself. She was comparing her stupid crush to David's seven-year relationship. The only thing that had lasted that long in her life was her latest hairstyle. The post-chemo buzz, she liked to call it. She had always kept her hair long before the disease. She had cried for two nights when it had fallen out. Now it bothered her if it touched the back of her neck. It seemed frivolous, somehow—like the reconstructive surgery her boyfriend and the plastic surgeon had tried to convince her to get after the operation. Lie back on that table; go back under that knife? *So I can fill a fucking bra?*

"It's strange," David was saying, as Tyler pushed the

horrible memories away. "Sometimes I look at Jasper, and I see the disease inside of him. I know he's still the same, but now there's this monster living in his bloodstream, this deadly killer just waiting to spring forth."

Tyler shivered. She wished she had made more time for her brother over the past few years. She had been too consumed by her own struggle, in the growing difficulties with her career.

"It's not the same as it used to be. The cocktails are changing the course of the disease."

"But not the nature of the disease," David said. "I think about all the people who are walking around with HIV inside of them, innocent carriers, spreading death to people like Jasper. We had been broken up for six months, Tyler. One sexual encounter, a stupid, drunken night in the bathroom of a dance club, that's all it took. This virus is so much smarter than its hosts. It doesn't need a second chance."

Tyler's face felt warm. Something was pricking at her thoughts, but she couldn't quite make it out. Something about viruses and hosts. Her thoughts were interrupted as the waiter finally brought David his vitamin drink. The drink was thick and dark brown, the same color as the waiter's shirt. Tyler wondered if it was a coincidence or some corporate strategy.

"So why did you want to see me this morning?" David asked, glancing over his shoulder toward the glass picture window that looked out onto the tree-lined, semi-urban street. "Were you just trying to kill time while you waited to see if your perp was going to show?"

"Actually, I just wanted to talk to someone on the outside. This case is really getting to me—deep down, under my skin."

David fingered his drink, concerned. "From what

you've told me, it sounds like there's a pretty heinous murderer on the loose."

Tyler nodded. After what she had seen at the Sleepy Hollow motel, she was beginning to believe that Vincent Moon was at least partially correct; Jack Collier did seem to be killing his way across the country. He had been seen getting on the bus in New York, he had left hair and urine samples in the bathroom at the motel— that latter of which matched a specimen of dried urine found on the bathroom seat in the lavatory at Penn Station. And he had even stolen the dead girl's Jeep.

But he had also left ten thousand dollars in her motel room. And fifty thousand in Justin Moore's apartment, along with a dead cat. Now he was potentially on his way to an alternative cancer clinic.

Was he planning some sort of violent attack? Was it some twisted plan of revenge, set off by his expulsion from Harvard coinciding with his professor's success at finding a cancer cure? And had he really sabotaged that miracle cure, turning it into such a deadly scourge?

Tyler was still no closer to understanding what made Jack Collier tick. She had even reinterviewed his former foster parents, but they had not been able to tell her anything new. There had been no contact between them and Jack since he had left New Jersey seven years ago. Since his real parents' deaths, Jack had effectively been on his own.

"There's still so much that doesn't make sense," Tyler finally said. "And it's not just the mysterious nature of the case that's getting to me. It's my reaction."

"That makes sense. It's probably churning up memories of your fight with cancer. You might be cured of the disease, but you still carry the scars."

He stopped, his cheeks reddening. "I'm sorry. Poor choice of words."

Tyler smiled. "It's okay. I do carry the scars. I look at them every morning when I get dressed. But it's more than that. I'm watching Moon preparing to take this kid down—and I mean *down*—and I want to stop it. I want the whole thing to *stop*. But I know it won't. It's like a train wreck that's already happened some time in the future, and I'm just steaming along the tracks—"

The sudden, shrill ring caught her by complete surprise. Her hand shot out, missing the orange juice by a fraction of an inch. She could hear Caufield's voice even before the phone had reached her ear. Her face paled, and she rose from her seat. She could not believe the timing. It was happening *now!* The entire café seemed to spin in front of her eyes.

"The train wreck?" David asked, watching her from his seat.

Tyler nodded. She was already moving past him, toward the door. "They've just spotted Jack Collier on his way into the clinic. He's carrying a backpack; God only knows what's inside. If Moon starts shooting . . ."

"I'll pay for the drinks," David called after her, but Tyler was barely listening. Caufield's words still echoed in her ears.

You'd better get over here quick, Dr. Ross. Moon's got enough firepower with him to start a small war. From the look on his face, I think that's exactly what he intends to do!

FOURTEEN

It was the longest ten yards Jack had ever seen. He stood on the curb where the taxi had dropped him off, staring at the low, boxlike building with the shuttered windows. A paved path led up to the front door, bisecting a manicured lawn that seemed out of place on a street of cafés, record stores, bars, and fast-food joints. There was a twenty-four-hour drugstore to the building's right, the front window display touting some new brand of antibiotic soap; a bright red pyramid of boxes rose from floor to ceiling, only partially obscured by a pizza delivery van parked halfway up the sidewalk. To the building's left was a similarly familiar sight, a McDonald's, complete with a colorful, fenced-in playground in the front and a bright yellow sign for the drive-through window located around back. The golden arches seemed almost radiant, backlit by rays from the rising sun. Jack could see people sitting on stools in the window, drinking coffee and eating breakfast sandwiches out of Styrofoam squares.

Jack turned his focus back to the clinic and squared his jaw. He knew there was a good chance Angie had traveled elsewhere since six months ago, but even the tiny chance that she was inside the boxlike building filled him with emotions: excitement, longing, passion, and most of all—fear. That she had changed, that she had somehow moved on, that she was so sick even the cure in his backpack wouldn't save her. Two years was such an incredibly long time. In the lab, time went around quickly, like test tubes in a centrifuge. But out here in the real world time dripped like melting glass.

He gripped the strap of his backpack like a pacifier as he started up the front path. Out of the corners of his eyes, he noticed motion on the sidewalk; there seemed to be an inordinate number of people on the streets for 7:30 A.M., but most were dressed in business attire, so they barely rated attention. He had grown so used to the money on his back, his paranoia had begun to wane. Three hundred dollars in a wallet, $190,000 in a backpack; over time, it just seemed like extra weight.

He reached the door to the clinic and pressed a black doorbell located halfway up the frame. The door was unmarked, and because of the shutters there was no way to see what went on inside. Jack knew from his own cancer research that alternative clinics were often shrouded in some level of secrecy. Since their methods were not recognized by traditional medicine, they often took precautions against public scrutiny; a certain level of press was necessary to bring in patients, but too much publicity about the actual experimental treatments could quickly get a clinic closed down. It wasn't that their methods were necessarily dangerous or irresponsible; it was simply that alternative cancer treatment, like magic, relied on a certain willingness on the part of its audience, a belief in results without any real understanding of the processes that led to those results.

Once you really looked behind the curtain, the Wizard was a midget, just like the rest of the little fuckers. His power lay in the fact that you believed he was powerful.

The door swung inward, and Jack looked at the local Wizard, trying to size him up without being conspicuous. The man was fittingly small, five-five at most, with a tuft of black hair and droopy, though amicable, features. His eyes were blue and mildly beady. He was wearing a white doctor's coat, a lumberyard of pencils bulging out of the chest pocket. He didn't look like a doctor exactly; he lacked the sense of authority and self-love.

"Can I help you?" he asked, his hand still on the door. Jack cleared his throat. He had thought this through during the long ride from the Sleepy Hollow Motel. He knew that Angie would not have checked in under her own name; she had to assume that Jack was going to come after her, and she wouldn't make it that easy. Besides, it was doubtful the staff at the clinic would let him search through their files without some sort of incentive. Alternative medicine was a private decision, and the clinic staff would be trained to respect that privacy.

That left Jack with a single avenue: bribery. He shifted his backpack around, and unzipped the front. The man's eyes bulged as he saw the stacks of bills.

"I've read about your work, and I'd like to make a donation. May I come inside?"

The man coughed, then nodded. Alternative cancer treatment was not covered by health care, nor did it attract a lot of attention from donors. It hardly mattered that Jack was a kid, dressed for the road. He was carrying enough money to keep the clinic afloat for months.

"I'm Dr. Kendrick," the man said, as he led Jack down a carpeted hallway. The walls were institutional yellow, the carpet a blend of natural-looking brown fibers. "I founded this clinic along with my partner, Dr. Alec Greenstock. If you're familiar with our work, I'm sure you recognize his name. He's the one who published the paper in the *Alternative Journal* last fall."

Jack had never heard either name before, nor had he ever read about the Helio Clinic. But he knew a fair amount about alternative therapies. His research at Harvard had borrowed from many experimental ideas, though his results had come entirely from hard science. Before he had focused on bacterial therapy, he had conducted a survey of the different areas of research, hoping to find the most promising avenue toward Angie's cure.

"I found the article quite illuminating," he lied, as they continued down the hallway. He just needed to get the man talking, and he was sure he'd be able to keep up his end. "I've been following Dr. Greenstock's research since my sister was diagnosed with stage four ovarian cancer two years ago."

They entered a vast lobby with light blue shag carpeting and high, cement walls. There were couches in the center of the room and a reception desk—staffed by a nurse in blue that matched the rug—near a door that led to the interior of the building. But the centerpiece of the lobby was an enormous aquarium that took up the entire front wall. Even from ten feet away, Jack had no trouble identifying the creatures swimming back and forth in the tank. Each was about two feet long, with triangular fins and long, muscular tails. They moved gracefully through the crystal clear water, painting elegant shadows across the thick glass.

"Baby sand sharks," he said, half to himself. Then a light went on inside his head, and he smiled. Angie was desperate, but she was smart. She had chosen the alternative therapy she had considered the most promising: "Live cell therapy—shark cartilage, live cells from shark tissues injected directly into cancerous tumors."

Kendrick nodded, as they continued across the lobby. "Our line of research dates all the way back to 1931, well before the current trend in shark cartilage therapy. The idea that living cells from one body have a capacity to bond with similar cells in another body was first discovered by the Swiss physician Paul Niehans. Injections of healthy embryonic cells from farm animals were used to target diseased organs in people, with fairly stirring results."

They had reached the reception desk, and the nurse pressed a button, unlocking the door that led to the rest of the building. She gave Jack a matronly look, then turned back to a magazine that lay open in front of her. Jack followed Kendrick into another hallway, passing closed wooden doors on either side. He could hear the mechanical beeps and whirs of medical machinery, but he could not identify the technology from the sound alone. He wondered if they were passing therapy rooms—if perhaps Angie was behind one of the doors. His heart pounded at the thought. He tried to keep his focus on the role he was playing.

"About ten years later," Kendrick continued, "German scientists began using tissue from embryonic umbilical cords to help regenerate damaged immune systems. Over the next few decades, the procedure was used to treat almost eighty thousand people, including Pablo Picasso, at least one pope, and a number of Hollywood celebrities. Dr. Greenstock and I have developed the methodology even further, and we're beginning to see some truly astounding results."

They reached an office at the end of the hallway, and Kendrick ushered Jack inside. The office was small and spartan, with a steel desk that looked like it had come from a military catalogue and a bookshelf neatly lined with oncology textbooks. Kendrick pulled two cushioned chairs from next to the bookshelf and sat across from

Jack, legs crossed, buggish eyes drifting unintentionally toward the backpack on Jack's lap.

"And you've focused on shark cartilage," Jack guessed, "because of the research that links it to tumor inhibition. From what I've read, shark tissue can constrict blood vessels that feed malignancy, perhaps the reason that sharks rarely develop cancer, no matter how many carcinogens you expose them to."

Kendrick smiled, pleased that Jack was familiar with the science. "Shark cartilage is just one of our many therapeutic advances. We're also using thymus extract, fetal umbilical cords from calves and goats, and embryonic livers from Rhesus monkeys. If you'd like to bring your sister in for a preliminary screening, perhaps we can work out a treatment plan."

Jack crossed his arms against the top of the backpack. "Actually, I believe my sister might already be one of your patients. That's why I'd like to make a donation to help your research. I just need to make sure my sister is here."

Kendrick paused, his smile wavering. He looked from the backpack to Jack's face. Of course, a kid carrying so much cash was suspicious; he was either into something illegal or incredibly eccentric. "As I'm sure you can understand, I'm not at liberty to divulge the names of our patients or their current prognosis. That's privileged information. But if you're really family, well, I might be able to make an exception. What is your sister's name?"

Jack could tell that Kendrick was hungry for the money; even so, this was going to be tricky. He unzipped the pack, and began to withdraw stacks of hundred-dollar bills. "Her name is Angie Moore, but I don't think she checked in under her real identity. My father is a radiologist, and he would never have supported her choice to try alternative therapies. He believes a more aggressive surgical approach is her only hope."

Kendrick raised his eyebrows. "For stage four ovarian? I can see why she opted for the alternative route. Well, I'd love to be able to help you out, but if you don't know what name she checked in under, I'm not sure how I can."

"What about photographs?" Jack asked. "Or maybe I could go through the medical charts themselves. I'm familiar with her physiological stats."

He leaned forward, placing three stacks on a corner of the steel desk. Kendrick looked at the money, then came to a quick decision. Thirty thousand dollars was equivalent to ten patients—without any chance of damage to his annual statistics. He rose and crossed toward the bookshelf. He retrieved a thick booklet, with a glossy plastic cover.

"This is our registration book for the past year. We photograph every patient when they first join our program. Since our therapy often lasts upward of nine months, our patients develop tight bonds with one another; this booklet acts as sort of a yearbook, so they can keep in touch after they return to their normal lives."

Jack took the book from him and began flipping through the pages. There were twelve color photos on each page, four rows of three. Most of the patients were in their late fifties or early sixties—though a surprising number seemed to be younger, and a few were even children, teens, and younger. "So your patients remain on the premises for the entire course of treatment?"

Kendrick had opened the top drawer of the desk and was delicately placing the thirty thousand dollars inside. "Yes. Along with the live cell treatment, all of our patients are on strict vitamin diets to lower the general toxicity in the system. We also offer coffee enemas at regular intervals. The caffeine has been shown to open up bile ducts and veins in the liver. And, of course, we monitor electrolyte and white count levels throughout the day."

Jack grimaced, as he thought about Angie subjected to such a lifestyle. But it was certainly no worse than chemo or radiation therapy. And of the alternative options out there, live cell therapy seemed the most promising. He did not regret the donation he was making to Kendrick's operation.

He continued turning through the registration book, his gaze moving from face shot to face shot. Every time he caught sight of a woman Angie's age he paused, hope rising inside of him. But each time he was disappointed: blonde hair, blue eyes, too short, too heavy. He was more than three-quarters through the book before his gaze settled for a brief second on a woman near the bottom corner. At first glance she seemed a decade too old, but something about her eyes caught his attention. They reminded him of the girl from the Sleepy Hollow Motel, smiling even though her face was so deadly serious.

"Oh, my God," he whispered. *Angie.* There were creases in her skin that hadn't been there before, and her black hair was shorn tight against her head; but it was definitely her. He quickly shifted down to the few sentences of writing beneath the photo. Karla Dawson, age twenty-four, a resident of New Jersey. Then his heart fell as he saw the red stamp at the bottom of her entry: *Released, 8/24.*

He quickly held the page in front of Kendrick. "This is her, but it says she was released in August."

Kendrick squinted at the photo. "Yes, I remember Karla. Stage four ovarian. She was with us for almost five months. She wasn't responding to the treatment as quickly as some of the others, so she decided to check out. I think she wanted to try another clinic, some place she had read about in one of the journals."

Jack stood, his hands trembling at his sides. "Do you know where she went?"

Kendrick shook his head. He quickly shut the desk drawer, perhaps afraid that Jack was going to take back his donation. "I'm sorry, I don't. But she did have a roommate while she was here, a young woman with lung cancer—Sandra Fox. She and Karla were quite close. Perhaps she knows more."

Kendrick came around the desk and opened the door. Jack clutched his backpack tightly against his chest as he moved out into the hall. He could feel the vacuum-packed petri dish at the bottom; he imagined the tiny streptococcus bacteria in their semidormant state, struggling to stay alive. The irony of the situation slammed into him; Angie was chasing down alternative cures, while he chased her—the real cure pressed against his chest.

He tried to control his thoughts as he followed Kendrick past another set of doors then down a new hallway. He knew there were a lot of clinics out there, and a lot of therapies that were much more brutal than shark cartilage and coffee enemas. He had to trust Angie's instincts, that she wouldn't try anything that would cause her real harm. She was dying, but she still had time.

He prayed she still had time.

"Here we go," Kendrick said, as he came to a door similar to the ones they had just passed. "Sandra's an early riser, so she should be awake. She's one of our most remarkable patients, and she's responded extremely well, though she came here in a very advanced state of the disease. We've been using sheep umbilical cords—"

Jack pushed the door open and stepped past Kendrick. A hospital bed against the far wall, a pair of IVs on either side of the headboard, a TV on a swiveled base hanging from the ceiling, and a small window, drapes halfway open. A sharp memory brought to life for Jack in the familiar, antiseptic smell in the air: *My mother died in a room just like this.*

He took a deep breath, his attention shifting to the woman in the bed. She looked to be about forty, but it was hard to tell because of her size. She couldn't have been more than eighty pounds, her limbs so thin they were barely more than bone. Her head was completely hairless, and her sharp ears made her look elfin, like some creature from a children's fable. She was sitting up on two thick pillows, reading a book. Although she was obviously in an advanced state of cancer, there was something incredibly beautiful and alive about her. Staring at her, Jack felt emotion welling inside him. Again, his mother, those last few days: the tubes running out of her body, the heart monitor clicking away, the doctors scurrying back and forth. He remembered sitting at her side, begging her not to die, not to leave him alone. And she had looked back at him with that incredible strength, the strength of someone who had already seen the other side. *I don't have a choice, Jack. I'm sorry, but I don't have a choice.*

Now, years later, in a different hospital room with the same smell in the air, he almost didn't want to speak for fear of shattering the moment.

The woman looked up, then smiled at Kendrick. "Now this looks like a therapy I'm really going to enjoy, Doctor."

Jack blushed, as Kendrick wagged a finger. "Sandra, play nice. This young man is not part of your treatment. He's here about Karla."

Sandra looked at Jack more carefully. Then she slammed her book shut, a wide smile on her face. "You're Jack, aren't you? Angie's Jack."

Jack's heart leapt into his throat. He stepped forward. "That's right. She told you about me?"

"Only every day. We'd talk about you over coffee enemas."

"Sandra—" Kendrick started, but Jack cut him off.

"Is she okay? I mean, was she healthy when she left?"

Sandra shrugged, tossing a glance at the IVs running into each of her arms. "She was able to leave. That should tell you something. She hadn't turned into a shark, no matter how hard Dr. Kendrick tried."

Sandra winked at Kendrick, who was standing awkwardly against the door. Jack took another step forward.

"Do you know where she went?"

"So you're finally going after her. What the hell took you so long?"

The question was like a gunshot to Jack's chest. He wanted to yank the petri dish out of his backpack and shove the strep A into her IV bottle. All the shark cartilage in the world didn't add up to an ounce of Jack's bacteria.

But he knew he couldn't cure this woman—not yet. He needed the bacteria in his backpack to cure Angie. Besides, after Dutton's *Science* article and the clinical trials that were assuredly going on at Harvard while Jack raced across the country, it wouldn't be long before all the alternative clinics shut down and patients like Sandra were treated with the real, and only, cancer cure.

"Please," Jack said, standing at the foot of the elfin woman's bed. "Can you tell me where she went?"

Sandra sighed. "Love is almost as nauseating as chemo. Angie went to Nevada. A clinic outside of Las Vegas called Bosley Inn. I know, it sounds like a whorehouse; it's run by a doctor named Liam Bosley."

Kendrick made a noise with his teeth. "Bosley. I know the man. Really experimental stuff. Heat therapy and holistic herbs."

Jack was barely listening. His head was spinning. Las Vegas was more than a thousand miles away. At least four days of steady driving. *Too long.* He'd have to find another way.

"I appreciate your help," he said, determination flowing through him. Again he thought about opening his petri dish, returning her aid with the ultimate gift. But then he thought of Angie, and he knew he had no choice.

When he stepped outside the clinic and into the fresh morning air, his entire body started to shake. He thought about flagging a taxi and heading back to the Jeep, parked three blocks away in a parking garage, his duffel in the backseat. But then the ground beneath his feet began to undulate in tune with his beating heart. He realized he had not eaten anything in almost two days.

Instinctively, he turned toward the golden arches. He was nearly staggering by the time he had circumnavigated the playground on the front lawn of the McDonald's. The scent of french fries and freshly microwaved animal by-products kicked life into his veins, and he pushed past a pair of teenage girls in jogging suits on their way out the glass front doors.

If he had paused to look at his reflection in the glass before entering the McDonald's, he would have seen a startling sight: a dozen men in camouflage paramilitary uniforms racing after him, semiautomatic rifles aimed directly at his back.

FIFTEEN

"Nobody engages until I give the order!"

Moon's voice echoed in Tyler's plastic earpiece as she jogged behind him. They were still five yards from the entrance to the McDonald's, and at least six FBI agents were ahead of them, all armed with government-issued assault rifles. The decision to wait until Collier had exited the clinic had been more strategic than cautious; the clinic was built like a warren, and Moon had wanted to avoid sending his agents into a labyrinthine hot zone. His original plan was to take Collier in the street, but Jack had surprised them all by rushing straight into the McDonald's.

"Set up a perimeter around the building," Moon relayed, as the first agent neared the glass entrance. "Myself and Dr. Ross will go in first. Densmore and Paget, follow us inside. The rest of you take up positions in the playground."

The agents closest to the McDonald's broke to either side, then dropped to their knees, rifles trained on the door. At that moment, the silence that seemed to grip the entire city cracked, and frightened shouts rang through the air. Pedestrians sprinted out of the way, and Tyler heard a car screech to a stop behind her, waved away by an agent talking into a walkie-talkie.

From outside, it didn't seem that anyone in the McDonald's had yet noticed the commotion; the sun was now high enough to cast an obscuring glare across the plate-glass front window. But soon the pandemonium would be impossible to ignore. The question was, how would Collier react? And what was he carrying inside his backpack?

Tyler's pulse rocketed as she thought through the possibilities. If he had the bacteria in some sort of airborne form—a package of spores, a spray bottle with some sort of liquid base, even a low-heat explosive device—they could have a true biodisaster on their hands. But Moon had not been willing to listen when she had argued that her team of scientists in Racal suits should have been the first to make contact. He wanted Collier himself, and he was willing to risk his own men to bring down the Karma Killer. The fact that Tyler was with him on the assault was as close to a compromise as he had ever managed.

"The kill code is Karma," Moon continued, and Tyler was amazed at how calm he sounded. "If I give the code, I want spine and head shots only. If he's still moving, he can still hurt us. Okay, approaching contact zone. Stand by."

Moon drew a .45-cal. revolver out of his shoulder holster as he reached the glass door. Staring at the huge gun, Tyler felt a sheen of sweat break out across her back. She was not wearing a side arm. It had been a difficult decision after the Sleepy Hollow, but she didn't trust herself anymore. If it was just her and Jack Collier, she wasn't sure she could pull the trigger. And that meant a handgun was more dangerous than it was worth.

She watched Moon's fingers whiten against the door handle. The world around her seemed to vanish as the adrenaline coursed through her veins. It had been a long time since she had been in a live-fire situation: Her last engagement had been in Atlanta, and that could hardly compare. In Atlanta, she had remained a hundred yards back in a command Humvee while the raid had gone down. She had heard the shots, had seen the cult members dragged out of the warehouse, but she had not met them face to face.

If Jack Collier went down, she would watch him bleed.

Moon paused with his hand on the door, turning to look at her over his shoulder. The lower part of his face was partially covered by the mouthpiece of his short-wave communicator. His eyes disappeared in the burst of bright sunlight reflecting off of his glasses.

"You stay two feet behind me and on my left. If you see any sign of a biothreat, give me a clear signal. Then give me a clear shot."

He yanked the door open and stepped inside. Tyler sprinted in after him. She could hear Densmore and Paget—African American, about the same age as Densmore, certainly the same barber—rushing behind her. Moon stepped to her right, angling around the waist-high counter that ran along the front window. The McDonald's opened up ahead of them: rectangular and geometric, three rows of white plastic tables bolted to a black-and-white-tiled floor. There were a dozen stools pulled up to the window counter, half of them populated, and at least two-thirds of the tables were likewise occupied. At the front of the restaurant was the cashier's stand, a long, white marble counter supporting three cash registers. Three lines, each five people deep, snaked out in front of the registers. Tyler spotted Jack at the front of the line extending from the first register. There was a tray on the marble counter in front of him, containing a vast amount of food. At least four hamburgers, two drinks, and an enormous carton of fries.

Moon made it three steps into the restaurant before someone saw him and screamed. Trays crashed to the floor; soda and ice sprayed across the tiles. A stool flipped over, followed by an overweight college student in gray sweats. Then the room went dead silent, as every head turned toward the encroaching team of FBI agents. Tyler kept her gaze trained on Collier. He was slow turning around, his backpack weighing heavily against his right shoulder. When he finally caught sight of Moon—gun raised and pointing right at him—his eyes went saucer wide. His young face, already pale, turned ash white. Moon waggled the gun to the right, and the people behind Collier quickly moved aside.

"Jack Collier," Moon shouted, "I'm agent Vincent Moon of the FBI. Keep your hands at your sides!"

Collier stepped back against the counter. His hip hit the tray of food, shoving it over the other side. The two drinks splashed against the McDonald's employee who had just rung him up, soaking the teenager's shirt.

"Hands at your sides!" Moon repeated, though Collier hadn't disobeyed. "Densmore, come around my right!"

Tyler heard Densmore's heavy breathing as he skidded past her. Two patrons in similar blue suits rushed out of his way as he came up the aisle parallel to Moon. Moon was still advancing a few feet at a time, his limp less pronounced than usual, his gun aimed directly at Jack's chest. Tyler had the sudden image of the gun going off, piercing a hole through Jack, the bullet ripping out the other side of his body and into the backpack. She could almost see the saran-wrapped package of dried bacterial spores inside, shredded by the force of the bullet, billowing up into the ventilation system of the restaurant.

"Moon," she said, half under her breath, "don't aim at his chest."

Moon ignored her, still continuing forward. Collier seemed to be in a state of pure shock, his mouth opening and closing. Finally, sound eked from his vocal chords. "Look, let's all just calm down—"

"Shut the fuck up!" Moon yelled. He stopped ten feet from Collier, his shoulders hunched slightly forward. "The man to my right is Agent Densmore. He's going to walk up to you and take the backpack off your shoulder. If you make a single move, I will shoot you directly in the face. Is that understood?"

Jack stared at Moon for a full second. Then a strange thing happened. The fear seemed to leave his eyes. Tyler didn't know if it was resignation or madness, but the kid was no longer intimidated by Vincent Moon. Tyler was not entirely surprised. Jack Collier had lived a hellish life.

"That isn't necessary," Collier said quietly. "I'll give you what you're after. All I want to do is keep what's mine."

Suddenly, he shifted the backpack off his shoulder and reached for the zipper. Densmore stumbled back, his rifle rising. Moon dropped to one knee, both hands on his gun. Before Tyler realized what she was doing, she launched herself forward.

"Jack," she shouted, slipping past Moon, praying that he didn't start firing. "Why don't you put the backpack down on the floor so we can talk?"

She could feel Moon's anger resonating toward her. She had intentionally disobeyed his orders. She reminded herself that they were equals. She was the scientist on the case, only she knew the possible danger that Jack Collier carried in his hands. She didn't want to end up a skeleton any more than Vincent Moon did.

"You can have the money," Jack said, looking right at her. "I don't give a fuck about the money. But I'm keeping the petri dish. Just give me another week, and you can have that back too."

Tyler paused, palms out in front of her. She had no idea what Collier was talking about, but she wanted him to know that she was going to listen and that she was unarmed. She was a scientist like him, scared to death because death was really just inches away, perhaps for both of them.

"What money, Jack?"

Jack raised an eyebrow, staring at her. "Who the hell are you? And what's with all the goddamn firepower?"

The kid was no doubt delusional. Tyler had to be extremely careful. "My name is Tyler Ross. I'm a scientist with the FBI."

Jack seemed to understand. "So they brought you along because of the cure. Well, it's mine, Ms. Ross. Not Dutton's. But I don't expect you to believe me. It doesn't matter anyway. You're not going to let me walk out of here even if I give you back the money."

"What money?" Tyler asked again. She had moved directly between Moon and Jack, and she could hear him shifting behind her, trying to get a new angle. The hairs on the back of her neck stood straight up; she had a feeling that any minute now, he was going to shove her aside and start firing.

She desperately didn't want that to happen. Looking at Jack up close, she saw he really was just a kid. Brash, not as scared as he should have been, perhaps even psychotic, but just a kid. Like her brother. Dealing with a world that had treated him like crap. Things had gotten so bad, he had deluded himself into believing that Dutton's cure was his own. Maybe that's why he had changed it into a killer—to really make it his own. Or maybe that had been an accident. Maybe the whole thing had been an accident.

"I know you're scared," she said, trying to make her voice sound calm. "I know you didn't mean to hurt anyone. We can work this out, Jack. Just put the backpack on the floor, and nobody's going to start shooting."

The last was for Moon and Densmore, who had crept a few inches closer, the rifle trembling in his hands. Jack looked from Tyler to the long barrel of the semiautomatic. Then he shook his head. He seemed truly bewildered. The fear crept back into his expression as he tried to understand what was going on.

"I *didn't* hurt anyone. Dutton doesn't need the goddamn money. He's rich as fuck."

Tyler glanced at Moon. What the hell was the kid talking about? Moon didn't seem to care. He was whispering into his mouthpiece. Obviously, he had changed the reception channel so she couldn't hear what he was saying. A chill moved through her. Perhaps he was giving Densmore the kill code. Any second this was going to erupt.

"Jack—"

"Look, you can take it all fucking back," Jack said, and suddenly he shoved his right hand deep into the backpack.

Tyler felt Moon grabbing her by the shoulder, shoving her down toward the floor. As she hit the black-and-white tiles, she saw Jack's arm jerk upward, tossing something in her general direction. Densmore shouted, falling back as he opened fire, trying to pick the object out of the air. Suddenly the restaurant was filled with green confetti.

"Hold your fire!" Tyler shouted, "Hold your fucking fire!"

She twisted out of Moon's grip. Jack was leaping over

the cash registers, the backpack once again slung over
his shoulder. The confetti still rained down, and Tyler
held her breath, praying it wasn't a bacteriological delivery system. Then she focused on the green strips and
realized it was money—shredded by Densmore's crack
aim.

"What the fuck?" she whispered. Then she saw Jack
hit the ground on the other side of the cash registers,
and she dove forward. Moon and Densmore held back,
still apprehensive of the cloud of minced cash. Tyler
touched the marble counter and vaulted her long legs
over the top. Jack was racing between two rows of microwave ovens toward the back wall of the restaurant.
She looked past him and saw the thick glass of the drive-
through window. There was a gangly, freckled teenager
sitting on a stool in front of the window, a microphone
in front of his lips. To his right was a bank of fryers:
cages full of crisp french fries dripped into vats of bubbling oil, suspended by articulated steel arms.

Jack was heading straight for the gangly teenager and
oversized window. Tyler rushed after him. "Jack, you've
got to give yourself up! They're going to kill you!"

Jack paused, a few yards from the teenager. The bank
of fryers bubbled to his right, filling the air with a thin
layer of steam. Jack turned halfway toward Tyler, his
hand again jammed into the backpack. Tyler's stomach
clenched as she watched his face.

"Come on, Jack. Don't do this. I know you didn't
mean to injure anyone."

Jack's hand whipped free of the bag. Tyler shifted her
eyes and was both shocked and relieved to see a .38-cal.
handgun. She had imagined something much worse.

"Just a few more days," Jack said, deadly serious, the
gun sliding through the air in front of him. "And then

I'll give myself up. That's all I'm asking—a few more days."

Tyler watched a single, angry tear drip from the corner of his left eye. She felt her mouth go dry. She could hear Moon and Densmore crashing over the cash registers behind her. Jack didn't have a few days; he had a few seconds. "Give yourself up right now. I'll do my best to help you—"

Her words were cut off by a flash of motion. She watched, stunned, as the freckled teenager from the drive-through leapt onto Jack's back. Jack agilely twisted to the side, then grabbed the kid roughly by the wrist with his free hand. He yanked the teenager off his back, aiming the gun at the kid's face; then he let him go. The kid staggered back, holding his bruised wrist.

Jack looked at Tyler for a full beat, then spun toward the drive-through window. He aimed the gun and fired three shots. The thick glass spiderwebbed, white cracks extending all the way from floor to ceiling. Suddenly, Jack burst forward at full speed, throwing himself shoulder first at the center of the glass. The glass shattered outward and Jack disappeared, his body spinning down toward the row of cars below.

"My god," Tyler whispered, starting after him. Then she heard a horrible scream from her left.

The teenager was standing in front of the row of bubbling fryers, still clutching his right arm. Tyler's gaze moved to his wrist. There were bright red sores radiating across his bare flesh. As she stared, the sores doubled in size, and began tracking upward toward his elbow.

Moon and Densmore were barreling closer; they hadn't yet noticed the teenager. Tyler held up her hand, shouting for them to stop. Moon glanced at the kid then grabbed Densmore by the shirt, holding him back. The teenager's body began to jerk spasmodically, the sores now touching the crook of his elbow. The skin around his wrist was almost totally gone, white bone glowing almost the same color as his cheeks.

Christ, Tyler thought, *he's going to die right in front of me!* Then her gaze slipped past his deteriorating arm— and a horrible idea struck her. Her jaw clenched, and she realized there was no choice.

As Moon and Densmore stared, she grabbed a grease rag from a hook on the nearby wall and wrapped it around her hands. Then she lunged toward the anguished teenager.

Using the rag as protection, she grabbed him by his right upper arm, and spun him toward the bank of fryers. She kicked one of the french fry cages out of the way, then plunged his right arm into the bubbling oil.

His scream tore into her ears, but she held his arm down, trying to ignore the hideous smell of burning flesh and boiling bone. The heat from the fryer singed her face but still she held on, an anguished moan rising in her throat. Finally, the teenager sagged in her grip, his body going into shock. She pulled his arm out of the fryer and lowered him to the floor. His arm was completely charred up to his elbow, but the skin above the joint was clean of bacteria. She had saved his life.

"Get a paramedic in here now!" she screamed at Densmore. The young FBI agent looked at Moon, who nodded. Densmore ran back toward the front of the McDonald's, while Moon crossed to Tyler's side. He dropped to one knee next to her, looking at the teenage boy. The boy was shaking against the floor, his eyes tightly shut.

"Is he going to live?" Moon asked.

Tyler nodded. Her head was spinning. "The boiling oil killed the bacteria. Another second and his whole body would have been infected."

"Collier just touched him," Moon said, looking toward the shattered drive-through window. The communicator in his ear was going off at a rapid pace, tinny voices trickling out as his black suits reported in. "It happened so goddamn fast. According to my men outside, he landed on a station wagon. The driver ran for cover, and Collier took the car. My agents are giving chase, but he took everybody by surprise. He's got a three-block head start. We might not catch him."

Tyler didn't know what to say. She watched as Moon rose painfully to his feet.

"You fucked up my operation," he said simply. "You're responsible for what happened here."

Tyler didn't have the energy to respond. Moon touched her shoulder with a heavy hand. "Still, that was quick thinking with the fryer. You're a very strong woman."

He looked away as Tyler turned and vomited across the tiled floor.

SIXTEEN

Ten frantic minutes later, Jack was still reliving the moment: his body hurtling through the air, his shoulder touching the fractured glass, his torso bursting out into the sunlight, enveloped in a wave of sparkling shards. Falling, spinning, twisting, his back hitting the top of the station wagon, denting the roof. People shouting all around him as he rolled over the edge, his knees crying as he landed, hard, on the pavement. The gun still in his hand, not aiming, really, but teasing, the dark barrel communing with the man in the driver's seat. The man begging for his life, crawling out of the car, then Jack behind the wheel. The station wagon peeling out of the drive-through and into the city traffic.

Jack's head swirled as he launched back into the present. He was hurtling down a one-way alley, windowless buildings flashing by on either side. A latticework of overpasses cast shadows across the road in front of him, mocking his speed with a strobe-light effect. He wasn't sure where he was heading, just that he had to put as much distance between himself and the FBI as possible. He had a head start, but that wouldn't take him very far. Soon every cop in the city would be looking for a twenty-six-year-old male driving a light blue station wagon. There would be helicopters in the sky and road-blocks on the highway. He had watched enough Fox television to know how it worked.

"Jesus Christ," he gasped, taking a sharp turn out of the alley and onto a two-lane street. Sweat was pouring down the sides of his face, and his hands shook against the steering wheel. He pulled between a Volkswagen bug and a brown compact, slowing to an inconspicuous speed. He had to regain control. He had to *think*.

Dutton had reported the stolen money; that much was obvious. But that didn't explain the severity of the FBI's response. The McDonald's had been crawling with fed-eral agents armed with assault rifles. It seemed as though they had been expecting Jack to be equally armed; when he had reached for the money in his backpack, they had hit the ground as if he had been carrying a bomb.

Jack came to a red light and pulled to a stop. He wiped sweat out of his eyes and felt something warm against his hand. *Blood.* There was a thin gash above his right eyebrow, another scratch on his left cheek. His clothes were covered with flecks of broken glass, and both elbows were scraped raw.

My God, my God, my God! He glanced at the pas-senger seat and saw Justin Moore's .38 sitting on the vinyl like a coiled snake. What the hell had he been thinking? He had pulled a gun on an FBI agent. He could have been killed. But it hadn't been a conscious action, he had just pictured Angie and reached into the back-pack.

His jaw clenched tight. He hadn't had a choice. If they arrested him, Angie died. The miracle cure wouldn't be available to the public until months after extensive animal and human trials. Even then, Angie would not seek it out, not as long as the world thought it was Michael Dutton's creation. She would not have believed.

The light changed, and Jack continued down the highway, his thoughts clearing. He had done the right thing. He was going to end up in jail anyway; if Angie lived, it would all be worthwhile.

He heard a sudden noise from above and looked up through the windshield. It was a low-flying plane, not a helicopter. He was still all right. But he had to ditch the car soon before he came to a police block. And he didn't want to simply steal a different one; he needed to go a long way, and with modern computers, stolen cars ended up on police lists extremely quickly. He had a better idea, something he had thought up while driving into Chicago. He got his bearings at the next light and headed toward the highway leading back into Indiana.

Meanwhile, his mind replayed the scene in the McDonald's, searching for some sense of scale. It still didn't make any sense. There was too much firepower, too much of a risk to innocent civilians. They had wanted him bad, all because of a quarter million dollars?

He pictured the female FBI agent—the tall woman with the short, blonde hair and pretty blue eyes. She had said something strange to him, repeated it more than once: *I know you didn't mean to hurt anyone.*

Had it been some sort of ploy?

Jack didn't think so. He could tell that the woman—Tyler Ross, she had said—was scared. She was under the impression that he had done something horrible, something that would warrant such a massive FBI response.

He again glanced at the .38. He felt nauseous, wondering what would have happened if his finger had slipped against the trigger, if he had shot the woman at point-blank range. He shook his head, bewildered. He had never hurt anyone in his life; there had to be some sort of mistake.

A possibility struck him. Maybe Dutton had made something up to get them to go after him. He had accused Jack of plagiarism and made the charge stick; maybe he had just upped the ante. Jack couldn't begin to guess what sort of lie Dutton could have told, but the professor was crafty. He had stolen years of Jack's work in a single weekend.

The only other possibility was that somehow, Jack really *had* hurt someone. He thought about Justin Moore, lying semiconscious on his bed. Then his thoughts switched to Kate, asleep in the Sleepy Hollow Motel. Maybe one of them had succumbed to some sort of accident, and Jack had been blamed. If so, he could try to explain himself to the FBI. Tyler Ross seemed like she would listen.

By the time Jack hit the highway, he had discarded the idea. He wasn't going to play into their hands. He had tried the straight path at Harvard, and it had gotten him nowhere. He didn't owe the FBI any explanation.

He switched lanes, gliding toward a turnoff on the highway a few hundred yards ahead. He was glad he had avoided a car chase; the station wagon had the maneuverability of a Sherman tank. Taking the exit ramp at sixty-five caused the thing to rattle like it was about to explode.

Thankfully, the wagon stayed intact as Jack navigated toward a brightly lit sign two blocks past the end of the ramp. He had first seen the sign on his way into the city earlier that morning when he had pulled off the highway for a bathroom break: BILL'S USED AUTOS.

On the other side of the sign was a glade of asphalt, one of the biggest parking lots Jack had ever seen. More than three-quarters of the spots were full, most of the cars American models with four- and five-figure prices scrawled across their windshields in chalky white soap.

Jack tried to compose himself as he drove into the lot, drawing to a stop in front of a low, glass-walled showroom filled with higher-end sports cars suspended on disk-shaped, rotating platforms. The showroom looked empty—aside from a group of salesmen in cheap-looking jackets standing by a coffee machine.

Jack shut the engine and retrieved his backpack from under the passenger seat. He thought about leaving the .38 in the car, then decided it was too dangerous. He placed it back beneath the dwindling stacks of cash. Even though it had kept him from getting arrested, he wished he had never taken the damn thing from Justin's apartment.

His knees wobbled as he stepped out of the station wagon, and he quickly dabbed the blood off of his forehead and cheek with a corner of his sleeve. He looked at himself in the windshield, straightening his jacket and shaking away the remaining glass. Then he headed for the showroom.

The second he stepped inside, one of the salesmen was moving toward him, a shark spotting a bloodied carcass. The man was perfect: mid-forties, balding, with thick, twitchy lips and a snaggletooth on the left side. Jack could tell from his eyes that he was hungry.

"Looking to upgrade?" the man asked, starting his pitch. "A young man shouldn't be driving around in a family mobile like that clunker outside. I've got a Corvette just your style."

The man was pointing at a sleek red convertible on one of the spinning platforms. Jack shook his head. "I'm looking for something a bit less flashy. One of the cars outside, maybe a Buick or a Pontiac suburban."

"Are you planning to trade in the wagon?" the man asked, obviously deflated.

Jack shook his head, as they walked back outside into the parking lot. "If it's okay, I'm just going to park it here until my mother can come pick it up for me. She's out of town until next Friday, but I'd be happy to pay you for storing the thing for me. Cash, of course."

Jack unzipped an edge of the backpack and watched as the man's eyes widened.

"My favorite way to do business," the man finally said. "I think something could be arranged."

"One other thing," Jack continued, as they approached a gray Skylark, circa 1984, that seemed perfectly unremarkable. "I'm in a bit of a rush. A few friends are planning a road trip this afternoon, and I don't want to spend the entire morning filling out paperwork. Again, I'd be happy to compensate you for rushing things through."

"Also in cash?" the man finished for him, touching the hood of the Skylark with an open palm. Maybe he knew something dirty was going on, but he didn't seem to care. He was about to make a hell of a sale. "Well, I don't see why that would be a problem. I wouldn't want to stand in your way; there's nothing like a good old American road trip."

Twenty minutes later Jack was choking on the smell of freshly cleaned vinyl as he pulled the Skylark out of the lot, his backpack ten thousand dollars lighter. He had to squint to see through the chalky remains of the soap on the windshield, and the radio only got AM, but he wouldn't have to worry about the Chicago police or the FBI. The station wagon was parked somewhere near the back of the used car lot, and he doubted anyone would notice when his "mother" failed to pick it up. In fact, he wouldn't be surprised if it became just another one of Bill's used cars.

Jack relaxed as he sped down the on-ramp. He was heading east now, the wrong direction, but for good reason. He needed to get to Las Vegas, and he didn't have time for the drive, especially now that the FBI was gunning for him. He needed a faster way to travel, and that left only one real option.

He had been avoiding airports because of the security risk. Now he knew his feelings had not been idle paranoia; there was a good chance they had been looking for him at the train and bus stations in New York. O'Hare was simply out of the question, but that didn't mean he couldn't fly to Vegas.

He had a good memory, and he could almost repeat what Kate had told him word for word: *It's not much of an airfield now, just a way station for Midwest drug couriers and salesmen too cheap to fly commercial.* She could have been exaggerating for effect, but she didn't seem the type. Jack still had a good deal of money left, and he doubted he'd have to show his ID to a drug courier with a twin-engine prop plane. Now that his duffel was unretrievable, his carry-on would fit snugly under the seat in front of him. He smiled, pleased with himself.

Las Vegas was three days by car, but it was only four hours by air. If the feds were smart, they might be able to figure out where he was going. But they wouldn't know how he was going to get there. That gave him a fighting chance.

He gunned the engine, merging back onto the highway. He wouldn't be back in Gary until late afternoon. But like the man said, there was nothing like a good old American road trip.

SEVENTEEN

Duke Baxter moved through the quiet hallways of the intensive care unit like a sixty-six-year-old man with a prostate the size of a grapefruit. His shoulders were hunched so far forward he felt like he was about to fall over, while his gnarled right hand gripped the portable, wheeled IV rack for balance. A long, white tube snaked down from the IV to the wide sleeve of his pale blue hospital smock. The tube was taped to the inside of his forearm, just a few inches above the pink registration bracelet that identified him as a long-term patient of the University of Chicago hospital system.

The doctors and nurses he passed as he trudged down the hallway barely looked at him, and he fought to control the smile tugging at the corners of his lips. Sick old people didn't smile, he reminded himself. In fact, most old people didn't smile, even when they were healthy. In seven years of marriage, he had never seen the old sore crack a grin.

He tried to imagine what she would have done if she had seen him chasing his story through the bowels of the U of C hospital. She knew how much he detested the damn places; "Heaven's waiting room," he'd always called them. The one time he'd needed surgery—a hernia at age fifty-nine—she'd practically had to drag him by his hair. He couldn't stand the thought of all the different germs and viruses floating through the air, the spittle from a thousand coughing patients painted like a thin film over every doorknob and toilet seat. He wished he was wearing gloves and a mask like all the doctors and nurses, the selfish bastards. But they weren't part of his disguise.

He passed a pair of orderlies standing next to a portable EKG, and didn't even rate a nod; his cover was that good. He had borrowed the smock and bracelet from his former next-door neighbor, a seventy-two-year-old woman with blue hair and a truly disturbing sex drive. The old sore had dubbed Betsy Lynn the human vacuum cleaner because of the stories that had floated around the apartment building after she had moved to Chicago, but Duke had always maintained a guarded friendship with Betsy because of the cakes and cookies she had dropped by when Marta first got sick. As long as she kept her other talents in check and kept the pastries coming, what the hell did Duke care about her reputation?

Betsy hadn't asked any questions when he had borrowed the smock and bracelet. Maybe she thought it was some kinky fantasy; she certainly wouldn't have guessed the truth. Like most of the other people from the apartment building, she considered his journalistic dreams the delusions of a lonely senior citizen. She couldn't have suspected that he was on the verge of greatness.

The truth was, he was minutes away from cracking the story wide open. Seven hours ago, Sheriff Carlson had tipped him off about the FBI operation outside the Helio Clinic, and he had arrived on the scene just as the ambulances were carting the burned teenager away. When he had tried to question the two FBI agents from New York, they had completely ignored him. The woman—her name was Tyler Ross, and that alone had taken him seven phone calls to figure out—had looked positively green as she had shoved him aside. The hulking man with the limp and slight hunchback had waved a .45 in Duke's face when he had tried to follow them to their cars. Duke hadn't been scared. He had served in WWII and faced down Nazis in Bordeaux; he wasn't going to piss in his pants because of a gimpy, gorilla-sized FBI agent. Well, maybe they hadn't been Nazis exactly, maybe it had been two weeks after the Germans had surrendered, but it was still WWII.

After the FBI agents had driven away, Duke had used his scanner to follow the ambulance to the U of C. He had made a short stop at Betsy's, then had returned to the hospital ready for some investigative journalism.

He had entered through the emergency room, counting on the fact that there wasn't anything less conspicuous than an elderly man in a big city ER. He had changed into the smock in a bathroom and found the IV rack in a deserted examination cubicle. Locating the ICU had been a bit more difficult; there weren't any maps in the damn place, and he had been forced to ask directions from a harried orderly in pink scrubs. She had suggested he take the elevator because of the IV. Five minutes later he had found himself in the heart of the beast, dodging microbes as he searched for the teenage burn victim.

He wound deeper into the ICU and came to a hallway lined with glass doors. The hallway was a bit noisier than the rest of the floor, the air filled with mechanical sounds: the beep of heart monitors, the hiss of respirators, the clickety clack of pumps and levers. Duke cringed as he glanced through the closest glass door at a middle-aged man plugged full of tubes and wires. He thanked God the old sore had died in their bedroom. For himself, he was hoping for something a little more dramatic: maybe a plane crash or a shark attack. Something exciting to keep the gossipy fools in his apartment building occupied.

He turned another corner and slowed to a stop. He was in another hallway, this one lined with wooden doors. There were a half-dozen people up ahead, more than a few in black suits, some with white plugs in their ears. Feds, no doubt, pretending to be in control of the situation. The main bulk of them were gathered around the last room at the end of the hall; a large, crew-cutted young man was stationed directly in front of the wooden door, arms crossed against his chest.

Well, Duke thought, *now what?* He was certain the teenager from the McDonald's was inside that room, but how was he going to get inside to question the kid? He watched as a nurse in green approached from the other end of the hall, pausing to show her ID to the crew-cutted agent. He scrutinized her photo like a real pro, then finally opened the door for her.

Duke cursed, leaning heavily against the IV rack. It appeared as though he had gone to all this trouble for nothing. *Look at you,* he could hear the old sore chiding, *all dressed up and it ain't even Halloween. What did you think; it was going to be easy?* Duke wanted to tell her to shut the fuck up, but of course she was dead, and as usual, he had no choice but to ignore her.

His thoughts were interrupted as one of the black-suited men broke away from the rest and headed right toward him. He thought the man was going to shoo him away, but he just headed past. Duke might as well have been a piece of furniture.

Relieved, Duke returned his attention to the G-man standing guard at the other end of the hall. He was busily developing a plan when the door behind the agent opened inward, and the nurse came out, followed by a young kid in a wrinkled McDonald's uniform. The kid looked to be about nineteen, with long, brown hair pulled back in a ponytail and acne all over his cheeks. The kid paused to say something to the agent guarding the door, then followed the nurse, moving down the hall in the other direction.

Duke smiled; God was tossing him a lob. He marched after the kid, trying to move as fast as possible without giving his health away. He used the IV rack to push his way through the gaggle of FBI agents mucking up the hallway, even nodded as he passed the one guarding the burn victim's door.

He finally caught up to the kid with the ponytail in front of a bank of elevators on the other side of the ICU. He waited until the nurse in green had walked out of earshot then cleared his throat.

"I like the uniform," he said, as the nearest elevator door slid open. "You got to pay for it yourself, or does it come with the job?"

It was the sort of ridiculous question that old people were supposed to ask. The kid broke a smile as he stepped into the elevator. He held the door open for Duke, then hit the button for the first floor.

"One of the many perks," the kid said. "But if it gets damaged, it comes out of my paycheck."

He glanced down at the soda stain covering the front of his shirt. Then he shook his head, a bewildered look on his face. Duke saw his opening.

"Quite a commotion out there in the hallway. Woke me up from my nap. Those guys in the suits look pretty serious."

The kid nodded, his ponytail bobbing up and down. He lowered his voice, as if telling a grave secret. "They're with the FBI. Like on TV."

Duke raised his shaggy eyebrows. "No kidding? The FBI? You in some sort of trouble?"

The kid laughed, then got serious. "Not me. It's my friend. He got hurt pretty bad. It was one crazy fucking scene. But I'm not allowed to talk about it."

Duke could tell by the way the kid bit at his lower lip that he wanted to talk; he was dying to talk. Duke just needed to give him a little push in the right direction.

"When you get to be my age, kid, ain't nothing left that can surprise you. I've already seen it all. I'm sure your story is good, but I can wait for the movie."

The kid looked at him, running a hand against the volcanoes on his cheek. Then he shook his head, his eyes glowing. "Sir, you might have seen a lot, but I'm pretty sure this tops it all."

By the time the elevator doors opened on the first floor, Duke had his story—and it was much bigger than he had suspected. He waited until the kid had rushed off toward the hospital cafeteria, then hit the button for the parking garage. On the way down, he tore the IV tube off of his forearm, his fingers trembling with excitement.

Jesus Christ, he was going to be famous. By tomorrow morning, his byline would be on the front page of every newspaper in the country. He thought about the old sore watching from above, eyes widening as she saw his face on the evening news. Then he laughed out loud.

He could already taste that fine Cuban cigar burning down against his gums.

EIGHTEEN

Vincent Moon leaned against the hood of a black government sedan, watching as the McDonnell Douglas helicopter descended toward the empty field in front of him. The copter jerked as the rotors fought against the heavy gusts of wind coming off of the grassy glade, and for a brief moment Moon thought the pilot would have to recircle for a second try. Then the struts finally touched down, and the experienced flyer instantly cut the engine. The rotors slowed, becoming visible, and the side door of the copter swung open, clanging against the machine's fiberglass fuselage.

Moon straightened his black lapels as he watched the small, compact man climb out of the copter and start across the field. The sight took him back twenty-five years. The field was different then, a rice paddy with stalks as high as a man's shoulder. And the helicopter was much less elegant, an insectlike construct of steel beams and bubbly Plexiglas eyes. But the man was the same: gunmetal gray hair, chiseled, weathered features, cobalt eyes.

Of course, his uniform had changed. His colonel's stripes had been exchanged for a dark, pinstriped suit, and his combat boots had morphed into shiny leather shoes. But he wore the outfit with the same sense of loyal dignity: He was a career soldier, still serving beneath the same God. Moon pushed away from the sedan as the stocky man approached, ignoring the shards of pain that ricocheted down his right side with the motion.

"Senator Conway," he said, stiffly courteous as he held out his right hand. "I trust you had a good flight from Washington."

There were more shards of pain as Conway shook his hand, but Moon's face did not change. He had learned to live with the pain, the same way people accepted allergies or arthritis. It was only late at night, when he lay twisted against a hard mattress, that he let himself think about the mass of scar tissue that ran along the base of his spinal column.

"We took off; we landed. I don't remember the rest." Conway had never been much for small talk, which was fine as far as Moon was concerned. He saw Conway as a superior officer, even twenty-five years later. He would not have felt comfortable talking to the man about the weather.

"I'd like to express my sorrow at your loss," Moon said, trying to find the right words. He didn't know how to play this role either; he had lost a wife and a dog over the past ten years, but he kept his grief on the inside, right next to the scar tissue. He would never remarry, but maybe one day he'd find a new pet. *The dog never asked how he was feeling.* "And I swear to God I'll bring the animal who did this to justice."

Conway nodded, glancing toward the sedan. He saw that the car was empty, that Moon had made the twenty-minute drive from Chicago alone.

"I understand you met the boy. Face to face. And that he got away."

It wasn't an accusation, but to Moon the words were

like a blow. "The operation was compromised by my partner, Dr. Ross."

"I'm not looking for an excuse, Vincent. I want you to tell me about the perp. What did you see in that McDonald's?"

Moon rubbed the back of his hand across his lips. His glasses felt tight against the bridge of his nose, but he didn't adjust them. "I saw a murderer. No remorse. Minor amounts of fear. He knows exactly what he did, and I think he has some equally brutal acts planned for the future."

Conway looked away, his jaw tightening. It was what he wanted to hear, but it still made him angry. Moon felt his stomach clenching; he had seen this expression before. In the rice paddies, in the jungle, even back at the base camp in Danang.

"And what about the media exposure so far?" Conway asked, still looking across the field. "Is everything still under control?"

Moon nodded. At least here he was on solid ground. "The press seemed to buy the story about the gas leak at Penn Station. And the McDonald's debacle has been written up as just another armed gunman meeting and greeting the public in a local fast-food joint."

"So you don't expect any surprises?"

Moon thought for a moment, then decided he shouldn't keep any secrets. It was hardly a real concern, but that was for his commanding officer to decide. "There is one unexpected annoyance. A reporter from a small newspaper called the Gary *Gazette*. But I don't think he'll be a problem."

Duke Baxter looked more like a columnist for some retirement community newsletter than a real journalist. Moon doubted he'd be able to put the story together, and even if he did, he probably didn't know the first thing about getting the world to notice.

"We'll get Collier before the story breaks," he finally concluded.

Conway nodded. Then he looked Moon straight in the eyes. Moon felt a chill move through him.

"I've never asked you for anything, have I, Vincent? In the twenty-five years since Vietnam, I've never made a single request."

Moon stiffened, his throat going dry. He knew exactly what Conway was getting at: *payback*. Twenty-five years ago something had happened that had bonded the two men together—the sort of bond that could only come out of Vietnam.

It had gone down three weeks before the end of Moon's tour. He had been out on patrol with four men from Conway's outfit, trudging through the jungle on a routine recon mission. There had been motion up ahead, and Moon had started forward to check it out. A moment later he had heard the gunfire; to his utter shock it had been coming from behind him. He had gone down in a spray of blood, two bullets tearing through his right side—one within centimeters of his spine. Just before he had gone unconscious, he had seen the shooter: a grunt named Danny Gonzalez, a fresh kid from Los Angeles. Friendly fire, they had called it on the medical report, a statistic, an accident.

Except this hadn't been a fucking accident. Two nights earlier, he and Danny Gonzalez had gotten into an argument during a card game. Moon had insulted the kid in front of his buddies from the barrio. Moon had known the minute he had gone down; Gonzalez had shot him on purpose.

The day he was released from the MASH unit—a permanent limp in his step, a hunch in his shoulders, and

pain that would follow him through the rest of his life—
he had gotten even. He had ignored his discharge orders,
had instead returned to his unit, walked into Gonzalez's
tent, picked a golf club out of a rack in the corner, and
had proceeded to beat the young man unconscious. He
would have continued beating Gonzalez to death if Conway hadn't entered the tent and wrenched the club out
of his hand.

Conway had known about the card game, and he had
sympathized with Moon. So he had made the charges
disappear; there had been no witnesses, and Gonzalez
was no longer able to complete a full sentence, let alone
finger his attacker. Conway had given Vincent Moon a
second chance and had spared his career.

Gonzalez spent the next four months in intensive care,
and the rest of his life in a wheelchair. Moon was hon-
orably discharged from the Marine Corps and was sub-
sequently recruited by the FBI. Conway had made sure
he had moved quickly up the ranks, and Moon had never
forgotten what his sergeant had done for him in Vietnam.

"No, sir," Moon finally said, his shoulders aching.
"You have never asked me for anything."

Conway's voice cracked with sorrow. "I'm asking
you now, Vincent. Do you understand?"

Moon nodded. He knew exactly why he was on this
case. Conway ran a hand through his gunmetal hair.
"This Tyler Ross—is she going to be a problem? I can
have her taken off the case."

Moon thought for a moment, then shook his head. "I
don't think that will be necessary. She's got an attitude,
but I can work around her. She's a woman and a scientist. She's severely outmatched."

Conway paused for a moment, digesting Moon's
comments. When he finally spoke, there was steel in his
voice.

"I don't want a trial, Vincent. No media circus. I don't want to see pictures of Jill—of what Collier did to her—on TV. I don't want to hear this monster's excuses or see him crying on *Barbara Walters*. I want him buried nine feet under mud. No coffin; just his broken, bullet-ridden body for the worms to eat. Is that clear?"

Moon breathed deeply. It was a strange thing to hear out in the open, but he had no reservations. He owed Tom Conway his life. "Absolutely. We don't know where Collier is right now, but I think I know how to find him."

"I want him dead, Moon." Conway was standing like a military colonel, not a state senator. Moon could almost see the rice stalks waving behind him. "And I want it done quickly."

Moon pressed the side of his hand against his forehead, a stiff marine salute. Conway returned the salute, then spun on his heels and headed back toward the waiting helicopter.

"He said she was his sister. I didn't think he was lying, at least not at first."

The little doctor was jerking nervously as he moved down the narrow hallway, leading Moon and Densmore through the center of the mazelike clinic. They had gone through this three times already, but Moon wanted to make sure he had bled Kendrick dry.

"And he just handed you the money?" Densmore chirped, hands clasped behind his back, skeptical. "Didn't ask for a receipt, didn't want to know where it was going. Just handed you thirty thousand dollars, and you didn't ask any questions?"

Kendrick shrugged, sheepishly. "This is not a typical business. Many of our grants are given without much protocol because of the nature of our research. I once had a check handed to me in the bathroom of the opera house because a man didn't want his wife to see him making a donation. We inject shark cartilage into tumors, gentlemen. They don't hold telethons for our sort of work."

Moon grimaced as they took a tight corner, his hands balling into fists. "Didn't you think it was an awful lot of money from such a young man?"

"He had a lot more in his backpack," Kendrick said. "I think it must have been more than a hundred thousand. I just assumed he was a whiz kid computer programmer or something like that, trying to find his sister—or whoever she is."

Moon pursed his lips, thinking. The money was still a mystery. Where had Collier gotten his hands on so much cash? Was it a down payment on the bacteria? Had he stolen it along the way? Or had he just been saving up for years, planning for his murderous rampage?

Moon assumed that Tyler Ross had her own theory about the money; but since the scene at the McDonald's, he had hardly spoken to her. Right now, she was back at the hotel, arranging to have Michael Dutton flown into Chicago to discuss the new scientific development: the fact that Collier had infected a young man with just the touch of flesh against flesh. Moon had not told her that he was returning to the clinic; she would only have gotten in the way.

"And after he handed you the money," Densmore continued, as they moved deeper into the building, "you took him to see your patient—Ms. Sandra Fox. And she told him where he could find his 'sister.'"

Kendrick stopped in front of a closed door, a nervous look on his face. "That's right." He paused, looking at the two FBI agents. "She's probably asleep. She takes

an afternoon nap after her course of treatment. She's in
a delicate state, so please don't upset her—"

"We'll handle the situation from here," Moon interrupted, towering over Kendrick. "Please wait for us in
your office. We'll resume our questioning after we've
interviewed Ms. Fox."

Kendrick paused a moment longer, then moved
quickly down the hall. Moon reached for the doorknob.

The room was silent, save for the gentle drip of the
twin IVs. The woman was fast asleep in the center of
the hospital bed, her egg-shaped head resting deeply
against a soft down pillow. Her body was tiny, like a
featherless bird, curled in a fetal position beneath a thin,
white blanket. The look on her face was almost cherubic,
and Moon hesitated a moment before locking the door
behind him.

He moved to the right side of the bed, his gaze shifting to the IV line that led from the hanging glass bottle
to the woman's right arm. Then he turned to Densmore.

Densmore glanced at the woman, a nervous look on
his face. Then he slowly reached into the inside pocket
of his jacket. He removed a long hypodermic needle
filled with transparent liquid.

"Are you sure this is safe?" he whispered, as he
handed the syringe to Moon.

Moon did not respond. The woman was dying of cancer. Kendrick was pumping her full of shark cartilage
and fetal umbilical cords. Her health seemed a moot
point.

He flicked a finger against the hypodermic needle,
making sure there were no air bubbles. Then he gripped
a section of the IV wire and pushed the needle into the
soft plastic. There was a quiet pop, as the needle burst
through. He depressed the plunger with his thumb,

watching as the transparent liquid dribbled down toward the sleeping woman's arm.

When the syringe was empty, he pulled it free and covered the pinprick hole with his finger. Densmore handed him a tiny piece of clear tape from a roll in his pocket, and Moon resealed the IV.

He stood back, waiting for the Pentathenol to sweep through the woman's bloodstream. He didn't think it would harm her; the chemical acted on neurotransmitters in the brain, and the woman was dying from tumors in her lungs. Either way, it was a risk Moon was willing to take. He was hunting a young man who had already killed ten perfectly healthy people.

A few minutes later Sandra Fox stirred, and red splotches appeared on her cheeks. Her eyes drifted open. Moon leaned forward, checking her pupils. Glazed and slightly enlarged; the Pentathenol had roughly the same effect as a dozen Valiums. In reality, there was no such thing as truth serum. But there were a hundred different ways to get her so fucked up she didn't care what she said—or whom she said it to.

"Ms. Fox," Moon said, gently. "We'd like to ask you a few questions about your former roommate. The woman who called herself Karla Dawson."

"Angie Moore checked out of the Bosley Inn four weeks ago," Moon said to Densmore, as he slammed down the receiver. They had commandeered Kendrick's office, telling the doctor to wait in the lobby until they sent for him. Moon was seated behind the steel desk, his shoulders hunched together as he leaned over the phone. Densmore was seated across from him, legs crossed, a computerized notepad open on his lap.

"Do they know where she went?"

"No. But it doesn't matter. We'll find her."

Moon drummed his fingers against the phone. His mind was moving fast, spinning through the details. So Jack Collier was searching for his dying girlfriend. That didn't make him any more human—it just added another dimension to his madness. He was an obsessed stalker, chasing the woman who had left him behind. He had gotten revenge on his professor by sabotaging his cure and killing his graduate students; now he was going to kill his ex-love—and anyone else who happened to cross his path.

"Do we go to Las Vegas?" Densmore asked eagerly. "Collier doesn't know she's not there, and they won't give him the information over the phone. It took a call from the Bureau to get them to cooperate with you."

Moon nodded. Collier would already be halfway to Vegas by now. If he was driving, he'd be there in two or three days. If he'd somehow found a flight, he'd be there by nightfall. "Yes, but we won't catch him there. He's smart enough to know we'll be waiting for him."

Moon cocked his head, the pain running up and down his spine. Collier was not a fool. He wouldn't try to enter the clinic through the front door. He'd find another way.

"The clinic is a red herring," Moon finally decided. "There's a better way to catch our perp."

Densmore raised an eyebrow. "Angie Moore."

Moon nodded; his lieutenant was shaping up to be an excellent agent. One day, he'd take Moon's place. He'd be the one they called when they needed something done right. "She's the key to catching the Karma Killer. With the money he seems to have gotten his hands on, he could have left the country by now. He could have disappeared. But that's not his plan. He's crossing the United States, searching for his girl. If we get to her first, then he's ours."

Densmore leaned forward, lowering his voice. "What

about Dr. Ross? Do we update her on what we've learned?"

Moon thought for the briefest of seconds. Ross would fuck everything up. She would not understand the stalker mentality; she would give emotional bias to a sociopathic urge.

"We don't tell Dr. Ross anything about Angie Moore. We follow this lead on our own. We leave Ross in Vegas, a stakeout that never ends. Meanwhile, we hunt down the lost little girl."

It was a wonderful plan. Ross would be out in the desert with Dutton and her test-tube junkies, while Moon hunted down the Karma Killer. This time, when the guns went off, there would be no woman getting in the way.

"We'll find Angie Moore," Moon said, rising like a storm cloud from behind the desk. "And when we do, she'll lead us to Jack Collier. And then this case will be over."

And my debt will be paid.

NINETEEN

"It's almost biblical, isn't it?"

Alone in the passenger cabin of the four-seater Cessna, Jack pressed his face against the cold, circular window, staring down at the jet black desert. At first he didn't see anything, just a pool of spilled ink stretching on forever. Then the plane curved gently to the right and suddenly the desert caught fire, a glowing ball so bright Jack had to blink to believe what he was seeing. He couldn't make out the shapes yet, just the shine of the city, its incandescent soul.

"It's like a halo crashed down from heaven," the gruff voice continued over the roar of the twin engines. "Broke in half and lit up the night. You gotta love Vegas, baby."

Jack turned toward the cockpit, smiling. The curved steel door was open, and the pilot was turned halfway around in his seat, his headphones off his ears and a bright smile on his face. His name was Grady, and he had bushy hair and a hawk nose. He was a big, friendly man, and Jack had taken an instant liking to him.

"How far are we from the airport?" Jack asked, as the plane bumped over a patch of clouds. The flight had been intense, the small plane responding to every change in wind or temperature. Jack had only flown once before, on a one-way ticket from Newark to Boston that had been included in his scholarship package. He had never been in anything as rickety as the old Cessna, and it didn't help that there were two parachutes hanging from the wall just a few feet away.

"We're only a few miles from McClane," Grady responded, finishing the wide turn. "But that's not where we're landing. The airfield is another thirty miles to the west, just outside the Carson City limits. A shack, a strip of asphalt, and a legal whorehouse five minutes away. Smugglers' paradise, Jack. Not like that shithole outside of Gary. This town knows how to treat its drug dealers."

Jack shifted his gaze from the parachutes to the pyramid of burlap sacks taking up the far corner of the cabin. Each sack weighed about forty pounds; Jack's shoulders still ached from lugging half of them on board. It was enough marijuana to supply a dozen high schools, a weekend's harvest from one of the premier dope farms in Indiana. Grady had exchanged two kilos of cocaine from New York for the marijuana, and there was a buyer waiting for him in Vegas with a backpack of cash twice as large as the one under Jack's seat. Jack hadn't passed judgment on the man because of his line of work: When people like Justin Moore chose to ruin themselves with heroin, it wasn't the fault of the men who provided the smack any more than it was the fault of the ones who supplied the syringes. Nor did the marijuana make Grady any less likable; it just put him in perspective. He had offered to help Jack get to the clinic outside of Vegas because he knew there would be money involved. Their arrangement was black and white, no question of motivations or intent.

Jack had watched Grady struggling with the burlap sacks in the airfield in Indiana and had known immediately that this was his ride. It had cost him ten thousand dollars and the Buick Skylark, but it was well worth it. Grady didn't ask any questions and had just as much reason to avoid the authorities as Jack.

"Will I be able to find transportation at the airfield?" Jack asked, gazing down at Las Vegas. Now he could make out the landmark hotels of the Strip, from the glowing pyramid at one end to the towering Stratosphere near the other. Downtown was a mesh of blinking stars, and it was all connected by belts of packed highway, a constant surge of cars feeding the city like the coopted circulatory network of a cancerous tumor.

Grady coaxed the Cessna over another bank of clouds, and Jack's stomach lurched toward his throat. Then the plane settled as it began its descent.

"I can help you find a car and some maps of the area," Grady offered. Although he hadn't asked any questions, Jack had found him easy to talk to—especially when the turbulence was bad. He had listened sympathetically as Jack had described his quest for Angie. "There's a phone near the runway, so you can call the clinic and get the directions. How are you planning to get inside?"

Jack hadn't said anything about the FBI, or the fact that they were probably waiting for him at the Bosley Inn. But Grady wasn't a fool, and this wasn't a commercial airline. *The burlap sacks weren't full of roasted peanuts.*

"Well," Jack finally responded, watching the blinking lights of the neon city. "First I need to find out if she's there. They won't tell me anything over the phone; I need to find some other way to talk to one of their employees."

Grady paused for a moment. The engines growled as the desert rose menacingly. "Jack, how many people do you think work in this clinic?"

Jack shrugged. He could only hazard a guess. "Maybe twenty. Twenty-five."

"Alone out there in the desert, surrounded by sick and dying patients. Gotta be tough on the psyche, don't you think?"

Jack wasn't sure what Grady was getting at. "I guess. Are you trying to tell me something?"

Grady smiled back at him. "Just that there might be an easier way to get the information you're looking for."

Jack raised his eyebrows. "You know about a back door to that clinic, Grady? Because I can't think of another way to talk to anyone who works there, short of parachuting through their roof."

Grady turned back to the controls. The Cessna dipped noseward, wind rushing through the cabin. They were dropping like a stone with wings. Below, Jack saw nothing but desert. Las Vegas had disappeared behind them, and they seemed to be heading toward a vast, sandy wasteland.

"You gotta remember where you are," Grady said, as the sound of the landing gear tore through Jack's ears, "and learn from the natives. In this town, you don't go chasing after your marks. You set down bait and wait for them to come to you."

Jack had no idea what the hell the drug dealer was talking about. "What sort of bait?"

"That's the easy part. If my hunch is right, the bait's already set."

If it hadn't been the middle of the night, and Jack didn't have the air conditioner at its highest setting, and he wasn't sipping out of a plastic bottle of fresh spring water, he'd have thought for sure he was looking at a mirage. For three straight hours he had been facing a stiff black desert horizon, and suddenly there it was, rising up out of the sand—just as Grady had predicted: CHEAP BEER.

The sign was in bold neon, and Jack didn't know whether it was the name of the place or just an advertisement. Either way, it didn't really matter. The long, ranch-style building was only twenty miles from the Bosley Inn. If Grady's hunch was correct, Jack was sure to find a few tired clinic staffers inside, working through their bullied psyches.

He took his foot off the gas pedal and let the sand-caked Volkswagen bug slow to a reasonable pace. The car stopped shuddering for the first time since the two-lane highway had changed into a single swath of packed dirt. The bug had cost him almost as much as the flight from Indiana; he now had less than $120,000 left in his backpack, but he was so close to Angie he could almost smell her perfume.

He edged to a stop between a pair of old pickup trucks, quickly surveying the parking lot. The lot was more than half full, most of the vehicles oversized and caked with desert dust. Jack wasn't sure who lived out here, other than those who worked at the Bosley Inn, but he guessed this watering hole was never empty and never full. As Grady had put it, if you lived in the desert, sooner or later you needed a drink.

Jack slung his backpack over his shoulder and hurried toward the neon sign. Frigid, conditioned air hit him as he pulled open the heavy front door, and it took his eyes a moment to adjust to the smoky atmosphere. The place seemed run-down, but still maintained a sense of rustic charm. The entire room was paneled in cheap wood, and there was a long bar with tattered velvet stools running the length of the back wall. A trio of poorly upholstered couches sat near an unlit fireplace across from the bar, and a scattering of tables intermingled with fake, potted plants sat randomly arranged across the sawdust-covered floor.

Jack counted at least fifteen people in the bar, mostly men. A few of the patrons were standing by the fireplace, three occupied the couches, and the rest were drinking quietly at the various tables. The mood was subdued; what little conversation trickled through the air seemed to consist of single syllables, often left floating alone in the thick drafts of cigarette smoke.

Jack started toward the bar, giving the clientele a closer look as his boots kicked up sawdust from the floor. Most of the patrons were dressed in jeans and cowboy boots, though a few were obvious tourists—maybe on their way home from one of the local cathouses. It was impossible to tell just from appearances if any of the men or women worked with cancer patients.

Jack began to despair as he reached one of the velvet bar stools. If he didn't come up with something soon, he'd be buying drinks for everyone at the bar, striking up forced conversations. It wasn't much of a plan; but at the moment, he didn't see another alternative.

He lowered himself onto the stool, thinking hard. Bare seconds later he was interrupted as a bartender appeared and set down a white frilly napkin. The man was rail thin, with oily brown hair and watery lips.

"I'd check your ID if this wasn't the middle of fucking nowhere. What'll you have?"

Jack ordered a beer. When the bartender moved toward the cooler, Jack noticed the television set hanging above the bar, turned to a college basketball game. The sound was off, the picture grainy; Jack could see the score was close, but he couldn't tell who was playing. Then the bartender returned, setting a glistening beer on the napkin.

"And how about a drink for the lady?" the bartender asked, looking over Jack's shoulder.

Jack turned and saw that a tall blonde had materialized behind him. Her arms were crossed against her ample chest, and she was grinning. "Don't tell me you drove all the way across the desert for a beer, honey. Want some company?"

Jack smiled back, relieved. Grady had also assured him that this would happen: every local bar had a local professional, and it was a certain bet that at least some of the depressed clinic staffers came here for more than the cheap beer. Maybe this was the opportunity that Jack was searching for.

"Have a seat," he said, trying to look older than he was.

The woman slid onto the stool next to him, and the bartender brought her a glass of orange juice. Then the thin man moved away, giving them room to talk.

"You're way too cute for a place like this," the woman started, leaning forward just enough to show her curves. "Wait, don't tell me. You just had your heart broken; you're out in the desert trying to drown your sorrows in sin."

Jack kept his eyes on the basketball game to keep them from drifting down her dress. "Something like that."

The woman didn't seem to mind his short answer. She was good at making conversation. Jack barely said anything, and her story came pouring out. Her name was Lori, and she was from Dallas, Texas. She had spent three years as a stripper in Las Vegas before moving out of the city. Yes, she had modeled before. No, she didn't hate her work because she loved men so damn much. Yes, she did bachelor parties, and no, she didn't have a boyfriend. The answers were all volunteered before Jack had asked the questions. Finally, she downed her orange juice in one long draft.

"So do you want to party, kid? Or just drink beer?"

Jack turned back from the television. It was time to make his move. "I'm actually trying to find someone. There's a medical research facility just ten miles from here called the Bosley Inn. My friend is on the staff there, and he comes in here all the time."

Lori didn't have a suspicious bone in her body. "The cancer guys. Yeah, they practically live here. It's a lot of pressure, working with the terminally ill."

Jack smiled inwardly. Grady had been right. Set down bait and wait for them to come to you.

"Are any of them in tonight?" Jack asked, hopeful. He was prepared to wait at the bar all weekend.

Lori scanned the room. Then she pointed at one of the couches by the fireplace. "The little guy with the glasses and the cowboy boots. Steve Pickney. A really nice guy when he isn't drinking. I've partied with him twice this week already. Is that your friend?"

Jack shook his head. The man had bright red hair and was wearing an awful plaid shirt. His cheeks were almost the same color as his hair, and there was a bottle of scotch on the couch next to him.

"No, but he might know my friend. I'll go over and talk to him."

"Sit tight," Lori said, rising from her stool. "I'll get him for you. I think I see a tourist by the door who needs some company."

Jack watched as Lori crossed the room. She said something to the red-haired man, who looked up toward the bar. Jack could tell from his expression that he was pissed off by the interruption. It would make things difficult, but Jack didn't care. His luck had been phenomenal so far.

Lori moved off toward the tourist, leaving Pickney alone. He grabbed the bottle of scotch and staggered toward the bar. When he reached the stool next to Jack, he jabbed a finger toward the beer in Jack's hands.

"You better be buying some beer to go with my whiskey, boy. I was just getting comfortable."

The smell of alcohol was overwhelming. Jack pointed to the stool. "Have a seat. I just need to ask a couple of questions; then you can have all the beer you want—on me."

The man lowered himself onto the stool, eyeing Jack suspiciously. "Lori says you got a friend who works at the clinic."

Jack shook his head. "Lori must have misunderstood. I've got a friend who's a patient at the clinic. A young woman named Karla Dawson. Do you know her?"

Pickney's eyes narrowed. "What the fuck you trying to pull? We don't give out information about our patients."

The bartender was looking over, alerted by Pickney's belligerent tone. Jack lowered his voice. "I'm not trying to cause any trouble. I was heading over to the clinic tomorrow to visit my friend. I was telling that to Lori, and she mentioned that you work there. I figured I'd ask if you knew her."

It was a reasonable story. The man's anger seemed to subside. He took a long swig from the bottle of whiskey, then shrugged his shoulders. "Well, that doesn't change anything. I still can't tell you anything about our patients."

Jack nodded. "Are you one of the clinic's doctors?"

Pickney laughed, an ugly sound. "Do I look like a doctor? I'm a tech. I work the meat cookers."

Jack's hands clenched at the brutal image. He had read about places like the Bosley Inn during his research.

"My friend sent me a letter describing the clinic's therapies. Hyperthermia sounds like a pretty difficult business. Cancer cells are more sensitive to heat than normal cells, but the trick is getting the heat to the right place without damaging the surrounding tissue."

Pickney stared at him, then turned to the bartender, ordering a beer. When the beer came, the man focused his attention on the TV. The basketball game was in the fourth quarter, and the score was tied. "You sound like a scientist."

"I've got a Ph.D. in biology," Jack said. He needed to get back to Angie, but he had to take his time, had to make this jerk comfortable. "I've done a lot of reading into cancer treatment. I think you guys are up there with the best."

Pickney shrugged. "Bosley's got a pretty good system worked out. We use fiberoptic cylinders to deliver microwave heat directly to the tumors. In some of the advanced cases, the doc implants magnetic rods right up next to the malignancies, which we heat up with radiation. Innovative shit. Maybe your friend will come out okay, if she's not too far along."

Jack watched Pickney go from the beer to the whiskey, then back again. Maybe it really was the pressure of his job, or maybe it was just a bar in the middle of the desert. "Her name is Karla Dawson. Sometimes she goes by Angie. A tall brunette—"

"Hey!" Pickney said, loudly. "I thought I already told you, I can't talk about our patients!"

Jack unzipped his backpack, stuck his hand inside. His fingers touched the hard barrel of the .38, then moved to one of the stacks. He withdrew five bills and laid them on the bar.

"I don't want to stay in this fucking desert any longer than I have to. If you'd just tell me if she's at the clinic,

I'll leave you alone. You get five hundred dollars for your trouble. Now that sounds like a fair deal to me."

Pickney stared at the money. He wavered for just a moment. "Yeah, I know Karla. She was with us until four weeks ago. There wasn't much we could do for her. Her cancer was way too advanced for heat treatment. Bosley put her on an herb diet, but it wasn't helping. She just kept getting worse."

Jack's stomach dropped. His lips trembled, and his head began to spin. "Did she—"

"She moved to Los Angeles," Pickney said, sweeping up the hundred-dollar bills. "Got a job at a café on Melrose, some place with a French name. 'Le' something or other. Invited us all to come by some time and say hi. Sweetest thing in the world—"

Pickney stopped mid-sentence, staring at the television set. Jack was running through the information in his head. Angie was still alive, but she was getting sicker. She had given up on the alternative route and had taken a waitressing job in LA. Jack could reach her before morning—

"Fuck," Pickney interrupted, gesturing toward the TV. "Isn't that you?"

Jack looked up. There was a black-and-white photograph of his face on the television screen. He recognized it from his yearbook. His cheeks turned hot, and he froze. *Christ.* The FBI had put his picture on television. He had to get the hell out of there.

"Hey, Chester," Pickney shouted. "Turn that up. We got a celebrity in here."

"That's okay," Jack started, rising from the stool, but he was too late. The bartender flicked a switch under the bar. The sound came on, and everyone in the vast living room turned toward the TV.

The black-and-white photo disappeared, replaced by

a live image, an old man Jack didn't recognize sitting in a TV studio. The man had shaggy white eyebrows and was wearing a bad suit. The man coughed once, then his voice blared out through the bar: "The FBI calls him the Karma Killer—but I call him the Scourge. See, the disease lives in his skin. All he has to do is touch you—and you die. Horribly."

Suddenly, a new picture appeared on the screen. A police photo of a skeleton lying on a beige mattress. Next to the skull was a pile of long, black hair.

"Her name was Kate Matti," the man's voice continued. "She's just one of ten victims so far. If he touches you, this is what happens—in a matter of minutes. He's a human plague, and he's out there somewhere. If you see him—run. Because if he touches you, you're dead."

The screen shifted back to the black-and-white yearbook photo. Jack stared at himself while the blood rushed through his ears. *Oh, my fucking God.* He couldn't get the image of Kate Matti's skeleton out of his head.

It was impossible. It had to be a lie. Jack's mouth opened and closed and he tried to find air.

I know you didn't mean to hurt anybody. He remembered the armed FBI agents in the McDonald's and the fear in Tyler Ross's eyes. Then he pictured the crew-cutted men in black suits at Penn Station.

Coming after him because he was a killer. A Scourge.

Holy fucking shit.

"Jesus!" Pickney gasped, looking at the hundred-dollar bills in his hands. Realization burst through his alcohol haze, and he threw the money at the bar. Then he stumbled back, his face pale.

"It's you," he croaked. "You're the Karma Killer. You got the death in your skin!"

One of the women in the bar screamed, and suddenly

everyone was backing away. The bartender was reaching for a phone, fear flashing across his cheeks. Jack rose, his backpack on his shoulder, his hands out in front of him.

"It's not true," he whispered. "It can't be true."

Please, God, don't let it be true. He looked at his fingers, at the pink flesh stretched over the bones beneath. He pictured Kate Matti's hands, the skin gone, the skeletal fingers curled against the beige mattress. *Please, God, please, God, please, God . . .*

The picture in his mind changed. He saw himself leaning over Kate's sleeping body, touching his lips to hers. *Touching his lips to hers.*

He turned and sprinted for the door.

TWENTY

The window was rolled down and Jack was screaming at the top of his lungs, his tortured voice reverberating across the desert sand. Tell me how? he screamed. Tell me why? *Tell me where I went wrong?*

The desert remained cruel and silent. The VW bug shook, the tires barely touching the dirt road as he sped on and on. His eyes were blurry with tears and the headlights were off; he was a steel missile hurtling through the darkness, praying to God that he'd just slam into a tanker truck and get it over with. Then he thought of the flames eating the skin off an innocent driver, and the tears flowed even harder, burning his cheeks like licks of orange flame. The TV had said he'd killed ten people. Ten innocent people reduced to skeletons because he had touched them. Kate Matti at the Sleepy Hollow Motel. Who were the rest? Who else had he touched?

Faces flew through his memory. Justin Moore? The old woman at Grand Central? Someone on the train? Someone at Penn Station? Some kid at the McDonald's? Dr. Kendrick? Grady?

Jack's foot came down hard on the brake pedal, and the tires skidded against the road, sending up a high cloud of dirt and sand. Jack collapsed against the steering wheel, his chest heaving. He had to regain control. He had to think.

The man on the TV had called him a scourge. He'd said that the disease lived in Jack's skin, and that he spread it with his touch.

The first question was obvious: Was it possible? Could Jack be carrying death in his epidermal cells? Or was it some new FBI trick. No, it couldn't be a trick. The television report was going to start a nationwide panic. Jack could still see the fear in Pickney's eyes; he could still hear the women screaming as he ran out of the desert bar. The FBI had wanted to keep this a secret.

So if it wasn't a trick, was it possible? Jack took deep breaths, rubbing the tears from his cheeks. He was a scientist, he had to rationally think this through. He closed his eyes, pretending he was back in his lab at Harvard, alone in the middle of the night with his test tubes and petri dishes. *Alone with his bacteria.*

He opened his eyes and looked at the backpack sitting on the seat next to him. His body started to shake.

My, God.

Streptococcus A lived inside human skin cells. It was transmitted primarily by touch. The untailored version was one of the most dangerous microbes on earth. It could eat skin and organ tissue at a rate of a few inches per hour. If left alone long enough—perhaps weeks, perhaps months—it could, feasibly, reduce a woman to nothing but bones.

But Kate Matti hadn't died over months. The man on the TV had said it had taken seconds. That didn't sound like necrotizing fasciitis.

Jack slammed his hands against the steering wheel, again and again. He had used strep A to make his miracle cure. Somehow, the bacteria had mutated again, had changed form to something incredibly deadly. And somehow, he was carrying that scourge in his skin.

"Why didn't it kill me?" he asked, out loud. His voice sounded strange bouncing off the interior of the VW bug. "Why couldn't it have just killed me?"

It wasn't a scientific question. It was a supplication to God. He had played with the bacteria at a genetic level; he had taught it to hunt down cancerous tumors. Now it was hunting down skin and organs. Even though he hadn't done it on purpose, it was his fault. He should have been the one to die. Instead, he had somehow become a carrier.

The guilt was massive, a thousand pounds against his back. He was a murderer. Kate Matti was an innocent young girl who had only wanted to help. He had reduced her to bone.

When you do something wrong, Jack, you've got to make it right. Karma, Jack.

Karma.

"How do I make this right?"

The desert wouldn't answer him. Angie couldn't answer him. It was up to him to figure out. Somehow, he had to make things right.

First, he had to turn himself in. If the FBI gave him a lab, maybe he could find out what went wrong. He could isolate the bacteria, sequence it down to its genetic level, and find out how it had once again become a killer.

He shook his head, surprised by his own idiocy. The FBI wouldn't give him a lab; they'd shoot him on sight.

The only chance he had was Tyler Ross. The FBI woman had been willing to talk. Maybe she'd still be willing to listen.

He put his foot back on the gas pedal, reviving the little car. At first, he considered heading straight to the Bosley Inn. The FBI might still be staking the place out. Then he had a better idea.

If the feds had moved into the area, they'd be staying at one of the area hotels. It wouldn't be hard to find, and they wouldn't expect him to come to them. If he was lucky, he'd get to Tyler Ross when she was alone.

Maybe she'd believe him. He hadn't meant to kill anyone. He was just trying to save Angie. His intentions were true. It wasn't karma, but it was something. Maybe, somehow, Tyler Ross would understand.

TWENTY-ONE

Tyler watched the moon dancing across the fetid surface of the kidney-shaped swimming pool—a glowing white orb flickering with each breath of wind that licked across the thick, greenish water. She was struck by the strange urge to stick her hands through the reflection, to shatter the orb into a million sparks of light. Then she pictured the putrid water eating away her skin, and she shivered, pulling her lamb's wool jacket tight across her chest.

"Are you okay?" Michael Dutton asked from the other side of a small, candlelit table. "Do you want my coat?"

Tyler smiled at him. They were alone on the patio of the rickety desert hotel, and it was now almost midnight. The last remaining table of FBI agents had retired an hour ago, exhausted from a long day spent camped out in bulletproof SWAT team vans.

"I'm just tired," Tyler responded, still looking at the swimming pool. "And confused. This case is like a boxing match. One minute, I feel like I'm on top of things, and then a jab hits me and I lose my center. It's been three days, and I'm no closer to figuring this out. It's like we're still back at your lab at Harvard."

The frustration was physically painful. After the debacle at the McDonald's, Tyler had nearly fallen apart. Although she had saved the teenager's life, the personal cost—both to him and to her—had been immense. She had sat by his side in the hospital room for hours until Moon had arrived with the information about the clinic outside of Las Vegas. Her mind had swirled at the thought of facing Jack Collier again, but her pride had not allowed her to quit.

During the flight to Nevada, she had contacted Dutton, then arranged for an FBI charter from Boston. Nobody understood this bacteria better than Michael Dutton, and if he couldn't figure out what the hell had happened at the McDonald's, what chance did anyone else have?

She turned back to the professor, watching as he downed his fourth vodka tonic. He was dressed for the cool night; a heavy forest green jacket that matched his eyes, dark jeans, and a white oxford shirt. He looked less tired than the last time she had seen him, but there was still a wildness in his eyes, only partially due to the alcohol. She had no idea what he had been going through back in Cambridge, but she could only assume it had been as hard for him as anyone.

"Then how about a drink?" Dutton said. "A few sips won't kill you."

Tyler shook her head. There was a bar on the other side of the pool, and the bartender already knew Dutton by his first name. While Tyler had watched the clinic from one of the bulletproof vans, Dutton had chosen to remain at the hotel, surrounded by biology texts and Caufield's preliminary reports. Tyler did not condone the drinking—but if it made it any easier for Dutton to submerge himself in the case, she wasn't going to complain.

As for herself, the truth was Tyler would have loved a drink, if she hadn't given up alcohol years ago as part of her strict, anti-carcinogen diet. She couldn't shake the feeling that they were wasting their time in the desert; she could have accomplished much more back in Feinberg's lab in Washington, especially with Dutton by her side.

"Maybe he'll show up at the clinic," Dutton said, his glass clinking against the table. "Maybe he didn't see the TV report."

Tyler shook her head. The stakeout was simply a formality since the story had broken on the evening news. Jack Collier wouldn't dare show his face now that everyone in the country was scared to death of him. Caufield was still outside the clinic with a handful of Moon's lackeys, but Tyler did not expect her cell phone to ring anytime soon. Moon had gone to bed hours ago, and in the morning he was going to relaunch his operation on a national scale.

"The story was carried on every station in the country. Our information line has received more than five thousand calls from people claiming to have seen him, everywhere from Trenton to Seattle. If he didn't see the story, he's sure to have seen the effects. I doubt he can step into a mall anywhere in the country without setting off a panic."

"None of these sightings has panned out?" Dutton asked.

Tyler shrugged. "It will be days before we can sort through them. We were taken completely by surprise by the story. Some reporter from Indiana figured it out on his own."

Dutton leaned back in his chair, his long legs crossed. He ran his hands through his sweeping auburn hair. "Well, he won't get too far, with the entire country looking for him. Some cop's liable to take him down well before we make contact."

Dutton did not seem displeased with the idea. Tyler chalked it up to residual anger; Jack had destroyed his cure, after all.

Tyler flashed back to the moment in the McDonald's when she had come face to face with Collier. She remembered how he had insisted that the cure was his, not Dutton's. And then he had said something else, something she still couldn't figure out: *Dutton doesn't need the goddamn money.* As if the hundred-dollar bills he had been carrying in his backpack had once belonged to his professor.

Tyler watched Dutton's face as he stared across the pool. She was struck again by his good looks and the rakish glow in his green eyes. It was true, he didn't look like a man who needed money. Not because he was rich, but because money wasn't important to him. He served a higher calling.

Jack was delusional; it was the only answer that made sense. But maybe the delusion wasn't entirely his fault. Maybe the thing he was carrying in his skin was affecting his brain.

"But why isn't it killing him, like the rest?" Tyler asked, thinking out loud. "Why isn't the bacteria attacking his flesh?"

Dutton glanced at her, then shrugged, almost disinterested. "He's found some way to protect himself. Turned himself into a living weapon."

It wasn't a very scientific answer. Tyler pressed her hands against her face, thinking. She pictured the scene in the McDonald's one more time, watched Jack reach out and touch the teenager, watched the teenager reel back, clutching his wrist . . .

Suddenly, a different memory shot into her thoughts. She was back in the café in Chicago, listening to her brother talk about unknowing people infected with HIV.

Innocent carriers, he had called them. *Spreading death.*

That was it. A carrier. *A host.*

"The strep A must somehow recognize him as its life source: a host. Something inside of its genetic makeup has programmed it to leave him alone so that it can survive indefinitely. But everyone else is fair game. Everyone else is food."

Dutton shifted uncomfortably in his chair. "Sure, maybe that's what he engineered it to do. So he could kill with just a touch. Easier than carrying around some bio bomb."

Dutton made it sound like it was the simplest thing in the world: genetically engineering a deadly bacteria to live harmlessly in one's epidermal cells. Well, Dutton was a genius, he had come up with the cure in the first place. Tyler needed to go much slower, to think it through step by step.

"It isn't spreading by secondary contact," she said. "He touches the money, then someone else touches the money, and that's okay. It only attacks when there's flesh-to-flesh contact. Or in the case of the Penn Station bathroom, contact with a deposit of living tissue—a urine particle on a toilet seat."

Dutton drummed his fingers against the table. The candle trembled, wax dripping down in a viscous river. "That makes sense. Bacteria are different than viruses. A virus spreads because it needs hosts to replicate. It will slack off one host, wait patiently in the environment until another host comes by and activates it—"

"But bacteria are more like predatory animals," Tyler continued for him. "Bacteria eat because they're hungry, not merely to survive. If they're somehow living healthily within Jack Collier's skin, they won't leave unless they come into contact with another food source."

She ticked down the list on her fingers. "The men in

Penn Station. The cat at Justin Moore's apartment. Kate Matti. The teenager in the McDonald's—"

"And my two lab students."

Tyler paused, surprised by Dutton's angry tone. This was a scientific discussion. "No, I don't believe Jack ever came into contact with the lab students. They caught the disease through contact with the strep A itself in the petri dish, the same way the pig in our experiment died."

Dutton looked at her. His eyes seemed to cloud up. "So they died because I told them to go to the lab and gather the samples. It was my fault."

Tyler felt a burst of sympathy. There was real pain in Dutton's voice. "No, you didn't know the strep A had gone bad."

"But Jack knows," Dutton said, the pain replaced by more anger. "He's spreading this on purpose. He's made himself into a scourge."

Tyler wasn't so sure. When she had entered the McDonald's, she had nearly been convinced that Jack was the killer Moon thought he was. Now she was beginning to have second thoughts. Would he really have genetically engineered a bacteria to ride inside of his skin, turning him into a living weapon? Wouldn't there have been an easier way to go on a killing spree?

"He didn't touch the kid in the McDonald's in order to kill him," she said, fairly confident.

Dutton nearly jumped down her throat. "Maybe he did. You said he had a gun, but he didn't use it on the teenager. Instead, he just grabbed his wrist. That sounds like intent to me."

Tyler rested her elbows on the table. The candle flickered between them, shadows chasing one another across Dutton's chiseled jaw. Finally, Dutton smiled, rubbing his eyes.

"I'm sorry. I'm a little emotional right now. This whole thing has hit me very hard. All I wanted to do was help people. Now my cure has been turned into this horrible plague, and it just makes me so angry. Jack has robbed so many people of a chance at life. It just seems so unfair."

Tyler saw her hands reach out, saw her fingers curl into his palms. He seemed to be in so much pain. She knew his history, knew that at this very moment his blood was flooded with vodka, but a part of her didn't care.

He's a project, she reminded herself.

But he's also a man who can understand what she'd been through. He had dedicated his entire career to understanding her.

"Seven years ago I was diagnosed with breast cancer," she said quietly. "I still remember the moment like it was yesterday. It was a Tuesday afternoon, my regular mammogram. Normally, my doctor took about ten minutes to read my films. That afternoon, I was waiting for twice that. I knew something was wrong."

It was almost stream of consciousness, but Tyler couldn't stop herself. The case was weighing on her and she was looking into Dutton's green eyes and she just needed to let it all come spilling out.

"She came into the waiting room and told me she had to redo the films. 'Don't worry,' she said, 'this is procedure and it doesn't mean anything.' But I knew it wasn't procedure."

Dutton's palms felt warm, the sweat beading beneath her fingers. But he didn't pull away.

"There was a calcification on the right side. The doctor did a manual exam—and felt the cyst."

Her eyes burned, the moment still just as powerful seven years later.

"I can remember exactly what I was wearing—my favorite colors, red and black. A striped silk blouse, an Italian knit vest, a mid-calf black skirt, black tights, and black shoes. I remember driving home in a daze, calling my boyfriend at the time, crying for hours and hours. Then the surgery. I was small-breasted anyway, and a lumpectomy would have been ridiculous. Besides, I just wanted the thing *off*."

Dutton's mouth opened, but no noise came out. His cheeks had paled, but Tyler did not want to stop. She knew he understood. He was a cancer specialist; he had spent years in a lab struggling to find a cure.

"The cancer hadn't spread, thank God. But I knew my life was never going to be the same. Six months of chemo, five years of hormones and waiting and fear. Now they call me cured, but I know it's always going to be with me. In my head, if not my body."

She waited for Dutton to say something. He looked bewildered, his strong features frozen behind the candlelight. She felt herself starting to blush. Was she out of her mind? She barely knew this man. But now that she had started she couldn't stop.

"To this day, I haven't worn black or red again. They were more than just colors, they were a part of my personality, a symbol of the control I had over my world. That control was taken away from me."

She stopped, her hands trembling. In another moment she was going to start crying. She needed Dutton to say something. She needed him to react. She looked into his eyes, waiting, hoping—and then it happened.

He leaned forward over the table and kissed her.

The door to his hotel room swung inward and Tyler felt herself half-carried over the threshold. Her flesh burned with desire as his lips worked their way down the side of her throat, but her mind remained blank; she knew this was foolish, that she was a federal agent working a case and he was a civilian under her supervision. If Moon found out, she could be suspended, perhaps even lose her badge.

But my God, it felt good. His teeth touched the edge of her collarbone as her jacket came off. His right leg slid between her thighs, his knee rising against her. They were halfway across the room, now, standing in front of a plush couch that faced a small kitchen area. There was a leather satchel on the floor by Tyler's feet, and two empty scotch bottles a few feet away. Beyond the bottles was the foot of the bed, the covers already pulled up, the pillows heaped together like a throne beneath the high wooden headboard.

This is happening way too fast. Tyler took a deep breath, telling herself that she had to stop, that she had to go back to her own room and lock the door. Then Dutton's lips pressed against hers and his tongue slipped into her mouth and her entire body started to pulse. She felt his hands move down her arms to her waist, then back up again, toward the buttons of her shirt—

She grabbed his wrists, pushing away. Her face had turned bright red, and she took a step back, nearly tripping over the leather satchel on the floor.

Dutton looked at her, confused. The desire was fierce in his eyes. "What's wrong? Isn't this what you want?"

Yes, damn it. It had been a year since she had slept with anyone. But no matter how much time passed, this moment didn't get any easier.

"Michael," she started, and then she stopped herself. There was nothing she could say that would make it any better.

Slowly, she turned to the side and undid the buttons of her shirt. As the soft material slid off her shoulders and fell to the floor, she watched Dutton's gaze move down to her chest.

Tyler thought she saw something flicker across his face, then quickly disappear. She prayed the perception wasn't real, that it was a figment of her own insecurity.

"You're so beautiful," Dutton murmured, stepping toward her.

She wished she could believe him. She looked down at her own chest, at the curved red scar that ran horizontally across the right side. Her small left breast seemed absurdly large next to the flat expanse of excavated skin.

She had never regretted her decision against reconstruction; but that didn't change how she felt every time she undressed for a man.

Dutton put a hand under her chin and lifted her head. "You really are beautiful."

His words were soft and smooth, but there was definitely something different in his eyes, now that he had seen what the cancer had done to her. Tyler swallowed, her jaw tightening. She reminded herself whom she was with. Dutton had dedicated his life to curing cancer. He was supposed to understand.

But she could see it in his eyes. Despite his words, he was repulsed by the sight of her mastectomy.

"Michael, I'm not sure—"

"It's okay," he said. Before she could respond, his hands were on her waist. He kissed her, and she closed her eyes, forcing herself to try and recapture the moment. Maybe it was all in her head. *Maybe he really didn't care.*

The heat had just begun to revive when she felt his hands tighten against her waist. Without a word, he turned her around, bending her over the edge of the couch.

Maybe he really doesn't care, she repeated to herself, but she knew now it was a lie. She had been in this position many times before.

She felt her pants slide down her legs to her ankles, then her panties pulled to the side. She felt him touching her with his hands, parting her. A second later he was inside her, thrusting forward. She found herself staring down at the leather satchel on the floor, her anger rising. The anger wasn't directed at Dutton, really, but at herself for letting him do this, for letting a moment's passion get in the way of reason.

She listened to him grunting as he thrust harder and harder, and tears rose behind her eyes. Her fingers clenched against the couch as she waited for it to be over. She focused on the leather satchel, counting the seconds, when something caught her focus.

The satchel was partially open, and through the haze of her tears, she saw something familiar inside. She blinked, concentrating—and suddenly her vision cleared.

Her eyes went wide, as she tried to understand what she was looking at. Her memory flashed back to the McDonald's and the cloud of green confetti that floated toward her as Jack leapt over the counter. Her shock turned to anger as she realized that an answer to one of the central mysteries of the case might have been close by all along.

Dutton, you fucking bastard!

The leather satchel beneath her was filled with hundred-dollar bills.

TWENTY-TWO

Just ten yards away, outside in the darkness, Jack Collier's world was collapsing. He stood on a foot-wide ledge by the hotel window, his fingers white against the cracked stone wall. There was only a three-inch gap between the drapes that covered the inside of the window, but those three inches were more than enough. He could see Dutton standing behind Tyler Ross, his pants down, his body rocking back and forth as she leaned over the edge of the couch. He could see the red splotches on her cheeks and the tears of pleasure in her eyes. He could see them fucking away any chance he had at redemption, at giving the world his side of the story.

He spun away from the window, pressing his back against the wall. He looked down at the patio twenty feet below, at the hard cement that surrounded the kidney-shaped pool. All he had to do was lean forward. All he had to do was close his eyes and let go of the wall . . .

No.

His lips pressed against his teeth. He could not give up, not like this. He had listened to the news on the car radio as he had searched the desert for the FBI hotel. The whole world thought he had done this on purpose.

He had to prove that it wasn't true. He had to try to put things right.

He couldn't let Angie die thinking that he was a killer.

He edged away from the window. The fire escape was another ten yards away, a short climb down to the parking lot where his VW bug was parked next to the vans and four-wheel-drive Jeeps. As he had assumed, the FBI had been easy to find—and they had not been expecting him. Certainly, Tyler Ross had been keeping herself busy. Now that Dutton had gotten to her, there was no way she'd believe Jack. Dutton was the miracle man, the famous Harvard professor who had cured cancer; Jack was a killer who had sabotaged that cure, turned it into living death. Every thrust of Dutton's body would poison her against the truth.

Jack was filled with a sudden rage. *Fuck Tyler Ross!* Jack didn't need her help. He'd never had any help, not in his entire life. He'd done everything on his own.

He started down the fire escape, his heart racing at the effort. He would find some way—there had to be a way! Angie was still out there.

As he dropped to the hard asphalt of the parking lot, he realized that there was only one chance, one way to fix things. He had to figure out what had happened to his miracle cure, and he had to reverse the effects.

The cure had taken him two years. Now he probably didn't even have two days. Even if the FBI couldn't find him, his face had become synonymous with disease.

"I can do this," he whispered. As long as Angie was out there, he had no choice. He'd figure out what had gone wrong, and he'd find some way to reverse the process. He'd save Angie, or he'd die trying.

If he gave up now, Michael Dutton would win—and Angie would die. The entire balance of Jack's world would be obliterated. And his mother would have died in vain.

Karma, Jack.

He could do this. He could make things right. All he needed was a lab.

TWENTY-THREE

Tyler shoved Dutton off of her, reaching for her pants. Dutton stumbled backward, still engorged, a shocked, petrified look on his face. Tyler ignored him, coming around the couch. Her tears had been replaced by fire. She dropped to one knee and grabbed the satchel by its handles. She viciously flipped it upside down, and suddenly the air was filled with hundred-dollar bills.

"There's more than twenty thousand dollars here," she hissed. She glared back at Dutton. He was hastily zipping up his dark jeans, a trapped look on his face.

"So?"

Tyler leapt to her feet. For a brief second she couldn't find her shirt. Then she saw it balled up next to the empty scotch bottles. "So where did you get this money?"

Dutton finished with his pants and crossed his arms against his naked chest. He didn't look half as handsome anymore, his hair mussed, streaks of sweat running across his belly. "I drove into Las Vegas this afternoon while you were on the stakeout. I hit it big at the black-jack tables. Hey, you didn't say I had to spend all my time in this shithole hotel."

Tyler finished with the top button of her shirt. Her

fingers were trembling, and she could feel the muscles working in her jaw. She wasn't sure, but she knew now that Dutton wasn't everything he claimed to be. His revulsion at the sight of her mastectomy was one thing, an inconsistency at best, a fault of character. But the money was too much of a coincidence.

"Jack Collier is carrying a backpack full of hundred-dollar bills. He implied that it was your money, that he had stolen it from you."

Dutton laughed, incredulous. "Come on, Tyler. He's a murderer. A psycho."

"Was it your money?"

Dutton's eyes flickered for the tiniest of seconds. "No, of course not."

Tyler pointed to the hundred-dollar bills on the floor. "Then this is just a coincidence."

Dutton exhaled, searching for his shirt. "I'm not going to stand here and listen to your accusations."

Tyler watched him, her eyes narrow. She was now almost certain that Jack had been telling the truth about the money. He had stolen it from Dutton. Maybe it was gambling money that Dutton hadn't reported; maybe there was another reason he had kept it a secret.

Christ, this changed everything. The fifty thousand dollars they had found at Justin Moore's apartment, the ten thousand more spread across Kate Matti's motel room. Jack had been using Dutton's money to fund his trip across the country.

"It isn't a down payment on the bacteria," she said, still watching Dutton get dressed. "It's your money. He even offered to return it. But he said the cure was his."

Dutton laughed, the sound harsh. Tyler stared at him. She felt the room starting to spin. *My God, was it possible?* Collier was twenty-three years old. Dutton was a professor at the top university in the country. He had twice been on the short list for the Nobel Prize. His name had appeared in nearly every scientific journal in the world. It couldn't be true.

Then she remembered the feeling she had experienced when she had first interviewed Dutton about the cure. He had been hiding something from her. She had ignored the hunch because she was attracted to him, because she wanted to believe in him. But now that attraction was gone. There was nothing to get in the way of her sixth sense.

"Tell me again, Professor. Why did you use your own DNA to make your cure? Why didn't you use screened blood from a blood bank?"

Dutton sat down on the edge of the bed. He didn't look at her. "I already told you. It was available and convenient."

"But it wasn't procedure," Tyler continued, hovering over him. "Before, you said you were in a rush to finish the experiment. Why? You could have gotten screened blood in a matter of hours. What was your rush?"

Dutton rolled his shoulders. "I was in the heat of discovery. It was an exciting moment. You wouldn't understand."

"Professor, did you come up with the idea to use strep A as a cancer cure?"

The question reverberated through the room. Tyler took a step closer. "Was it your idea? Or was it Jack's? Did you steal this cure from him?"

Dutton's jaw tightened. "Get the fuck out of my room, Dr. Ross!"

Tyler stared into his green eyes. They suddenly seemed almost reptilian. She stepped back, awed by her own new theory. It changed everything. If Jack Collier had developed the cancer cure, then why would he have sabotaged it? Why would he have turned it into a deadly plague?

The answer was obvious. She kept her eyes on Dutton's face. "He didn't do this on purpose. Maybe he didn't even know about it. He thought we were after the money and the cure. He didn't know about the deaths or about the disease."

My God, it made so much sense. It was like a bright light exploding in Tyler's head. The dead cat, the poor girl in the motel, the men in Penn Station—Jack hadn't killed any of them on purpose.

"So where is he going?" she asked. Dutton was ignoring her now, his arms across his chest. "Why is he running?"

After the scene at the McDonald's, the answer was academic. He was running because the FBI wanted him dead. But he had been heading across the country before the FBI had gone after him. First New York, then the clinic in Chicago, then to the desert. *Another alternative cancer clinic.*

"He's looking for someone," she said, thinking aloud. "He took a sample of the miracle cure with him. He didn't know it had gone bad. He's trying to save someone—someone dying of cancer."

Dutton rubbed a hand through his hair. For a brief moment Tyler actually thought he was going to tell her something; then he turned toward her, and there was a thin, tight smile on his lips. "An amusing theory, Dr. Ross. Painting a murderer as a saint. I doubt Mr. Moon will share your fantasy. And that's exactly what it is, a fantasy. I created the miracle cure. I am a tenured professor at Harvard University, and it was my lab. *Now get the fuck out of my hotel room!*"

Tyler's fists shook at her sides. She could not believe she had let this man inside her body. She wanted nothing more than to retrieve her .38 and put a bullet in his skull. He was a liar and a fraud; she was certain of it. But she needed proof. Any action against him now could cost her badge. And he simply wasn't worth it.

Without a word, she turned and stalked out of the room. She had to get to Moon right away. Jack wasn't the murderer they thought he was; if Tyler could talk to him, she knew she could bring him in without harm. With his help she would find the evidence she needed to expose the truth. To bring Dutton down.

She reached the door to Vincent Moon's room, then paused in the hallway, making sure her shirt was tucked into her pants. Then she slammed her fist against the wood.

There was a long pause, and Tyler tried again. She heard tired footsteps on the other side, then the sound of the latch. The door swung inward, and she found herself staring at a young man with a short, blond crew cut. She recognized one of Moon's lackeys, a kid named Johanson.

"I need to speak to Mr. Moon," she said briskly. "It's extremely important."

Johanson rubbed sleep from his eyes. "He's not here, ma'am."

"Do I have the wrong room?"

The kid shook his head. "No, I mean he's not at the hotel."

Tyler grabbed the kid by his T-shirt and yanked him halfway out of the room. "Well, where the hell is he?"

Fear flashed across Johanson's face. "I'm not supposed to say."

Tyler stared into his eyes. "You do not want to fuck with me right now."

There was a tiny pause. "He left for Los Angeles two hours ago."

Tyler raised her eyebrows. "Los Angeles? Why?"

Johanson shook his head. He looked like he was about to cry. "I swear, I don't know. I just drive one of the vans."

Tyler shoved him back into the room and stormed down the hallway. *Los Angeles?* Moon had lied to her. That was a very bad sign. Without her around to stop him, there would be no limit to his barbarism. If Moon got to Collier before she could tell him what she had just learned—she shivered at the thought.

She prayed to God that Jack was nowhere near LA.

TWENTY-FOUR

"Sir, there's no smoking on this flight. I'm sorry, but it's an FAA regulation."

Duke stared at the Nordic goddess from behind his Cuban cigar. She must have been at least nine feet tall, with a figure straight out of the pages of a glossy magazine. She was standing in the aisle of the first-class cabin, her hands on her impossibly small waist.

"It ain't lit," Duke countered, shifting against the faux leather seat. "I just like to roll it around a bit, get the taste going."

The goddess smiled curtly, giving him that patronizing grin young people use when they think someone is too old to notice what an ass he is making of himself. She was about to say something else when recognition flashed across her plasticine features.

"Weren't you on TV this morning? *Good Day Chicago*?"

Duke's chest swelled. He could get used to this. Traveling first class, getting recognized by stewardesses with names like Olga and Ingrid. He smiled around the cigar. "That's right. Duke Baxter, journalist at large."

"Well, Mr. Baxter, you'll have to take the cigar out of your mouth for the duration of the flight. It's disturbing to the other passengers."

Duke's cheeks reddened as she continued down the aisle. He could hear the old sore laughing in his ears. What did he expect, she was going to throw herself into his lap because she had seen his wrinkled mug on some morning talk show? Duke yanked the cigar out of his mouth and placed it gingerly in his front shirt pocket. It was going to be a long flight.

The seat beneath him trembled as the airplane pulled away from the gate. The first-class cabin was crowded with early morning commuters, most in business attire with leather briefcases and laptop computers. First class was not quite as lavish as Duke had expected, but the seats certainly were larger than coach, and the stewardesses seemed a hell of a lot prettier. It didn't compare with the intimacy of his pickup truck, but then, the yellow eyesore would never have survived the trip out west.

There was a loud rumble as the pilot checked the engines, and then the 727 made a sharp turn onto the runway. They would be airborne in a few minutes. Duke knew it was foolish, but the moment before takeoff always put him in an introspective mood. Today, the sensation was more pronounced than usual, probably because he had finally achieved something that was worth the introspection.

At sixty-six, he had arrived. His story had hit the airwaves at ten last night, and already he had completed six interviews, negotiated a major hardcover book deal, and received phone calls from three different Hollywood agents. There was talk of a movie, and one editor at the *Gazette* had even mentioned the idea of a Pulitzer nomination. Not bad for a guy whose biggest previous story had to do with a shoe store robbery in a shopping mall outside of Gary.

After the excitement of last night, Duke could have simply sat back in his apartment, lit up his cigar, and finally enjoyed the adulation of the skeptical bags who lived in his building. He had almost done it too—lit up the cigar, blown a ring of light blue Cuba over the photograph of the old sore he kept by his bedtable. But just as he was about to snip off the end of the stogie, the phone had rung, and suddenly the bright light of his career had gotten a whole lot brighter.

At first he had thought the kid had been pulling his leg. The story had seemed too good to be true. But then Duke had made the connection to the events at Penn Station, and he had realized that it was a real lead. The kid had seen him on TV, gotten his number from the directory, and wanted to help him get the story straight.

Duke decided this was as good a time as any to go over the details once again. He bent forward, his fingers searching beneath his seat for his small carry-on. He cursed as a divot in the runway sent his head bumping against the tray table in front of him, and then the plane was lurching upward, racing toward the sky. Duke's fingers found the clasp to his bag, and he quickly retrieved his notebook.

As the plane continued at a lurching angle—right up the old sore's heavenly skirt, it seemed—Duke opened the notebook and read through the few pages of notes he had taken during the short phone call. The deeper he dug into the kid's story, the faster his heart pumped in his chest.

The kid had given his name as Justin Moore and had claimed to be a friend of Jack Collier's. Over the past few days, he had been questioned extensively by the FBI and had even been threatened with legal action—though he also claimed to have no connection to any of the deaths and didn't know the first thing about the skin-eating bacteria. The reason for the FBI's interest seemed quite clear, however.

Three days ago, on Thanksgiving morning, Jack Collier had visited Justin in New York. According to the kid, Collier had been searching for Justin's sister, a young woman by the name of Angie. At the time, Justin had not known his sister's whereabouts, and Collier had left to follow his own lead, a cancer clinic in Chicago, located across the street from the McDonald's where the FBI assault had occurred.

Justin's story would have ended there, except yesterday night, after Duke's report aired on national TV, Angie had called her brother from Los Angeles. She had wanted to know if he thought the story could be true. Justin had not known what to tell her, except that Jack had been in his apartment and that the remains of his pet cat were now sealed in a plastic bag in an evidence cabinet at FBI headquarters.

But Justin didn't believe Jack was a murderer; it was his loyalty to his friend that had driven him to call Duke. Moreover, Justin didn't trust the FBI, especially an agent named Vincent Moon who had apparently roughed him up during an interrogation.

Justin had a right to be concerned. In the process of putting together his story, Duke had done a little research into all the players involved—including the two FBI agents who were tracking Jack Collier. Tyler Ross was a pretty straightforward agent, extremely good at her job and well respected in the Bureau. But Vincent Moon was another story. He wasn't simply respected; he was feared. He had killed more suspects in the course of arrests than any other agent in Bureau history. And as Justin's own experience illustrated, Moon's investigative methods were notoriously brutal. Three years ago, he had even been suspended after interrogating a pair of kidnappers suspected of molesting a number of children in the Boston area. Moon had gotten creative with the suspects, using a fire extinguisher to demonstrate the violent nature of the molestation—and its lasting psychological effects. Moon's subsequent suspension had been lifted after the two suspects had confessed to the crimes from their hospital beds.

Understandably, Justin was afraid of Vincent Moon and hoped that Duke could somehow clear Jack's name. Duke didn't need his notes to help him remember the last part of his conversation with the kid; he knew the words like they were lines from his upcoming movie script:

"And how do you expect me to do that?" he'd asked.

"Simple," Justin had answered. "Go to LA, find my sister, and she'll lead you to Jack. Ask him yourself what the fuck is going on."

The airplane lurched through a pocket of turbulence, and Duke shut the notebook, deep in thought. He tapped the cigar in his pocket, a smile tugging at his lips.

He knew what the old sore would have said: *Enough is enough. You got your byline. Now go home and act your age.*

That's exactly why he was on his way to LA. The minute he started listening to the old sore's advice, he would be ready to join her in the cemetery plot outside of Gary. He was going to California to finish this right.

He would track down the ultimate interview—an exclusive with the Karma Killer himself.

TWENTY-FIVE

Jack was lying on his back in the warm grass, staring at the sky. His arms were outstretched and the backpack was resting on his stomach, and he was just lying there, feeling the rotation of the earth. He knew there were people around him, some just a few feet away; girls in short skirts and tank tops on their way to class, jocks with sweatshirts and lettered jackets, professors with manuscripts under their arms—all the colors of the university rainbow. He also knew that any minute someone was going to recognize him, and then the air would be filled with screams. The police would come and then the FBI. The hum of helicopters would mingle with the screams, and suddenly he'd be in the center of someone's crosshairs, his spread-eagled body bisecting a circular lens like a Da Vinci print. A finger would tighten against a trigger and a high-caliber bullet would find him. The bullet would cut through skin and bone, and he would die there, lying against the warm grass.

He turned his head, his cheek tickled by the blades of green. He knew he had to get up; he had to keep moving. The six-hour drive from the desert was a blur, but it had been the short walk to the center of the pristine campus that had taken the strength out of his legs. Passing so many young, smiling people, keeping his head down so they wouldn't see his eyes, pretending not to notice the newspapers in the racks at every junction in the pathwork of the idyllic, parklike quadrangle.

He was a walking plague, his skin was poison. He was AIDS and cancer and ebola and every fear that modern America carried in its media-driven soul. He was a killer and he deserved to die.

But he couldn't die, not like this. He rose slowly onto his elbows, his palms digging into the grass. An enormous stone building loomed in front of him, with arched doorways and painted glass windows. The map he had gotten at a kiosk near the entrance to the university had called the architectural style Romanesque, and it did seem that the building had been plucked out of the landscape of some Italian master. Even the iron lion's head knockers on the ornate wooden doors had a fanciful quality; if it had started to rain, Jack half believed the knockers would melt away, gray paint pooling on the stone steps below.

Of course, it never rained; this was LA. Jack tucked his backpack under his arm and stood, wiping the grass from his pants. He was overdressed for the weather, but he refused to take off his gloves or coat. He knew that secondary contact did not seem to spread the bacteria, or there would have been hundreds of skeletons instead of ten. But he did not want to take the chance of brushing into someone. He could not handle more corpses on his conscience.

He waited a few moments to make sure the entrance was clear. Then he strolled forward, his gloved hands deep in his pockets. He reached the enormous double doors and pushed against one of the lion's heads, propelling himself inside. A rush of cool air hit him as he stepped into a vast atrium. The ceilings were at least twenty feet high, and the walls were covered in ornate wood paneling. There were hallways leading off in every direction, at least eight that Jack could see from his vantage point. There was a security desk to his right, staffed by a single guard in a light blue uniform. The man was reading a magazine, and he didn't even look up as Jack moved past.

Jack reached the center of the atrium and paused, glancing down the halls on either side. To the left he saw classrooms, most of them still dark, though a few students were gathered about twenty yards away, talking quietly in front of a corkboard hanging from the wall. Most likely there were test grades pinned to the board, and the students were the eager top tenth percentile. Jack knew the type—because he had always been one of them. Arriving well before the first eight o'clock class to see where he stood in the general order of things, whether he was still at the top, or whether someone had finally dethroned him.

He turned to the right, away from the students. At the end of a similar hallway was a stairwell, lit by fluorescent strips of light. He knew by instinct that this was the right direction. He had spent most of his life in buildings like this. At Harvard, they called it McCaffrey. Here, it was the Adler Biologic Research Center.

He headed toward the stairwell, the sound of his boots echoing in his ears. The fluorescent lights grew brighter, strengthening his resolve. This was his territory; this was his world. Outside he was a kid, but in this building he was a god.

He reached the stairwell, shutting the glass door behind him. Cement steps led up and down, and again the decision was academic. With each step, he descended lower into the belly of the building, his senses tuning themselves to the familiar sounds and sensations. The cool breeze of internal ventilation systems, the quiet beeps and hisses of high-priced equipment, the clink of test tubes and beakers. It was early morning, but there was no sense of time here. The concept of a deadline was something Jack brought with him.

He reached the bottom of the stairs and pushed through another glass door. Now the hallway was more like a cinder-block bunker, and there was the distinct smell of antiseptic cleansers. Jack's excitement grew as he approached a pair of heavy steel doors. Above the doors was a sign with bright red letters: WARNING— LEVEL-TWO BIOLOGY LAB, LII PRECAUTIONS MANDATORY.

There was an electronic combination lock next to the doors, but a small green light above the lock indicated that the lab was in use and presently unsecured. Jack pressed the metal handplate next to the lock, and the doors swung inward on electric hinges.

Although the layout was different from his lab at Harvard, the atmosphere was uncannily similar. The ceilings were low and paneled, and there was the hum of air moving through ventilation corridors somewhere above the panels. The rectangular room was divided into at least a dozen parallel aisles by high metal counters, and the gleam of tempered glass and stainless steel was everywhere.

Jack stepped a few inches into the first aisle, his eyes taking everything in at once. To his right was a low-tech work area, with two sinks, a test-tube rack, and an open drawer full of masks, gowns, and rubber gloves. Next to the open drawer was a large blackboard listing each of the aisles, with student's names and blanks where each individual could sign in. Jack noticed that there was only a single name signed in at the moment: Brett Castor, Ph.D., in aisle nine. Jack stood dead still, listening, and heard the sound of a sink turned on and off somewhere deep within the lab.

Heart pounding, he headed straight for the cabinet of sterilized gear. He grabbed a white surgical mask and a pair of rubber gloves. Then he took one of the test tubes out of the rack and filled it halfway with water. He purposefully left the tube uncorked, then stuck both gloved hands under the faucet, wetting his arms down to the elbows.

Just as he was turning off the faucet, he heard the sound of sneakers against cement. Someone—presumably Brett Castor—was moving toward him down the aisles. Jack made sure the mask was pulled all the way to the bridge of his nose, then held the test tube tightly in his gloved hand and turned to meet the stranger.

He had barely made it to the end of the first aisle when he saw the young scientist. Castor was tall and gangly, with a shock of blond hair and deep-set eyes. Though the lab was safety level two, he was wearing shorts and a T-shirt: no gloves, no mask, no precautions of any kind. Obviously, he had not expected to run into anyone so early on a Saturday morning.

He didn't notice Jack until they were only a few feet apart. He looked up, startled, nearly tripping over his bright red high-tops.

"Whoa," he said. "I didn't know anyone else was working here today."

"Are you Brett Castor?" Jack asked, gesturing with the test tube. Droplets of water sprinkled to the floor between them.

"That's right. You one of Professor Gatley's new charges?"

"Fred Lamont," Jack said, winking from behind his mask. "Listen, Brett, you know anything about suspending hantaviruses in a phosphate buffer? 'Cause I'm having a hell of a time keeping these bastards inactive."

Castor's eyes shifted to the test tube of clear liquid. It took him several long seconds before he got the words out.

"Did you say hantavirus?"

Jack nodded enthusiastically. More water splashed to the floor. "The prof has me working on this in his other lab. It's a new pet project of his. The hantavirus came from a freezer in Utah, and we're trying to get a sequence out of it. But first I need to suspend the sucker in this liquid form. Got any ideas what I'm doing wrong?"

Castor stared at him like he was insane.

"Are you sure you should be carrying that around like that? I thought hantavirus was a level-four pathogen."

Jack nodded. "Sure is. That's why I'm wearing gloves."

He waited a beat, then laughed. "Kidding, Brett. In its liquid form it isn't supposed to be that dangerous. At least that's what the professor said."

That was more than enough for Brett Castor. He gave Jack a wide berth as he moved past. "Love to help, Fred, but I was just on my way to breakfast."

"Maybe when you get back?"

Castor was already halfway to the double doors. "Sorry, I'm taking the weekend off. But good luck with that. Really."

Jack smiled behind his mask, as the double doors clicked shut. He knew his comment about the professor's assurance would seal the deal. Not all professors were as bad as Michael Dutton, but most had a tendency to treat lab students like lab rats; and in the world of laboratory science, it was every rat for himself.

Jack tossed the test tube into a nearby sink and hurried to the closed double doors. To the right of the doors was a lever, beneath a bright red emergency flag. Jack yanked the lever down and heard a series of mechanical clicks.

He smiled again, heading back toward the interior of the lab. The emergency lever was a standard safety precaution of a level-two laboratory. In the event of a dangerous chemical spill, a lab student could seal the laboratory from the inside; only a professor with a master keycard could now gain entry. There was the chance that somewhere on campus, a prof's computer was now receiving an emergency report—but that was a risk Jack was willing to take. It was a Saturday morning, and he didn't know a single professor who worked this early on a weekend. That was the whole point of choosing a life of academia, after all.

Jack moved quickly through the lab, searching for the equipment he was going to need. The task ahead was monumental, but in his scientist's mind he was already working through the practical details—lining up the puzzles like targets in a rifle range.

He stopped in an aisle halfway across the lab, eyeing a bank of genetic-engineering equipment lining the metal shelf. His gaze skipped past a centrifuge, a conventional microscope, a handful of gel electrophoresis machines, to a pair of cabinet-sized electron microscopes. He knew that each microscope cost upward of a hundred thousand dollars; housed within the steel cabinets were powerful electromagnetic generators, strong enough to magnify a sample down to its basic structure.

Jack dropped his backpack on the floor and lowered his mask. Everything he needed was right here in front of him. It was time to go to work.

He shut his eyes, forcing his mind to clear. He would need every ounce of brainpower to figure this out. He had to forget about the FBI and the skeletons; he had to purge thoughts of Tyler Ross and Michael Dutton. He even needed to wipe Angie from his thoughts. There was no longer anything beyond the confines of this lab. His entire world was framed by a pair of electron microscopes and a locked pair of level-two safety doors.

Jack stretched his fingers inside the rubber gloves. The way he saw it, his task had two equally challenging parts. First, he needed to find out what had changed the strep A into an accelerated killer. He assumed the FBI had been trying to solve the same question for the past few days—but that didn't frighten him. The mutated strep A was his creation; he had spent two years nurturing it from an idea to a reality. He would see things the FBI could not.

Once he had found out what had gone wrong with the bacteria, he would then have to find some way to change it back to its original state. If the strep A had infected his body, he'd have to cause a new infection—create a bacteriological domino effect that would affect the strep cells throughout his system.

He reopened his eyes and approached the metal shelves. He opened an equipment drawer and quickly found a sterile syringe, a twist of rubber tubing, and a finger-long glass vial. He quickly tied the tubing around his arm, then tapped two fingers just below the crook of his elbow. He gritted his teeth as he jabbed the needle into his vein.

This was where it had all begun—a syringe filled with Jack's blood. He carefully emptied the dark liquid into the vial, then carried it to the conventional microscope. A moment later he placed a slide beneath the lens, holding his breath as he pressed his eyes against the eyepiece.

The sight made him sick to his stomach. He knew now that everything the old man on the news had said was true. The bacteria was in his bloodstream; that meant it was also in his skin, in his saliva, in his soul. It had turned him into an unknowing host.

He forced himself to concentrate, to ignore the pangs of guilt sweeping through him. He stared at the tiny single-celled bacteria, wondering if it looked different, if the changes were somehow visible. A few seconds later he shrugged, stepping away from the microscope and retrieving the vial of what was left of his blood. It didn't matter how the bacteria looked. What mattered was how it had changed.

Originally, Jack had engineered the bacteria to seek and destroy cancerous tumors. He had done so by inserting a genetic sequence from his immune system into the bacteria's genome, turning it into a hybrid of strep A and a human killer T cell. He had added to the bacteria a method of recognizing cancerous tumors—a previously unknown receptor for a ligand shared by 90 percent of malignancies. Using that receptor as a guide, the bacteria should have been seeking tumors as a food source.

But now the bacteria was searching flesh and organs. Somehow it was disregarding the receptor—or the receptor had changed to something much more common, something contained by skin and organ.

This gave Jack a perfect place to start: he would use PCR-polymerase chain reaction—a cutting-edge process that isolated genetic sequences—to fraction out the DNA that coded for his tumor receptor. If he didn't find anything, then he'd know the receptor was gone, somehow replaced by a new guidance system. He would then need to uncover what had taken the receptor's place.

He carefully spilled a drop of his blood into a microcentrifuge tube and began searching the drawers for the chemicals he would need to begin his experiment. He placed the microcentrifuge tube into the PCR machine and cycled the sample through a variety of severe temperature changes. After the reaction was complete, he loaded the sample onto a gel plate; electricity fired through the plate would allow him to "see" the genetic sequences within the bacteria and thus determine what had happened to the tumor receptor DNA.

All sense of time and place vanished as he worked; he could have been at Harvard or on Mars. He knew that dozens of highly trained scientists had done this exact experiment in the FBI labs—but his advantage was clear, defined by a single vial of chemicals just inches from his hands. Only *he* knew the correct primer, the mixture of molecules that would search out the receptor DNA within the bacteria. Dutton would not have been able to figure it out from his notes, and Tyler Ross could never have stumbled on it by herself. The primer was Jack's ace in the hole.

An hour after he had started, he plugged the first gel electrophoresis plate into the power supply. After the charge had coursed through the snippet of DNA, he removed the plate and placed a sample beneath a UV microscope. What he saw confused him, and he decided he needed a closer look. He removed the sample, then crossed to the pair of electron microscopes. He placed the sample into the base of the nearer scope and flicked a switch on its side. The rectangular machine trembled as the internal generator powered up.

A computer screen on top of the scope blinked to life. The electron microscope did not have an eyepiece; instead, the visual information was transmitted digitally, after being fed through a complicated array of software. Jack hovered over the tiny screen, flicking the glass with his fingernails. It was an old ritual: transferring his hope and heart to a cold piece of machinery, adding an edge of magic to this domain of pure science.

On the third flick the screen blinked, then bursts of green appeared, followed by a row of numbers. Jack hovered close to the machine, his mind quickly analyzing what he was seeing.

Strange. It was a genetic sequence, but not a sequence that he recognized. He should have been looking at the code for his tumor receptor, but this was a strip of DNA he had never seen before.

Could it have been a naturally arising mutation? He moved closer, running the tips of his fingers across the picture. He shook his head. The unknown strip of DNA was from a human source. What's more, there were markers between the chemical bases that pricked at his memory; these markers had something to do with the human immune system.

He leaned back against the counter, his mind spinning. Somehow the bacteria had incorporated into its genome a new genetic sequence that was somehow linked to the human immune system. It wasn't the strip of DNA that Jack had originally added to the streptococcus; it was something else, something unknown. How was it possible?

Could Jack have implanted the genetic material without knowing it? His jaw tightened, his arms crossing against his chest. No, there was a much simpler answer. An answer that suddenly made sense. Someone else had tinkered with his cure.

It wasn't hard to come up with the most likely suspect: Professor Dutton. He was the only one with the knowledge, access, and ability. But why? He had already stolen the miracle cure. Why mess with a miracle?

The answer was again obvious. Dutton had done everything he could to erase Jack from the project. He had even gotten Jack expelled from Harvard. But there was a clue that would always link Jack to the miracle cure. Jack had spliced his own immune system DNA into the bacteria's genome.

Dutton must have wanted to obscure Jack's DNA fingerprint within the bacteria. He must have tried to splice his own immune system DNA into the strep. And something went wrong. Instead of hunting and eating tumors, the bacteria was now eating flesh.

His anger rising, Jack hit a series of buttons on the side of the electron microscope, saving the genetic sequence onto a floppy disk. He then removed the disk from a drive connected to the microscope's base. The data in hand, he moved down the aisle, searching for a link to the lab's computer system. It took him less than a minute to locate a laptop terminal inside an unlocked lower drawer.

He shoved the disk into the laptop, then connected to the lab's mainframe. He frantically hit keys, dialing up the National Institute of Health (NIH) genetic database in Washington—the GenBank—where all known genetic sequences were stored for research purposes. Jack had checked unknown sequences through the GenBank many times before; within seconds, the computer would give him a list of possible matches—if any existed.

The next few seconds felt like an eternity. Jack stared at the screen, his fingers hovering over the space bar. The NIH seal glowed a bright blue against his cheeks, and the whir of the computer's hard drive harmonized with the hum from the ventilation corridors up above.

Finally, the computer emitted a series of beeps. The NIH seal was replaced by a paragraph of text. Jack's anger turned to shock, as he read and reread the words.

He had been right; the unknown genetic sequence was human in origin. It wasn't a natural mutation, nor was it something Jack had inadvertently added to the bacteria. And he was fairly certain it had not come from a sample from a blood bank or from any screened source.

Jack shook his head, blown away by what he had just learned. Everything made sense now. The vicious nature of the bacteria. The way it was feeding on skin and organ at an incredible pace. The reason it had not harmed Jack, had used his body as a vehicle in its search for food. It was all because of this genetic sequence, this fragment of DNA. According to the GenBank, this sequence was more than a simple conglomeration of chemical bases: it was the source of a disease that affected the immune system.

"Lupus," Jack whispered. "Dutton implanted lupus into my cure."

Lupus, a systematic autoimmune disease that caused the immune system to attack the human body. Characterized by skin sores, organ and muscle deterioration, sometimes at an incredible rate. Now that the lupus sequence was incorporated into the strep A's genome, the result was a new, hybrid bacteria—flesh- and organ-eating, but with the fierceness of the human immune system gone haywire. It wasn't harming Jack because Jack's DNA was still inside the bacteria; the bacteria recognized him as if he were part of itself. *A brother, a cousin, a host.* But everything else made of organic cells was fair game.

Jack stared at his hands, bewildered. He was carrying a bacteriological form of lupus in his body. Dutton had ruined his cure, turned it into an infectious autoimmune disease. Why?

Because he doesn't know. The lupus was obviously undiagnosed. Dutton was dying of a hideous disease; he just didn't know it yet. His body was going to turn itself inside out within a few years, but for now he was symptomless. He had added his blood to Jack's cure, thinking that he was going to erase any trace of Jack. Instead, he had turned the cure into a killer.

Jack's hands turned into fists. He knew exactly what he had to do, and now he had the means to do it. He could clean the bacteria up, remove the sequence for lupus, then reinfect himself with the new bacteria. A laundered plasmid could be transferred from bacterium to bacterium through single-cellular sexual transmission—like firecrackers in an organic chain.

He could turn himself from a killer to a cure.

Jack's body felt light as he rushed down the aisle. He could undo the damage Dutton had wrought. He could fix his cure, and then he could still save Angie's life. The FBI would come after him, and they'd probably kill him well before they believed his story. But if he could save Angie, it would be worth it.

He reached the end of the aisle and saw a phone hanging from the wall next to a pair of oxygen tanks and plastic safety masks. He grabbed the phone, then pulled a crumpled piece of paper out of his back pocket. He had torn the paper out of a phone book in a rest stop just outside of LA and had circled a single number halfway down the first column. The café had not been hard to find; luckily, this wasn't a big year for French on Melrose, and only one place seemed to fit Pickney's brief description.

Jack's heart slammed as he dialed the number. He did not know what time it was, but he guessed it was at least late afternoon. He still had many hours of work ahead of him, but there were no mysteries left, only details. It was time to make contact.

A young woman's voice answered after two rings. Not Angie, but similar in age. "Le Grand Café. Can I help you?"

Jack had trouble speaking, his mouth was so dry. "I'd like to speak to Angie Moore."

She would be using her real name now. She would not expect Jack to be looking for her at a café on Melrose Avenue.

"She's not in today, but if you wait a minute I'll connect you to her shift manager."

Before Jack could respond, he was put on hold. He cursed inwardly. What if Angie had left LA? What if she was heading to another cancer clinic? Jack did not think he'd survive much longer. No amount of cash could make him anonymous.

A young man's voice chirped at him, replacing the sickly sweet hold music.

"This is Doug Sampson. What can I do for you?"

Jack considered hanging up, then he decided he had no choice but to plow on. "I'm a friend of Angie Moore's from out of town. I'm trying to catch up with her. Do you know where she is?"

"I'm sorry, I can't give out her home number. But she'll be working the late shift tonight if you want to try back."

Jack exhaled, relieved. It would take him at least that long to reinfect himself with the tailored bacteria. "Actually, I think I'll stop by in person. Could you leave a message for me?"

There was a brief pause on the other end. "Sure. Shoot."

Jack's lips trembled, but he tried to keep his voice steady. "Tell her that Jack's coming by tomorrow morning to explain everything. Tell her that she shouldn't believe everything she hears on TV."

It was a strange message, but Jack didn't care. The young man on the other end seemed to take it in stride.

"Anything else?"

Jack thought for a second. He glanced back at the laptop screen, at the glowing photo of the lupus sequence from the electron microscope.

"Yeah, one more thing. Tell her that I miss her, and I'm coming to take her home."

"I'll make sure she gets the message."

Craig Densmore tightly gripped the receiver, signaling frantically with his right hand. Moon ignored him, instead concentrating on the video monitor in front of him. Droplets of sweat beaded across his forehead as the seconds ticked by. Just before the line went dead, a red banner flashed across the screen: <Trace complete.>

"We've got him," Moon said, slamming his fist against the table.

Densmore whooped, returning the receiver to its cradle. The apparatus was twice the size of a regular phone, with half a dozen wires sprouting from its cobalt blue base. Two of the wires were attached to the monitor in front of Moon, and two more ran into a microwave transmitter sitting in an open steel briefcase on the floor. Even though the line had gone dead, the transmitter was still active, receiving a continuous broadcast from a similar transmitter attached to the main phone in the café on Melrose Avenue.

Moon pressed buttons on the keyboard attached to the monitor, and a map appeared across the screen. A bright red circle indicated the source of the phone call.

"UCLA," he said, rising. "One of the buildings just south of the quadrangle. We don't have an exact fix because they're on a centrex system. But it shouldn't be hard to track down."

Densmore was rocking back and forth in front of the transmitter. His eagerness was palpable. Neither he nor Moon had slept in days, and they were both riding high on government-issued amphetamines, little red pills that could keep an agent going for seventy-two hours or more without rest. Moon had learned the usefulness of controlled chemical ingestion during his tour in Vietnam. Even the jungle was bearable at a thousand RPMs.

"Should we alert the SWAT teams?" Densmore asked. His young voice echoed off the sheer cement walls. The cell-like room was directly across the street from the café. It was really just an empty stockroom upstairs from a Chinese restaurant they had co-opted earlier that morning. The furnishings were sparse, and the smell of frying vegetables rose up from the floor; but there was a window overlooking Melrose and enough outlets to power the communication equipment.

"No. We'll take the chopper and six of our best people. And, of course, our new toy."

Moon threw a glance toward the right side of the room, at the enormous wooden crate that took up most of the far corner. The crate was four feet high, five feet across, and covered with government markings. It had arrived from New York just twenty minutes before Jack Collier's phone call. Moon had been across the street at the time, watching Densmore and two FBI techs install the transmission equipment in the café manager's office. The staff at the trendy French eatery had not put up much of a stink once Moon had explained that they were tracking a homicidal serial killer with his eyes on one of their employees.

"He won't stand a chance," Densmore said, reaching for a large duffel bag that was hanging from a hook on the wall. He placed the duffel on the table between them, and went to work on the zipper. A second later he had retrieved two AR-7 sniper rifles and handed one to Moon.

Moon felt a surge of adrenaline as he ran his hands

across the stock of the precision armament. The rifle was four feet long, carried a cartridge of fifty .49-cal. armor-piercing shells, and was fitted with a 400X magnification scope. Moon had trained with a similar weapon in Vietnam; in jungle conditions he could hit a brain base at over three hundred meters. In LA, in broad daylight, he could have put a shell up the ass of a butterfly at twice that distance.

He looked from the rifle to the crate in the corner, and a smile moved across his lips. A spate of pain moved across his shoulders, but his smile didn't even waver.

"What about Angie Moore?" Densmore asked.

Moon yanked the cartridge out of the rifle, turning it over in his hand.

"She stays under house arrest. She doesn't go anywhere near that café. If he somehow gets away from us at UCLA, that's where we'll take him down."

Moon raised his head, light from the window glancing off his glasses. From this angle, he could just barely see the outdoor tables of the café across the street, resting in the shadows of a bright red overhang. He raised the rifle to his shoulder, aiming the barrel a few inches past Densmore's nose. He pressed his eye to the scope and read the license plate of a car parked just a few feet from the front of the café.

"But he isn't going to get away from us," he said quietly. "He's not that good."

He lowered the rifle and again looked at the wooden crate. He almost wished he had not sent for the equipment from New York. He would much rather have thrown caution to the wind and finished this in person. But perhaps he would still get his chance. Collier had outplayed them once before; Moon would not underestimate him again.

"I don't care what he's carrying in his skin," he said, knocking the ammo cartridge against the table for good luck. Then he snapped the cartridge back into place. "He bleeds like the rest of us."

TWENTY-SIX

The man was halfway into his swing, the steel club raised high above his shoulder. His head was down, his chiseled face obscured by the brim of a dark green Marine Corps baseball cap. There were two Secret Service men by his golf bag ten feet away, standing there like the most expensive and least useful caddies on the eighteen-hole course. Both of the agents looked bored and hot, rings of perspiration staining their matching gray shirts.

Tyler moved quickly up the manicured hill toward the trio. It had taken twenty minutes to cross the private course by foot, and her body was drenched in sweat. Like the Secret Service agents, she was not used to the LA weather, but she was thankful she was able to do this in person rather than by phone. The problem with a phone was that it was way too easy to hang up.

She reached the top of the hill and slowed to a determined stroll, her eyes pinned to the man with the golf club. He was built like a fire hydrant, hard muscles visible beneath the light material of his brightly colored golf outfit. Flecks of iron gray hair were visible beneath the edges of his hat, and the skin on the back of his neck was weathered like bark. He was completely focused on the pockmarked white ball by his feet, and his eyes glowed with the intensity of a lifelong athlete. Tyler could imagine what it would be like to see those same eyes staring at her down the barrel of an M-16.

She considered letting him finish his stroke before interrupting; then she thought about Moon and his equally dangerous eyes.

"Senator Conway!" she shouted, as she reached the edge of the green. "I need to speak to you right away!"

The two Secret Service agents saw her first. They rushed between her and Conway, both grabbing for the holsters hanging around their waists. Tyler quickly yanked her badge out of her shirt pocket and flipped it open. The seal flashed in the LA sun.

"My name is Tyler Ross, and I'm a federal agent. I was given the senator's location by the director of the FBI."

It was a minor lie. Arthur Feinberg had pulled in a favor from Washington and had provided her the good news that Conway was in his home state for the Thanksgiving break. A call to his wife in LA had pointed Tyler to the private golf course.

Conway stepped between the two Secret Service agents, the golf club hanging against his hip. His jaw was stiff, but there was genuine curiosity in his eyes. He jerked his head to the side, sending the two agents back toward his golf bag.

"I know who you are, Dr. Ross. But shouldn't you be in Nevada right now, searching for my daughter's killer?"

Tyler's stomach curled into a tight ball. She could feel the venom in Conway's voice. Not directed at her, of course, but at Jack Collier. That venom and that voice were much more dangerous than the man's cold eyes. *That voice had ordered many deaths before.*

"Sir," Tyler said, slipping her badge back into her pocket, "I believe there's been a grave mistake made in the course of our investigation. I have new information concerning Jill's death and the source of the killer bacteria."

A dark cloud crossed Conway's cheeks.

"I've already got all the information I need. I have confidence that you and Agent Moon will bring the situation to an acceptable conclusion."

Ice ran down Tyler's spine. She knew exactly what Conway meant by the words. It was Vietnam talk: *acceptable conclusion.* It meant a body bag and a handful of spent shell casings.

"With all due respect," Tyler said through her teeth, "you need to listen to what I have to say."

Conway stared at her, shocked by her tone. Nobody spoke to him like that. He paused for a full beat.

"All right. You've got three minutes. Then I'm going to return to my game, and you're going to get the hell out of here."

It came out fast, the words close together. Tyler told him about Dutton's money and Dutton's inability to explain a key component in the development of the cure. She repeated what Collier had said at the McDonald's, and how it now seemed based in truth. She did not couch her idea in terms of a theory because she knew in her soul that it wasn't.

Conway's expression was unreadable as he listened. When she finished, he tapped his golf club against his leg.

"So you believe that Collier didn't do this on purpose," he said.

"It was Jack's cure," Tyler said. "He would not have deliberately sabotaged it."

Conway lifted his baseball cap off of his head and

wiped the sweat from his hair. Then he shook his head. "Where is your evidence, Dr. Ross? Michael Dutton is one of the most respected scientists in the world. Jack Collier is a punk with a criminal record."

Tyler's lips tightened. "Jack Collier is a kid, even younger than your daughter. And if anyone's to blame for this horror, it's Dutton."

Conway paused for a full beat. Then he shook his head. "My daughter is dead, and Jack Collier is carrying the disease that killed her. He needs to be stopped."

Tyler trembled as she came to a sudden conclusion. It was time to step forward. "Senator, your daughter's death was an accident. But what's going to happen to Collier if you don't call off Moon will be murder in cold blood. And I do not intend to stand by and watch you order a young man's death."

The golf club glimmered as Conway turned it in his hand. "Tread carefully, Dr. Ross."

But Tyler was beyond being careful. "I'll go to the press, Senator. I'll put the entire story on the evening news. An elected official using the FBI as his personal hit squad."

Conway's cheeks reddened. "This is going to cost you your badge."

Tyler shivered, but inside she was bristling with energy. She felt alive. "I don't care. It's the right thing. Now help me find Moon."

Seconds passed in silence as Conway's fingers whitened against the golf club. His eyes bored into Tyler, but she refused to turn away. Finally, Conway's face sagged. He signaled toward the two Secret Service agents.

"My phone. Now."

One of the agents rushed forward with Conway's cellular. It was twice as large as the commercial models, fitted with antiscanning technology and a magnified transmitter. Conway dialed, then pressed the phone to his ear.

Tyler watched his face as he conversed with someone on the other end. His cheeks tightened as he caught her gaze. Then he shrugged his shoulders, snapping the phone shut.

"Vincent's gone off radio contact. Even your director can't reach him now."

Tyler's throat went dry. She had never heard of an agent going off radio contact during a case. There was *always* a way to make contact. "You're saying there's no way to reach him?"

Conway lowered his voice. "It's something I taught him in Vietnam. You don't go off radio because of the enemy; you do it when you're worried about the people on your own side. If you're out of contact, nobody can order you to drop a mission. Nobody can get in your way."

Tyler felt fury billowing through her. Was she the only one left with a sense of perspective? These men were acting like they were still in Vietnam.

"So how do we stop him?" she asked, fighting to control herself.

"We don't. It's in Moon's hands."

Tyler wanted to hit him with a golf club. "Senator, that's not an *acceptable* answer. If Collier dies—and then I prove that all this was an accident—well, it's not just my career that's in jeopardy."

Conway's Adam's apple jerked beneath the skin of his neck. Finally, his fingers attacked the cell phone's keypad.

"If he's using one of the choppers," he said, pressing the phone back against his ear, "I can find out where he's heading. The captain of the flight division served under me in two wars."

A moment later, the steel had returned to his eyes. "Moon's on his way to UCLA. One of the biology labs on the quadrangle."

A biology lab. Tyler was stunned and impressed at the same time. Jack Collier hadn't given up, and he hadn't run. Instead, he had headed straight to familiar territory. Tyler could think of only one reason why he was at UCLA. *He was trying to cure himself.*

"Senator," she said, praying that it was not already too late, "I need to borrow your phone."

TWENTY-SEVEN

Six inches of glistening steel, tapered to a point so sharp it could pierce the membrane of a single human skin cell. A tempered glass tube filled with viscous, light yellow liquid, speckled with tiny flecks of white.

Jack held his breath as he stared at the syringe floating in a dish filled with warm water. The dish was sitting on top of the steel counter, somewhere between the two used gel-electrophoresis plates and a junkyard of empty chemical vials and expended test tubes. Jack's gloved fingers shook as he touched one end of the syringe. He watched it bob up and down in the water, watched the tiny clusters of life inside the yellow liquid quiver as they continued to expand into microscopic civilizations. In just a few more minutes, the bacteria would reach a critical mass—ready for the assault on his system. He would take the syringe and inject the yellow liquid directly into his bloodstream, and the transformation would begin.

His knees felt like jelly and there was a loud ringing in his ears. He had been working in a trancelike state for hours. He had never concentrated this hard before in his life, and he knew he was on the verge of cracking up. His skull hurt, his eyes barely seemed to fit in their sockets, and that damn ringing was driving him crazy.

But the syringe floating in front of him told him that it was all worthwhile. Once he had injected the newly tailored strep into his bloodstream, it would start a chain reaction that would travel instantly through his cells. The new plasmid would be transferred from bacterium to bacterium, reengineering the strep A, turning it back from a killer to a cure. Soon after, the change would become permanent; Dutton's lupus would be replaced by the correct receptor, and the bacteria would no longer seek flesh and organ. It would once again be guided by the killer T cell DNA. It would hunt only tumors, and Jack's touch would become one of life, not of death.

It was an enormous thought, one he could barely get his mind around. He would become a vehicle for the cure for cancer. All he needed to do was hold Angie in his arms, kiss her on the lips, and she would be saved. For two years, this had been his dream. It was beyond monumental.

Perhaps it would even make up for the ten skeletons that still danced through his memory. He let his trembling fingers drift through the warm water, the skin pruning like an aging piece of fruit. If only the ringing would leave him alone. If only he could have a moment of fucking silence—

He jerked his head up, coming to a sudden realization. The ringing was not coming from inside his skull. He turned and looked at the phone hanging from the wall at the end of the aisle. He grinned at himself, amazed that he hadn't realized it before. The phone had been ringing for at least the past twenty minutes.

Then his grin disappeared, as he wondered what it might mean. Could it be the FBI, trying to contact him? Did someone know he was there?

Paranoia, he thought. Like in the train station and at

the bus depot. Except it hadn't been paranoia; his fear had been justified. He looked back at the syringe, his nerves firing through his skin.

The phone rang on and on.

"Damn it."

He slowly crossed to the wall. His eyes flickered over the oxygen tanks and rubber masks hanging from pegs a few feet away, then settled on the hunk of annoying plastic. He considered yanking the offending device from the wall; then decided it couldn't hurt to find out who was on the other end. If the FBI was outside ready to come in, then he wanted to talk to them. Maybe they would listen to his story. They wouldn't believe, but maybe they would listen.

Then he pictured Tyler Ross as he had last seen her, bent over the edge of a couch with Michael Dutton standing behind her. Jack's lips curled back from his teeth.

He yanked the receiver off the hook and pressed it against his ear. "I think you've got the wrong number," he said. He was about to hang up when a woman's voice sliced through the air.

"Jack, it's Tyler Ross from the FBI."

Jack's face went cold. His hand froze against the receiver, and he blinked rapidly, trying to stop the floor from reeling. For a brief second he thought it was his imagination, an auditory hallucination conjured out of fear and stress.

"You've got to listen to me, Jack. They're coming to kill you."

Jack could hear the sound of a car's engine in the background. "How did you find me?"

"It doesn't matter. You have to get out of there."

It was a strange thing for an FBI agent to say. Jack thought about slamming down the phone, but something inside of him made him wait. He was curious, and he was scared.

"Why the hell should I trust you?"

There was a pause on the other end. "Because I believe you, Jack. It was your cure all along."

Jack fell back against the wall, stunned. The emotion welled up in his chest, and for a moment he lost the ability to breathe. He closed his eyes, but he could still see Tyler Ross and Michael Dutton in the hotel room. Now she said she believed him, but how could he trust her?

"Well, I don't believe *you*. How do I know this isn't a trick?"

"No trick, Jack." Her voice cracked, and he could sense the tension in her words. "I know that it was your idea to use strep A to destroy cancerous tumors. I know you didn't sabotage the cure, and I know you didn't mean to kill anyone."

Jack fingered one of the oxygen tanks hanging from the wall. He was confused, and he still wanted to hang up. But finally someone was saying what he needed to hear. Still, he couldn't trust *her*. Not after what he had seen.

"And what about Michael Dutton?"

The question came out contemptuous, and Tyler seemed taken aback. She couldn't know that he had seen her with his professor. He waited for her reaction.

"Dutton is a liar and a fraud. He tricked me just like he tricked you."

Jack's eyes widened. A bitter taste rose against his tongue. "Where are you?"

"On the freeway. I'm heading toward you. But I don't think I'm going to make it in time. Some other FBI agents are going to get there first. A man named Vincent Moon will be in charge."

Jack glanced nervously at the syringe still floating in the dish of warm water. Now he didn't know what to think. Tyler Ross was making a lot of sense. What's more, he could discern something in her voice—a certain kinship. He couldn't explain it, but it was definitely there.

"So what do you want me to do?" he asked. "Turn myself over to them when they get here?"

"No."

Tyler's abrupt answer shocked him. There was real fear in her voice.

"Why not?"

"Because Vincent Moon doesn't want to bring you in. He wants to kill you. I'm the only one on your side. You've got to turn yourself over to me, personally, so I can keep you safe until we work this out."

Jack rubbed a gloved hand through his hair. "What do you want me to do until you get here? Hide under a microscope?"

Tyler didn't laugh at his joke. "You have to get out of there—"

There was a sudden noise from the front of the lab, and Jack jerked the phone away from his ear. He froze, listening. The sound came again, a mechanical, heavy noise, muffled by the locked double doors but distinctive nonetheless. It was the tenor of a lawnmower engine.

"Jack!" Tyler's voice squeaked through the phone. "What's going on?"

He put the phone back against his ear, staring toward the front of the lab. He couldn't see past the next aisle, but he was certain there was something going on just beyond the double doors. "I hear something. An engine of some kind."

"Shit," Tyler cursed. "Vincent must have sent for the probe."

Jack didn't like the sound of that. "The what?"

"It's a remote-controlled robot. About four feet high, bulletproof, running on treads like a tank."

"You've got to be kidding."

He heard the engine rev again, followed by metal scraping against a cement floor. "Whatever it is, it's getting closer."

"Is there another exit?" Tyler asked. She was nearly screaming now. He could hear a siren blaring through the phone and pictured her screeching from lane to lane.

"Not that I know of," Jack responded. He was starting to panic. He looked again at the syringe. Another minute and it would be ready—but if he didn't get to Angie, it wouldn't make any difference. "Is this probe thing armed?"

Tyler paused on the other end of the line. "It can be fitted with a tear gas launcher and a .50-cal. machine gun."

Jack's face paled. "Jesus."

"You've got to find cover," Tyler said. "A place to hide."

Jack's gaze tracked past his syringe to the two electron microscopes, and he suddenly had a better idea.

"Tyler, how does this probe receive its commands? Microwave, radio, or infrared?"

She seemed surprised by the question.

"Radio waves. In the five-hundred-megawatt bandwidth."

Jack felt a burst of energy. He still had a chance. "Listen carefully. If I find a way out of here, I want you to meet me at Le Grand Café on Melrose Avenue. I'm going there to find someone. Do you understand?"

"Jack," Tyler started, "I'm going to be at UCLA in less than ten minutes."

"I don't fucking *have* ten minutes—"

Jack never finished his sentence, as suddenly, a massive explosion rocked through the front of the lab. He dropped the phone and staggered backward, driven by the wall of sound.

He didn't need to see the double doors to know that they had just been turned into a heap of molten scrap metal.

TWENTY-EIGHT

Vincent Moon hunched over the control console, his face glowing in the dull blue light of the enormous viewing screen. He could feel Densmore's warm breath against the nape of his neck, and he fought the urge to drive the back of his skull upward into the young agent's chin.

"Give me some fucking room," he hissed. Densmore's shadow quickly receded from the console. An amused murmur moved through the team of agents standing in a semicircle behind the young agent, but Moon silenced them with a flick of his left hand.

He leaned closer to the screen, watching as the lab opened up in front of the probe's 3-D camera. The thin joystick felt like a toy between his thick fingers, and he was having a hard time getting used to the jerk of the robot's treads against the hard cement floor. The C-4 plastique explosives they had used to knock down the locked safety doors had left a trail of twisted metal and still-smoldering debris across the entrance to the basement lab, and Moon had nearly upended the compact tank twice since it had worked its way inside.

He grimaced as the probe smacked into one of the steel counters, sending a rack of test tubes crashing to the floor. He would much rather have sent his team of agents inside the lab, armed with assault rifles and carrying tear gas grenades. But he did not want to risk any dramatic casualties, especially now that the media was keeping a watchful eye on the developing case. An FBI agent turned into a skeleton could cost Moon his job.

"Come on," he said, as he pulled back gently on the joystick, navigating the probe away from the counter and back into the center of the aisle. "Work with me, you little trash can."

"Sir," he heard from behind him. It was an agent named Crobert, out of breath from running down the stairs. The other agents parted to let him through. "The campus police are in the building's lobby. They heard the explosion and want to know what's going on."

"Tell them this is now FBI jurisdiction. The first rent-a-cop that comes down that stairwell will spend the rest of the weekend in a holding cell with my boot up his ass. Then he'll be charged with obstruction."

He moved the probe deeper into the lab. It passed a row of beakers sitting on a low shelf, and he could see the machine's reflection stretched across the curved glass, a robot in a carnival funhouse. He ran his eyes over the phallic tear gas launcher, pointing upward from the probe's waist, tilted at a forty-five-degree angle. Then he looked at the .50-cal. machine gun perched on a swiveled, dome-shaped base on the top of the trash can. The base could turn 360 degrees in less than a second, while the high-powered weapon was capable of spraying over a hundred rounds of armor-piercing bullets in a single revolution. *One beautiful piece of armament.*

Moon pushed the joystick forward, and the probe drove past the beakers to the end of the first aisle. It was moving much smoother now, the treads churning rapidly against the floor. Moon could not see his target yet, but he knew he was getting closer. There was no way out of that lab except the double doors, and that meant passing the probe. The second Jack Collier appeared on the view screen, he would be ripped to shreds by a rain of 50-cal. bullets.

For now, it was just a matter of smoking the Karma Killer out. Moon's left hand hovered over a panel above the joystick. There were two buttons on the panel, one red, one black. Densmore had stuck a flick of tape beneath each button: GAS. GUN.

Moon's people were not known for their creativity. But it wasn't creativity that was going to take Jack Collier down. It was a .50-cal. machine gun and a few million dollars of well-spent taxes.

Moon grinned as he slammed the red button with his thumb.

TWENTY-NINE

There was a loud, metallic pop, followed by a high-pitched whistle. Jack watched the first steel canister arc toward him, its missile-shaped body spinning in tight, rapid spirals. The canister hit one of the counters a few aisles down, then ricocheted back into the air. It hurdled the next aisle, glanced against the wall, then smacked into the floor, bouncing twice before it rolled to a stop just ten yards from Jack's feet.

Jack stared at the object in frozen dread. Move! he screamed at himself. *Move! Move! Move!* But his feet felt soldered to the floor.

Then the top of the canister burst off and a geyser of thick white smoke poured upward into the air. Jack's heart started again and he whirled backward, clamping his hands over his mouth and nose. His eyes caught sight of the oxygen tanks and safety masks hanging by the phone. He leapt toward them, wincing as a second canister flew overhead, followed by a third. He yanked the closest oxygen tank free and quickly fastened the mask over his face. The mask consisted of a transparent face shield, with a rubber mouthpiece and velcro straps that ran around the back of the skull. Jack pulled the straps as tight as possible, sealing his lips over the bitter rubber.

A rush of cool air touched his throat, and he spun back around.

The noxious smoke was now so thick he could barely see his hands in front of his face. He stumbled forward, his feet hitting one of the canisters and sending it skittering across the floor. He could hear the lawnmower engine getting closer, the heavy treads dragging the probe toward him at a constant pace. He only had a few more minutes before the thing would turn the last corner, trapping him in aisle twelve.

He reached the counter where he had spent the past ten hours, his hands fumbling through the test tubes and beakers. He finally made contact with the edge of the dish of warm water; then he grabbed for the syringe, soaking himself up to the elbows.

Despite the safety mask, his eyes were now beginning to sting; the tear gas was everywhere, trickles of white slipping under the transparent face shield and burning his cheeks. In a few minutes he wouldn't be able to see anything at all. He had to move fast.

He shoved the syringe into his pocket and turned toward the pair of electron microscopes. He could hear the probe just a few aisles away, moving closer and closer. There was the sound of shattering glass as a test-tube rack fell from a counter, followed by the crackle of wood being crushed by heavy tank treads. Jack's terror magnified as he pictured the thing Tyler had described, some sort of sci-fi creature hunting him down with deliberate intent.

He reached the first electron microscope and ran his hands over the steel casing, searching for some way to break the thing open. The microscope base weighed at least fifty pounds and was the size of a small table. He got his fingers beneath a seam near the floor, pulling as hard as he could. Pain shot through his fingers, and he had to let go. He couldn't do this with his bare hands.

He spun back toward the shelves, yanking open cabinet drawers. Trays of various shaped objects spilled to the floor. Pipettes, epinods, scissors—and screwdrivers, a dozen different styles and sizes. Jack grabbed the largest flat head he could find then turned back to the microscope.

He got the flattened end into the seam, and put all of his weight into his wrists. There was a groan of metal, and then he heard a bolt snap. He furiously worked the screwdriver up and down, cursing the engineers who had done such a good job putting the damn thing together. Another bolt snapped, and now there was a few inches of space, enough to get the screwdriver halfway through the casing. He leaned with all his strength, levering the case upward. There was a loud snap, and the top of the casing cracked free. Jack fell back, landing on his ass against the hard floor.

He brought both feet up and slammed his heels into the microscope, knocking the top of the casing away. A circuit board of wires, transistors, and capacitors glared at him. A large power generator, the size of a loaf of bread, took up one corner of the expensive machine, sporting a bright red warning label: THIRTY THOUSAND VOLTS. DO NOT OPERATE WHEN CASING IS OPEN.

Jack smiled. He looked at the switch on the side of the microscope, still in the off position. Then he rose to his feet. Acidic tears streamed down his cheeks, but he barely noticed. The probe sounded like it was right on top of him, the roar of the engine echoing off the walls and paneled ceiling. He looked down the aisle but still saw nothing but white smoke and the sparkle of shattered glass.

He frantically began searching through the racks of chemicals above the shelving unit, tossing vials and beakers to the floor. He read through label after label, turning the syllables over in his mind, picturing the molecules in his head as they had been drawn in the pages of his Harvard textbooks. His panic rose as he reached the last two vials in the shelf, and then his eyes flashed across two of the most beautiful words in the world: MAGNESIUM SULFIDE.

Jack cheered inwardly, spinning back toward the open electron microscope. He unscrewed the vial's safety cap as he touched the scope's power switch with the toe of his shoe. He listened to the whir of the machine powering up, saw a few sparks rise from the exposed wires, held the vial out in front of him—and realized, suddenly, that the lab had gone dead silent.

Oh, fuck!

Jack turned his head, looking down toward the end of the aisle. The probe was standing in a shroud of white smoke, its cylindrical steel body perched atop four parallel sets of treads. The robot was four feet high, and it looked remarkably like a trash can—except the trash can had a .50-cal. machine gun mounted on its head.

Jack watched as a camera affixed next to the machine gun swiveled toward him. The glass lens winked at him like a malevolent eye. There was the metallic click of a safety being released, and suddenly the machine gun was spinning around, the long barrel arcing through the air at incredible speed.

Jack's reflexes took over and he threw the vial of magnesium sulfide into the open electron microscope. There was an immense crackling, as the highly conductive chemical splashed across the internal generator. A burst of white sparks erupted into the air, and Jack dove for the floor. Just as he hit the hard cement, the entire world seemed to detonate, a holocaust of noise ripping over him in waves.

He rolled onto his back. The machine gun was swinging back and forth, spitting flame as it fired randomly into the shelves, walls, cabinets, and floor. Bullets ricocheted off steel and cement, shattering glass and tearing huge holes in the ceiling. Jack scrambled out of the way, finding shelter behind the second electron microscope. The machine gun ignored him, the probe jerking all the way around until it was firing in the completely opposite direction. The phone hanging from the wall exploded into a thousand plastic shards, then a line of bullets zigzagged toward the ceiling.

Jack laughed out loud, keeping his head down. Even above the noise of the machine gun, he could hear the open electron microscope hissing as the electricity melted its insides into a heap of molten wires. He could hardly believe how well his idea had worked. He pictured the FBI agents out in the hallway watching through the video camera as their probe spun maniacally away from its target, the machine gun firing off entirely at random. He wondered how long it would take them to figure out what had happened.

His physics professor at Harvard would have been duly impressed. Just as Jack had calculated, the magnesium sulfide had caused the high-energy generator in the electron microscope to release a massive electromagnetic burst, completely disrupting the radio transmission to the probe. Whatever the FBI was using as a remote control had been rendered useless, and the robot was now acting on its own, following random commands from its damaged circuit boards. On a smaller scale, it was the same technology that the army had used in Baghdad and Kosovo to knock out the enemy's power plants and computer systems.

Huddled behind the other microscope, Jack didn't have time to pat himself on the back. First, he had to find a way out of the lab. He could count on the deranged trash can to keep the FBI at bay until it ran out of ammo. That gave him time to think, and that was all Jack had ever needed.

He had barely begun to categorize his escape options when a ceiling tile, loosened by the machine-gun fire, dropped to the floor in front of his face. He looked upward, through a grated screen, and into the dark recess of the biosafety level-two ventilation corridor. It would be a tight fit—and a long crawl—but it was a way out.

He checked to make certain the syringe was still in his pocket, then made sure the probe was still facing the wrong direction. He took a deep breath, then leapt like a cat onto the nearby counter. He rose to his full height and smashed his fists into the ceiling, sending two more panels crashing toward the floor. He grabbed the metal screen with both hands, ripping it free. He felt a rush of clean air against his facemask. Without pause, he hooked his arms into the dark corridor and strained his lank muscles.

Just as he pulled his head into the corridor, he heard the probe spinning back toward him, the rain of bullets arcing toward his heels. He screamed inwardly, and in a single motion, hauled himself the rest of the way. A second later he was completely inside the corridor and moving forward.

The sound of the machine gun dwindled as he crawled deeper into the darkness, the cool air pushing at him from behind. He didn't know where he was heading—but the ventilation system had to reach the outside world at some point. There would be filters to dismantle and probably a locked hatch to break through, but Jack would get out alive. Nothing was going to keep him away from that café on Melrose.

He had gone another five yards before he realized that

he had forgotten something. He stopped mid-crawl, yanking the safety mask from his head, blinking rapidly in the darkness. He suddenly felt naked.

He had left the backpack full of Dutton's money in the lab. For the first time since this had all begun, he was back to being a poor kid from New Jersey.

He grinned. He patted the syringe in his pocket, and again started forward through the corridor. "Fuck the money," he whispered to himself.

THIRTY

Moon stood watching the ten-million-dollar heap of junk lurch back and forth at the head of the aisle, the machine gun rattling impotently on an empty ammo belt. His fury washed through him in waves, and he lumbered forward, the AR-7 sniper rifle clenched tightly in his hands. Densmore and the rest of the half-dozen agents gave him a wide berth, gingerly picking their way through the devastation. The lab looked like a Vietnam aftermath, riddled with bullet holes and bathed in scalding white smoke.

Moon leaned forward, flicking a switch on the side of the probe. The thing ignored him, jerking straight into the wall, chips of cinder raining to the floor. Moon cursed, then flipped open a steel panel on the side of the robot. He set his sniper rifle on the floor and removed his .45 from his belt.

"Consider this a dishonorable discharge," he snarled, his voice reverberating against his rubber gas mask. He placed the barrel of the gun against the robot's control board and pulled the trigger.

The report echoed through the lab. Shards of circuit board fountained into the air, and the probe finally went dead. Moon reholstered his gun, then turned toward the demolished aisle. His shoulders sagged at the sight, pain angling down his spine.

The operation had been a total disaster. The damage to the lab could run well into the millions, and the media was going to have a field day. When Conway found out—and he would find out—he was going to rip Moon a second asshole. But this was nothing compared to Moon's personal sense of failure. Jack Collier was a fucking twenty-three-year-old kid. He had now escaped from Moon twice—and made him look like an idiot in the process.

"Anybody have any clue what happened here?" Moon lashed out, retrieving his sniper rifle from the floor.

"I think he used this machine to short out the probe," Densmore answered. He was hovering over an open metal case that looked like some sort of high-tech computer. There was brown smoke rising from the inside of the machine, speckled with bright yellow sparks. "Smart little bastard, isn't he?"

Moon didn't respond. He was already looking upward, at the missing panels in the ceiling. So that was how Collier had gotten out. When the view screen had gone blank, Moon had lost track of the perp; while Moon had prepared his team to enter the active zone, Collier must have crawled out of the building through the ventilation corridor. It had only been ten minutes since the probe had malfunctioned, but he would be long gone by now. If Moon had brought more agents, he could have established a perimeter, he could have locked down the entire building, but that would have required clearance from the director and, worse, the involvement of Tyler Ross.

"All right," he finally said, swallowing back the bile in his throat. "Our perp is back on the move, but this time we know exactly where he's going. Densmore, get our second unit over to the café on Melrose. Have them establish a loose watch from the street. Nobody makes contact with the target until I get there."

Moon ran his hands down the stock of the sniper rifle. He was going to finish this *himself*. He watched Densmore extract his cell phone, then pause before dialing.

"You think he's crazy enough to go to the café?" the young agent asked. "He's got to figure we'll come after him."

Moon nodded behind his gas mask. In a strange way, he was beginning to understand Jack Collier. "He'll know it's a trap, but he'll go anyway. He isn't afraid of us. And at this point, he has nothing to lose."

He turned his back on the wreckage. His large fingers were white against the sniper rifle. The more he understood Jack Collier, the more he hated the little shit.

Twenty minutes after Moon had left the building, Tyler Ross stepped through the demolished entrance to the lab. The bitter scent of tear gas burned the back of her throat, and she drew a handkerchief out of her jacket pocket. She clamped it tight over her mouth and nose, then found a cabinet full of masks and gloves.

As she worked her way deeper into the lab, Tyler's horror grew. The crowd of UCLA security officers and California troopers in the lobby of the building had been unable to give her any information, and there was no way to know yet whether Jack was still alive. Moon had not checked in with Conway or the director and was obviously still maintaining his radio silence.

Based on her initial observations, Tyler had to admit that things didn't look good. Then she turned a corner and found herself face-to-face with the decimated probe. The robot was leaning forward on one tread, its control panel hanging wide open. Tyler recognized the entry

hole of a .45-cal. weapon in the direct center of the machine's circuit board.

"Christ!" she whispered.

The place was a war zone. She scanned the rubble,
trying to figure out what had happened. From the looks
of things, the probe had malfunctioned, either that or
Moon had gone completely insane. Knowing the man,
she wasn't ruling the possibility out.

Thankfully, she did not see any signs of fresh blood.
Or any hint of Vincent and his men. Maybe Jack had
somehow escaped. But how? Was there another exit
from the lab?

Then cool air pulled at Tyler's handkerchief, and her
gaze drifted to the ceiling. She saw the missing tiles and
the dark ventilation shaft. *Jack had improvised.*

She took a step toward the ventilation shaft, and her
foot caught on something soft, covered in a pile of broken ceiling tiles. She bent to one knee and dug through
the rubble. A moment later her hands touched vinyl, and
she retrieved a bulky black backpack. She yanked the
zipper open and gazed down at the stacks of hundred-
dollar bills.

She grimaced, thinking of Dutton, then cautiously
shook the bills free. She jerked back, as a .38-cal. pistol
clattered against the floor. Then she noticed the zippered
front compartment. There was something oblong and
heavy inside.

She carefully undid the zipper and removed a bullet-
shaped metal canister. She recognized the object as a
vacuum-sealed container. Jack must have used it to store
the original strep. As she'd guessed, he'd been carrying
it with him the whole time. He had thought it was his
cure—not a weapon.

She rose, her gaze tracking across the counter. Amid
the shattered test tubes and overturned chemical vials,

she saw two expended gel-electrophoresis plates and a number of microscope slides, some smeared with dried blood. Sparks flowed through her body as she thought about Jack Collier working furiously in this lab, chasing a second miracle, driven by a true understanding of the disease that had scarred Tyler's life. Had he succeeded? Had he recreated the miracle cure?

Tyler reached for her cell phone, speed-dialing Caufield's number as she headed toward the door. She was going to need help if she was going to save Jack's life.

The truth was, it wouldn't make any difference whether or not Jack Collier had cured himself—if Moon got to him first.

THIRTY-ONE

Alarm bells were going off in Jack's head as the pretty young woman led him through the open French doors and out onto the patio of the café. It wasn't anything she had said; it was her wide, seemingly genuine smile. This was Saturday night at an expensive restaurant—on one of the trendiest streets in LA. Jack was wearing jeans and a dirty jacket, his face was marked with black soot and flecks of broken glass, his hair was sticking up from his head in spastic, sweaty locks, and he was sporting wraparound sunglasses he had found in the glove compartment of the VW bug. Even though the hostess claimed to be a friend of Angie's, why was she being so damn nice?

"You're lucky," she said, as the warm breeze pulled at the straps of her tight black tank top, "the club crowd hasn't arrived yet, so our best tables are still available."

Jack quickly surveyed the patio. The circular grotto was tiled in marble, and only moderately crowded. He counted fifteen wire-frame tables set in a semi-ellipse around a polished green statue, a waist-high replica of the Arc de Triomphe. As the young woman led him around the arc, he noticed trickles of bubbly water dribbling over the corner turrets, running in gleaming streams into a pool carved around the statue's base. Then a spotlight blinked on from somewhere inside the café, and Jack saw that it wasn't a statue, it was a fountain; and it wasn't water, it was pink champagne.

"Here we go," the hostess said, as they passed to the other side of the arc. "Right by the street. You can count the Ferraris as they drive by."

Jack lowered himself into an uncomfortable chair. There was a railing to his right, looking out onto the sidewalk. A group of four men stood by a jade green SUV parked by the curb, all dressed for a night on the town. Their shirts were nearly as shiny as their moussed-up hair.

Jack turned away from the street. The hostess peered down at him, that smile still pinned to her lips. "Angie should be here any minute now. Can I get you a drink while you wait?"

Jack saw her eyes waver, and the alarm bells chimed even louder.

"No thanks," he responded. "If I get thirsty, I'll just lick the arc."

She didn't laugh; she simply turned and skipped back across the patio. Now Jack was fairly certain: This was some sort of a trap. The hostess had been told to stall him. Maybe she was in the café right now, calling the FBI. Jack should have jumped the railing and raced down the sidewalk; he should have hopped back into his VW and headed straight for Mexico.

He looked back toward the slick men by the SUV. One of them was talking loudly in a European accent, his hands waving through the air. No, Jack was not going to run. If this was a trap and **he** ran, he might never see Angie again.

He had to put his trust in Tyler Ross. A woman he had only met once, who had already—in a way—betrayed him before. Now she had told him that she believed him; that alone made her different. She had also warned him about the probe and about Vincent Moon, the FBI agent who wanted him dead.

If she came to this café, he would turn himself over to her; otherwise, he was waiting for Angie. He really didn't have any other options.

He turned back toward the patio, watching the other patrons in the reflected light of the pink champagne. Fifteen, maybe twenty people, most of them near his age, many of them beautiful. Faces that could be on television and in magazines, perhaps a few that were. He tried to picture Angie making her way through this crowd, carrying a tray of brightly colored drinks with stupid names. Waiting for the day when the cancer would take her away—all alone, surrounded by frivolous beauty.

Jack's jaw clenched, and he reached into his pocket and carefully retrieved the syringe. He held the syringe in front of his eyes, peering through the thick yellow liquid. The white conglomerates of bacteria were twice as large as before. Critical mass, he thought to himself. *Eager to get out and propagate.*

He lay his right arm flat on the table and rolled up his sleeve. He tapped the syringe against the side of the table, making sure there were no air bubbles inside; then he placed the needle against his pale skin, right above the elbow joint.

Three women in blue miniskirts and high heels were watching from two tables away, but he ignored them, shoving the needle deep into his vein. One of the women said something and the others laughed, as Jack gently depressed the plunger. Surely they thought it was heroin or some designer drug, nothing they hadn't seen before on this street in this town.

If they had only known.

Jack removed the needle, held his other hand tight over the spot of blood that appeared. He closed his eyes and leaned back in his chair, feeling a warm tingle wash through him. The sensation started in his shoulder, swept down his back toward his legs. He imagined the bacteria moving rapidly through his circulatory system, passing easily through the cell membranes in his veins to the muscle, flesh, and organs around. Coming into contact with the strep bacteria already there, transmitting the genetic material from cell to cell.

A smile crossed his lips. His body had become a bacterial orgy. A massive, organic petri dish. In a few minutes, the new strep A would colonize his system, and his touch would carry a miracle.

Suddenly, he heard a loud crash, followed by a rain of curses. He opened his eyes and saw a busboy hovering over the women two tables away, apologizing profusely. A tray of shattered glasses lay on the floor at his feet. One of the women was berating him, a manicured finger aimed at his face. The poor man's back was to Jack, and he could see the wrinkled skin above the man's black uniform turning bright red in embarrassment. The color was a stark contrast to the stringy white hair springing from the man's head.

Jack's eyebrows rose, as a sudden thought struck him. The man seemed way too old to be a busboy.

Then the man turned in his direction. Jack's heart froze, as he recognized the face.

THIRTY-TWO

Vincent Moon's entire world had been reduced to a circle of gray, two centimeters in diameter, bisected by two bright red perpendicular lines. Shapes inside the gray shifted like ghosts, but the bright red lines never changed, they remained hard and cold and real. The bright red lines were God. Where they bisected, there was meaning and power.

There was truth.

Moon shifted forward, his elbows touching the hard wood of a windowsill, his spine twisted forward against the ancient pain. Suddenly, the gray cleared, the ghostly shapes took form. He saw the curved windshield of a sports car, then the grooved cement of a sidewalk. He leaned a few inches farther against his elbows and saw a flash of movement, a woman walking along a railing. Then the railing itself, curved iron winking in the streetlights. Then the circle slid past the railing into the shadows of the patio.

Moon's heart started to race, the circle trembling. He saw long, bare legs beneath a metal-framed table, then the hem of an expensive miniskirt. He saw a Perrier bottle on top of a table, magnified so fiercely he could count the bubbles inside. He focused for a brief moment on a pair of brightly painted lips, moving up and down in anger, a young woman berating someone for reasons unknown. Then he was past the woman and suddenly he froze.

"There you are," Moon whispered, "you stupid little fuck."

The sharp eyes and high cheekbones were unmistakable. Moon shivered, his excitement building like a Pacific wave. He fought to steady his hands. He could feel the sweat pooling against the chair beneath him, and he realized he needed a moment to compose himself. He pulled his head back, breathing deeply. He paused to survey his surroundings.

He was leaning halfway out the second-floor window overlooking Melrose Avenue, and the patio of the French café was just thirty yards below. The cell-like room was empty behind him, save for a portable phone sitting on the table a few feet away. The phone line was open, a direct connection to Densmore, who was waiting patiently in the backseat of an SUV parked in front of the café. Four of Moon's best men stood in front of the SUV, disguised as civilians. At a single command, they would swarm over the railing of the patio and secure the target.

But they would never get that command. The target was too dangerous; a single touch of his skin could turn one of Moon's men into a skeleton. More important, Moon had a score to settle. Jack Collier would not end up in the court system or achieve the dubious fame of a medical enigma. This would not become a sideshow. This was going to end here.

Moon's hands tightened against the AR-7 sniper rifle. The tremor was gone from his fingers, replaced by cool determination. He pressed his right eye back against the scope. His left eye remained open, just as Colonel Conway had taught him. There was sweat running down his back and his spine ached from the weight of the rifle, but he was already entering a state of near religious tranquility. The rifle had become an extension of his body, the focus of his soul. The pain in his shoulders and spine disappeared, and he could no longer feel his legs. Nothing existed beyond those bisecting, bright red lines:

Five.

Moon steadied his breathing, the rifle frozen in his hands. A bomb could have gone off in the room behind him, and he would not have blinked. In the jungle, they called this the Zone. A place beyond thought, beyond ethics, beyond emotion. A place of pure action. The Zone.

Four.

He shifted his hands a bare centimeter to the left, adjusting for the wind that licked at his cheeks. He saw a bead of sweat track down from Collier's hairline, followed the glistening ellipse with the scope as it moved across the kid's young flesh.

Three.

There could be no escape now. The Karma Killer's luck had just run out. Moon's entire body tensed as he let the ellipse of sweat disappear from the circle, as he focused his vision on the center of the bisecting red lines.

Two.

The crosshair tattooed itself across Jack Collier's forehead, a bare inch above his left eye. From this angle, the bullet would cleave his skull in half, spreading his brains across the patio. The kill shot.

One.

Moon's mind cleared, as his finger tightened against the trigger.

THIRTY-THREE

It happened so fast, it was like watching a movie filmed through a strobe light. Jack never had time to react because his mind lagged a split second behind—unable to comprehend.

The old busboy who wasn't a busboy was rushing toward him, brandishing a pad of paper and a pen, his bushy white eyebrows rising above watery, hound-dog eyes, his lips pulling back to reveal the worst set of dentures in the free world. He was moving fast for a man his age, driven by some inner fire Jack never had a chance to understand. His shadow spread across the wire frame table as his body obscured Jack's view of the street, and suddenly his voice burst forth.

"My name's Duke Baxter, and I'm here for your story—"

And before Jack could respond, even before the last syllable of Duke's life had stopped resonating against Jack's eardrums, there was a crack like a massive leather belt pulled tight. The old man's body lurched forward, his chest rupturing down the center, a fountain of dark blood spraying across Jack's face. Duke's eyes popped open and his hands flew toward heaven and he arched back, constricted by agony. Then his knees gave way and he collapsed. His chin hit the table, flipping him to the side, and his body crashed against Jack's knees. The chair beneath Jack gave out, and he suddenly found himself lying flat on his back.

My God! My God! My God! Jack could feel the weight of the old man's body against his legs. He tried to wriggle free, and a sharp pain moved through his left shoulder. He touched the spot with his other hand, and his face turned white. A chunk of his shoulder was missing. Warm blood spouted from the wound, and he could feel shards of bone sticking through his jacket.

The real agony came a second later and with it clarity. The high-caliber bullet had passed through Duke Baxter's torso, and had hit Jack right above the collarbone. He closed his eyes, groaning, his head falling back against the marble floor. The blood was pumping against his palm, propelled by the contractions of his heart. In another minute he would bleed to death.

He heard sirens and screams drifting toward him from the street, followed by the thunder of footsteps. He didn't know whether people were running toward him or away. But it didn't matter. He was going to die, here in this café. He'd never see Angie again.

His teeth came together and his eyes shot open. No, god damn it, he wasn't ready to die. He clamped his hand tight against his shredded shoulder, trying to staunch the bleeding. He mustered all of his remaining strength and slowly raised his head.

"Jack! Stay still!"

He looked toward the voice and watched a woman hurdle the low railing that separated the patio from the sidewalk. He immediately recognized her cropped blonde hair.

Then he saw the ring of men behind her, most of them wearing dark black suits. They had automatic rifles and shotguns and revolvers, and every barrel was aimed at Jack's head.

"Christ!" he whispered, as Tyler Ross's shadow spread across his chest. The blood continued to pump against his palm.

She dropped to one knee by his side, looking him over. He could see the concern on her face—and deep in her azure eyes, the fear. She had seen the skeletons up close; she had seen the horror of his touch. She could not know, for sure, that he was cured. She could only believe.

As Jack faded away, he felt her hands cradle the back of his head, her body folding over him like the protecting wings of an angel.

THIRTY-FOUR

Oh, Christ! Vincent Moon's eyes went wide, and he pulled back from the sniper scope, his heart rocketing in his chest. He could hear the sirens and the shouts from the street below, growing louder by the second. He couldn't believe what had just happened. Collier had been directly in his sight, a perfect kill shot, and just as he had pulled the trigger—

Fuck! Fuck! Fuck! Someone had compromised his mission. Someone had gotten in the way, saving Collier's life. Still, Moon did not intend to give up. The little fuck wasn't going to get away that easily. Not again.

Moon jammed his eye back against the scope. He struggled to steady his trembling hands, focusing down on the café, ignoring the frantic chaos, the overturned tables, the hysterical bystanders—

There. The scope's crosshairs flickered past a pool of red to Collier's legs, then up his prone body toward his chest. But before Moon could find another kill shot, a shape obscured his view—a long, female body, and a flash of cropped blonde hair.

"You goddamn bitch!"

Tyler Ross was halfway on top of Collier, one hand

pressed against his wounded shoulder. Her other hand
was up in the air, her badge flashing in the sunlight. She
was shouting something at Moon's approaching agents,
perhaps ordering them back, perhaps demanding an ambulance or a chopper. By touching Collier skin to skin,
she had proved that he was somehow cured of the killer
bacteria and no longer a risk. Moon's agents would have
no choice but to let her make the arrest.

But Moon wasn't down there on the ground, and he
didn't have to listen to Tyler Ross.

"I won't let you compromise my mission," he hissed
at the shape in his crosshairs. "I won't let you stand in
my way."

Rage flowed through him as he moved the crosshairs
to the center of Tyler's back, estimating the spot directly
above Collier's heart. The high-caliber bullet would pass
through both of them. Afterward, he would claim that
the confusion had obscured his view, that he had been
trying to save Ross from the Karma Killer.

He didn't want to kill her, but it was her own damn
fault. He steadied his aim, let his finger tighten against
the cold trigger—

"Moon, hold your fire!"

Moon paused, as the unfamiliar male voice echoed
through the room. He lifted his head up from the scope,
but kept the rifle steady. Then he glanced behind him
toward the door.

Wide, heavyset, a barrel of a man. It took Moon a
moment to recognize the puggish face. Then another moment to place the name: Martin Caufield, Tyler's second
in command. Caufield was one step into the room, and
there was a .38-cal. pistol held loosely in his right hand.
Moon's eyes narrowed, and he kept his voice low, a near
monotone.

"I am in command of this apprehension, Mr. Caufield. You have no authority here."

Caufield shook his head, and the .38 lifted a few inches from his side. Not trained on Moon exactly, but certainly a presence.

"Dr. Ross has control of the situation at the scene," Caufield growled. "She's taking the suspect into custody. Now put the rifle down!"

Moon felt waves of anger moving through him. How dare this fucking lab rat order him around! Moon turned back to the window and placed his eye hard against the scope. He quickly relocated the kill shot, the single square inch of flesh in the center of Tyler Ross's back.

"Dr. Ross is in imminent danger," he commented. "I'm going to try to save her life."

Moon heard the metallic click of the .38's safety being released.

"Don't make me shoot you, Mr. Moon."

Moon blinked, sweat running into his eyes. His lips tightened against his teeth. He felt his world beginning to crumble. This was *his* case, damn it. This was *his* suspect. This was *his* debt.

He knew full well that Colonel Conway would never forgive him for his failure. Their relationship had been forged in the jungle, and jungle rules applied. Failure equaled dishonor. And dishonor was unacceptable.

Dishonor was unacceptable.

Moon took a single breath, a decision made. With a sudden motion, he swung away from the window, the sniper rifle rising through the air. He saw Caufield react with surprising speed, crouching low in the doorway; and before Moon could get a single shot off, the .38 lurched once, twice, and the air was lacerated by sound.

Something punched Moon hard in the middle of his chest, sending him crashing backward. He gasped, the rifle clattering to the floor. Blood sprayed out of him as he tried to find his footing, and then the window ledge slammed into the back of his knees. A second later he was falling, his own screams drowned out by the hideous sound of rushing air.

He spent the last few seconds of his life wondering what it was going to feel like when he hit the ground.

THIRTY-FIVE

"Jack."

"Jack."

"Jack."

Tyler ran her fingers across his cold cheek, the tears welling in her eyes. He looked so thin and fragile in the hospital bed, his eyes jerking frantically beneath his eyelids, his skin so pale it was hard to tell where Jack Collier ended and the sterile white sheets began.

"Jack, come on. Stay with me."

His body shook, a tremor rising from deep beneath the bandages that covered his ruined left shoulder. The surgeons had worked on him for six hours, and still there was nothing definite they could tell her. Would he lose the use of his arm? Would the collateral damage be too much for his system? Would his heart collapse from the strain?

"Jack, it's Tyler Ross. You're going to be okay."

She prayed to God that it was true. But the truth was, the doctors weren't sure. And it wasn't just the wound to his shoulder, it was something else, something going on in his bloodstream. Something that had to do with the tailored strep A.

Tyler held her palm against his skin. When she closed

her eyes, she could still see him lying there on the marble floor. She could still hear the footsteps behind her, the armed agents charging forward on Moon's command. One more second, and they would have finished what Moon had started. She couldn't allow that to happen.

She had trusted her instincts.

"Jack, it's all over now. Nobody's going to hurt you."

It was partially true. Now that Tyler had proven, with her touch, that Jack was no longer carrying the disease, he was not in danger of being shot. Vincent Moon's death had saved the Bureau the trouble of suspending him for the murder of Duke Baxter, the man who had first broken the story of the Karma Killer. And Martin Caufield's self-defense testimony had been enough to open an investigation into Moon's handling of the case from its outset.

But certainly Jack was not yet in the clear. As long as Dutton maintained that the cure was his own, Jack's word and Tyler's beliefs would not be enough to clear him of nearly a dozen murders. Jack would have to prove, in both a lab and a courtroom, that he had created the cure; and until that happened, there was the specter of Senator Conway hanging over him. Even with Moon dead, the senator would not give up his vendetta easily. Tyler assumed that she, too, would feel his sting sooner or later.

Even without Conway's involvement, she doubted she would ever carry a badge in the line of duty again. She had already asked Feinberg to clean off the desk next to his, and she was looking forward to the sanctuary of the FBI laboratory. Caufield, who had been taken off active duty pending the outcome of his self-defense plea, was going to join her in her research. The samples of Jack's blood she had stored in the hospital's freezer would provide them both with years of work, and perhaps, with Jack's help, a second shot at the miracle cure.

The final loose end left was Jack himself. Tyler lifted her hand from his cheek, ready to call the doctor again, when Jack's left eye fluttered open.

"You're awake," Tyler said, trying not to sound shocked.

Jack offered a weak smile. It was enough to tear her heart open. "I'm not in the café anymore, am I?"

Tyler shook her head. She looked at the monitor by Jack's bed and saw that his vitals looked good. She knew the surgeons would be on their way down the hall, perhaps as surprised as she was. The fact that he had awakened did not mean he was going to survive, but it was still a good sign. He wasn't ready to slip away yet. Everyone had underestimated this kid. It was the story of his life.

"I have to ask you something," Tyler said. It was the last mystery in her investigation, something that had been bothering her for a long time. "Why did you use your own blood to tailor the bacteria rather than screened blood from a blood bank?"

Jack didn't need to think. The answer was the simplest thing in the world. "I wanted a piece of myself in the cure."

Tyler exhaled. *Of course.* Agent Densmore had filled in the pieces after Moon's death. Jack's girlfriend, Angie Moore, was the reason Jack had dedicated himself to finding the cure. She had been the one he had been chasing across the country. He wanted to use his own blood because the science was personal to him. It had never been objective.

"Angie's on her way, Jack. She'll be here soon."

The change in Jack's face was incredible. His cheeks flushed, and his breathing became strong. He struggled a few inches off the pillow, then dropped back down, exhausted by the effort. *The fine line between love and obsession.* Tyler wondered if this was the real reason Jack was still alive; his heart would not stop until he had seen Angie again.

"But you'll have to keep the reunion short for now," Tyler said, wondering if she'd ever feel that sort of love. "You need your rest."

There was a rustle of motion beneath the hospital blanket. Jack's right hand slipped free and his fingers touched Tyler's bare forearm. A strange tingle moved down her spine. Jack smiled at the look in her eyes.

"Just give me enough time to hold her hand," he whispered.

As if somehow, a single touch could change everything. Tyler was about to press him on the matter, when there was a quiet knock on the door behind her. Tyler turned as Caufield stuck his puggish face inside.

"Dr. Ross, I'm sorry to interrupt. I tried to send him away, but he's intent on seeing Jack. I can still get rid of him, just say the word."

Tyler had a dull feeling inside as she asked the necessary question. "Who is it, Mr. Caufield?"

"Dutton. He says he only wants a few minutes."

Tyler looked at Jack, fragile beneath the hospital blanket. Anger touched every nerve in her body. She started to tell Caufield to send the bastard away, when Jack met her eyes.

"Send him in."

THIRTY-SIX

Jack could hear them whispering behind the hospital door, Tyler's voice harsh and commanding, Dutton responding in single syllables. She was threatening him, telling him that she would be right outside, that Jack was under her protection. It was a strange, new feeling—someone watching over him. It almost balanced the pain emanating from his reconstructed shoulder.

He tried to lift his head from the pillow as the door shifted open. The effort was too much, and only his eyes tracked Dutton as the professor moved slowly into the room. The weathering lines on Dutton's face had deepened into canyons, and his hair seemed thinner, sticking up from his head in desperate twists. His suit looked slept in, and there was a slight tremor in his hands as they smoothed the wrinkles from his slacks. Only his eyes seemed the same, still cold and green and Harvard.

He stopped a few feet from the foot of Jack's bed. His gaze moved from Jack's face to the bandages covering his shoulder, then to the IV bottle hanging above his head. Jack wondered if he was calculating the chances of Jack's survival.

"You may not believe this," Dutton said, quietly, "but I never meant you any harm."

Jack would have laughed if he wasn't afraid that the exertion would send him into cardiac arrest.

"You only wanted to ruin my life and make me disappear. But I'm still here, Professor."

Dutton glanced back toward the door, making sure it was shut. Then he turned back to Jack. His jaw had gone tight. "Listen, you little fuck. Don't think for a second that anything has changed. I *deserve* the cure. I spent my entire life in that lab. That Nobel is mine, and I'm not going to let you take it away from me."

Dutton stopped himself, running a hand through his hair. Then he lowered his voice. "You must realize the best thing now, for both of us, is to work together. I'll admit that you assisted me in developing the strep A. We had a disagreement, and you stole from my safe and went on the run. Something went wrong with the bacteria, but it wasn't either of our faults."

Jack could hear the resignation in Dutton's voice. He knew that Jack had tinkered with the mutated bacteria or Jack wouldn't be in this hospital; he'd be lying dead in a quarantine autopsy lab. And if Jack had tinkered with the bacteria, then he had obviously discovered that Dutton had added his own blood to the strep. More importantly, he probably knew *why* Dutton had added his own blood. That meant Dutton had no choice but to try and bargain.

"You realized that my signature was in the cure," Jack said, his throat hurting from the cellular memory of an intubation tube. "So you tried to obscure my blood with your own. You knew I could use my blood's genetic markers as proof."

Dutton waved a hand in the air. He was trying to appear in control, but his desperation was obvious. "It's the miracle that matters, Jack. Look, you can share some of the credit. I can make the plagiarism charge go away.

You can return to my lab and we can put this behind us. Otherwise, well, it's still your word against mine."

Jack closed his eyes, nauseated by Dutton's pleas. But interestingly, he didn't hate Dutton anymore. In fact, he no longer felt anger toward his professor at all—only pity.

"My blood is in the cure, Professor. And your blood destroyed the cure."

There was a moment of silence, as Dutton looked at him, confused. "What do you mean?"

Jack was too tired to explain, and Dutton would know soon enough. If Jack had to go to court, if he had to prove that the cure was his and that Dutton had turned it into a scourge—all he needed was a simple blood test. Dutton's poisoned DNA would reveal his lupus—and his lie.

Jack took a deep breath, then exhaled. "It's called karma, Professor. And it *will* eat you alive."

Jack kept his eyes closed as Dutton stared at him, waiting for more. Jack kept his eyes closed as Dutton finally stormed out of the room, shutting the door hard behind him. He kept his eyes closed as angry, muffled voices echoed from the hallway, Tyler sending Dutton far, far away. He kept his eyes closed as the door came open again, as someone stepped quietly inside. He kept his eyes closed until he heard his name drifting at him in a soft, female voice.

"Jack, my God, Jack."

When he finally opened his eyes, he was staring at a dream. Newly shorn sable hair and full, bow-shaped lips. Thinner than he remembered, but even more beautiful. He was staring at a dream—and to his surprise, he knew exactly what to say.

SKEPTIC
HOLDEN SCOTT

DR. MIKE BALLANTINE is a man of science, fact, and logic—until he sees his best friend, the Governor of Massachusetts, obliterated before his eyes. Until a bizarre specter appears before him. Until a beautiful CIA agent named Amber Chen tells him about an executioner emerged from the depths of the Chinese Revolution, bringing to America a murderous art that is part magic, part science, and pure evil. Now, as Mike and Amber desperately try to unravel a mystery of biomedicine and murder, they face the most chilling revelation of all: that the worst weapon ever invented is not a bomb, a missile, or a toxin—it's a ghost . . .

"A truly original thriller—part medical, part paranormal, and totally gripping."   —Nelson DeMille

"Riveting . . . Brilliantly told. The suspense is relentless and builds to an ending that leaves you astounded and wondering why someone didn't think of this before . . ."
                    —Jack McConnel, M.D., cofounder of
                        the Institute for Genomic Research

"Ingenious, fascinating, and thoroughly original . . . SKEPTIC raises the bar for the medical thriller. Holden Scott ventures into exciting new territory."
                    —F. Paul Wilson, author of *Nightkill* and
                        The Barrens and Others

**AVAILABLE WHEREVER BOOKS ARE SOLD
FROM ST. MARTIN'S PAPERBACKS**

DONOR
CHARLES WILSON
USA Today bestselling author of *Extinct*

Young ER Dr. Michael Sims feels that too many of his patients are dying without cause. Shannon Donnelly, the Congressman's beautiful daughter, believes the police are wrong in ruling her father's death a suicide. Now they're teaming up to uncover the truth about a terrifying medical experiment involving nerve regeneration and organ transplants. It's backed by millions of dollars. It's protected at the highest levels of government. But there are no volunteers, no donors. There are only ordinary people who check into this Mississippi hospital . . . and discover that death wasn't the worst thing they had to fear. Getting "chosen" is. . . .

"With his taut tales and fast words, Charles Wilson will be around for a long time. I hope so."
—John Grisham

"Charles Wilson is a wizard plotter."
—*The Los Angeles Times*

**AVAILABLE WHEREVER BOOKS ARE SOLD
FROM ST. MARTIN'S PAPERBACKS**